BLUE WOLF BOOK TWO

BLUE SHADOW

BRAD MAGNARELLA

ISBN-13: 978-198651-079-0

ISBN-10: 1-986-51079-4

Cover art by Ivan Sevic

Cover titling by Deranged Doctor Design

Wolf symbol by Orina Kafe

THE BLUE WOLF SERIES

Blue Curse
Blue Shadow
Blue Howl
Blue Venom
Blue Blood
Blue Storm

1

El Rosario, Mexico

Miguel Bardoza giggled as his bare feet beat down the hard-packed dirt road at dusk.

"Get back here!" his sister called in Spanish from behind him. "It's not safe! There are trucks!"

The six-year-old boy paused long enough to look around before sticking his tongue out at her and scampering farther ahead. There were no trucks. Maria was just being bossy. She was trying to act like their mother, even though she was only three years older than him.

"Miguel!" she yelled, storming into a fast walk that wasn't quite a run.

"Miguel," the boy mimicked over a shoulder, then broke into more laughter, all while making sure to stay a safe distance ahead. She would tell on him when they got home, but to make her furious like this was worth it.

They were returning from their grandparents' on a long road that ran along one end of town. Miguel loved going to their house, partly because Grandpa would do coin tricks for him after dinner, then let him keep the coin. That night Grandpa put a whole peso in his mustache, but when Miguel dug his fingers through the thick, graying bristles, the coin wasn't there! Chuckling, Grandpa pulled the peso from Miguel's curly hair and presented it to him. Miguel could have burst. Grandpa had never given him that much money before.

"Don't tell your mother," he'd said with a wink.

Whether Grandpa had meant his actual mother or his sister, Maria, Miguel wasn't sure. That was why he was running ahead of her now. His shorts lacked pockets, so he was having to hold the peso in his right fist. He couldn't make it disappear like Grandpa, and he didn't want Maria finding it.

"Miguel!" she yelled again. "Do you want the monsters to get you?"

He slowed a little. There were no such things as monsters. But although he knew this—or at least he'd heard his father say it enough times to believe it was *probably* true—the woods on the far side of the field they were passing did look kind of scary in the growing dark. Scary enough for something big and hairy to jump out from behind the trees and chase them, even.

"There aren't any monsters," Miguel said, more to reassure himself than anything. He clung tightly to his peso and edged to the far side of the road, his large eyes roaming the dark trees.

"Are too!" Maria shot back. "And they eat bad little boys."

Now he knew she was lying. But he was still anxious to get to the road ahead that would take them away from the woods and back to their house behind the church in the center of town. He was almost to the end of the field when he ventured one last look toward the trees.

His breath caught in his throat, and he jerked to a sudden stop.

A figure he was sure hadn't been there a moment before was standing across the field, near the trees. Miguel's brain struggled to make sense of the fat silhouette with the wild hair and big nose. He didn't know anyone like that in El Rosario ... but there was something familiar about him.

Maria, who hadn't seen the figure yet, was still scolding Miguel as she closed the distance. Miguel wanted to tell her to be quiet, but couldn't seem to find his voice. When the figure stepped from the shadow of the trees, his colorful costume came into full view. Miguel's fear turned so suddenly to excitement that a little pee spurted from his bladder, but he barely noticed.

A whole peso, and now this!

"Maria!" he called back. "Maria, look! It's Baboso the Clown!"

"There's no Baboso out here, you little liar. The festival ended last week."

But it *was* Baboso, his favorite of the Brothers Payaso. He couldn't stop smiling as he bounced up and down. "Look!" he repeated.

But Maria refused to follow his jabbing finger as she arrived beside him. Instead, her hand clamped around his wrist. "What do you have in your hand?" she demanded. "Did you take something from Grandma and Grandpa's?" She tried to pry his fingers from his palm.

Miguel glanced down at his fist, but he was too excited

to worry about the peso. He waved his free hand and shouted, "Baboso! Baboso!"

The clown with the big dumb smile raised a white glove and waved it slowly back and forth. Miguel found that so hilarious, he laughed until tears leaked from the corners of his eyes. That made Maria follow his gaze. Her grip loosened around Miguel's wrist enough for him to jerk his hand away.

"Baboso?" she whispered.

Miguel ran to the side of the road, stopping at the field's edge. He would have been content to watch the clown's antics from there, but when Baboso lifted his other hand, a treat bag dangled from it. Inside the bag were fat nuggets of foil-wrapped...

"Chocolates!" Miguel yelled.

He was ready to take off toward the clown, his fear of the woods forgotten, when Maria seized his wrist again. This time, there was no discussion. Her mouth set in a determined line, she began tugging him up the road toward home, away from his favorite clown.

"No!" he screamed. "Baboso! Chocolates!"

He tried to bite her arm, but she smacked the top of his head. "It's not Baboso," she hissed, powering her lean legs into a run.

He might have been faster than Maria, but she was stronger. Miguel made himself dead weight and looked back. The clown hadn't moved. His grinning face shifted in and out of view beyond the field's weathered stalks. And he was still holding up the bag of chocolates.

"It *is* Baboso!" Miguel insisted, trying to brake with his heels now. "It *is*!"

Maria grunted and smacked the top of his head again.

Miguel hollered and rubbed the spot, almost the same place where Grandpa had fished out the peso earlier. That gave Miguel an idea.

"Look what Grandpa gave me," he said. "A whole peso! Look!"

He opened his hand so the peso jostled around his palm. Maria glanced down at it distractedly. When it fell from his palm and onto the road, she paused to kneel for it. Miguel gave a mighty tug and jerked away from her. In the next instant he was racing at full speed toward Baboso.

"Miguel!" Maria screamed.

But he had too far a head start. She would never catch him, he thought as he crashed through the stalks in the field. He weaved around them, hardly able to contain his excitement as the clown and that wonderful swinging bag of treats grew larger and larger.

"Chocolates," Miguel cried. "Chocolates for meee!"

"Get back here!" his sister called, but sounding very far away.

When Miguel was almost to him, the clown raised a finger to his lips and stepped back into the trees. Miguel giggled through his panting breaths. Baboso was always playing silly games. Miguel slowed slightly as he entered the trees and looked around for the clown.

"Miguel!" came his sister's faint cry. "It's not Baboso..."

How could the clown have disappeared? Miguel thought. He'd been right here a second ago.

"It's a monster..."

When the clown appeared beside him, Miguel saw what his sister meant. His eyes. Something wasn't right about his eyes. Miguel had never seen a dead person before, but he imagined that's what their eyes looked like.

They stared down at him, blood-spotted and unblinking, even as the clown continued to grin. His top teeth were pointed and made of metal.

Miguel backed slowly away, his stomach tight and a little sick. He didn't want the chocolates anymore. He didn't even care about the peso.

He just wanted to be home with his dad and mom.

Baboso made no move to chase him. He simply followed with those dead eyes.

Miguel spun and ran. He was almost clear of the trees when a large gloved hand closed around his wrist.

2

I braced myself against the edge of the sink, took a deep breath, and opened my eyes. For half a second I expected to see arctic-blue irises peering back at me from a stubbly, sun-browned face—the curse gone as suddenly as it had appeared. But no dice. Two weeks since the old woman in Waristan had marked me, and Jason Wolfe remained the Blue Wolf.

I ran a taloned hand between my peaked ears. The thick hair that spiked back up looked electric blue under the bathroom's fluorescent bulb. I squinted toward my yellow eyes before pulling my lips back. My muzzle wrinkled from rows of serrated teeth highlighted by two-inch canines. It still seemed impossible, but the proof was in the reflection.

I've killed with these teeth.

The thought stirred something powerful and predatory inside my chest. My heart began to thud harder. Before I could suppress the feeling, my ears canted away from the mirror: boots coming up the hallway. An instant later the door to the dorm room shook with knocking.

"Yeah?" I called, relaxing my lips from my canines.

"Here to give you a lift to the Legion compound," a man's voice answered from outside.

I grunted and checked my watch. He was early. I straightened from the sink and looked over myself a final time. I was wearing a black jumpsuit Centurion had designed for my seven-foot, four-hundred-pound frame, as well as boots that fit over my massive clawed feet. My eyes lingered on the breast of the suit where the Centurion shield gleamed silver.

The door shook with more knocking. "You coming?" the man called in a southern accent.

I scowled at the Centurion insignia and left the bathroom. A flight helmet with what looked like a breathing apparatus sat atop the dorm's dresser beside my gloves. The jutting apparatus didn't circulate oxygen, though; it was designed with the sole purpose of concealing my muzzle. Reginald Purdy, Centurion's head of program development, had assured me their technology division was working on something less obtrusive to hide my face. In the meantime...

I palmed the helmet and was preparing to push it over my ears when the impatient knocking sounded a third time. Swearing, I tucked the helmet under an arm and pocketed the gloves. Yanking the door open, I glared down at the Centurion associate.

"I heard you the first time," I growled.

The thirty-something man was wiry with shaggy muttonchops. His trucker hat read WOMEN WANT ME, FISH FEAR ME. He had been poised to say something, but now his jaw went slack. A vinegar scent of fear spiked from his skin. If he was transporting me, he had security clearance into the Legion Program, but hearing that the program would be commanded by a massive wolfman and getting an eyeful of said wolfman were two different things entirely.

"M-Mr. Purdy is waiting," he said at last.

"Purdy told me 0800," I said, looming over him. "And it's quarter till. I've got a locker to pack."

Muttonchops had caught me at a bad time—dealing with my temperamental wolf nature on top of the moral dilemma I faced in transitioning from a decorated special ops officer in the U.S. military to what amounted to a mercenary. I was disgusted at myself for giving Centurion United that kind of leverage over me, and I didn't bother hiding my disgust now.

Muttonchops swallowed and adjusted the utility belt that separated his fatigue pants from the tactical vest he wore over a black tank top. "Fine, I'll give you two minutes," he said, trying to disguise his fear with authority. "You're not ready by then, we'll take off without you."

Bad choice of words. Before Muttonchops or I knew what was happening, my taloned hand flashed forward, grabbed him by his tactical vest, and slammed him high against the wall. His hat fell off to reveal a rust-colored mullet.

"What's your name?" I snarled inches from his reddening face.

"R-rusty," he managed.

"Well listen up, *Rusty*. You don't give me orders, and you sure as hell don't talk to me like that. You've got no rank on me, one. And two, you're a little parasite more interested in cashing a paycheck than serving your country like a real soldier."

"Hey, man, I've got a mortgage ... kids to feed."

"The next time you come for me, it will be at the appointed time. If you're early, you wait. And if you've got something to say, you damn well make sure it's not insulting before opening your mouth. We clear?" When Rusty sputtered and wrestled with my fingers instead of answering, I shook him and roared, *"Are we clear?"*

"Captain Wolfe," someone called.

I turned to find Reginald Purdy hurrying down the corridor in one of his dark pinstripe suits. The smile lines of his aging African-American face were arcing up in question. "Is something the matter?" he asked.

I lowered Rusty back to the floor. "Not anymore."

Purdy's eyes moved between the Centurion associate and me. "Why don't you wait in the car?" he said to Rusty, who wasted no time putting Purdy between us as he collected his hat and hurried down the corridor.

I took a calming breath. "Sorry."

Purdy studied me for another moment, the pinch of his lips beneath his thin gray mustache telling me he'd read the situation. "Listen, I know this is a big adjustment for you. You're not in the military anymore. You're dealing with a different culture, different personnel. And you're here for no other reason than to see your humanity restored and to return to your fiancée. I understand and accept that. But I assure you, the work you're about to do is vital."

"Hunting monsters," I grunted. After what I'd experienced in the last two weeks, I shouldn't have sounded so skeptical.

"Indeed, it's a need that's not currently being met. At

least not with the kind of force and expertise a company like Centurion can bring to bear. Which is why we're anxious to begin."

"Good way to put it."

Barely fourteen hours earlier I had been in Florida, meeting with the mother of my former civil affairs officer, Calvin Parker. I had steered conversation far from the cause of his death—a dragon's lethal ice blast—instead sharing with her the privilege of having served with her son. The visit meant a lot to her, and I meant every word. Parker was one of the really good ones. I had wanted to stay longer, but the experimental drug worked for minutes, not hours. And with hair sprouting over my back, I'd had to leave the wedge of sweet potato pie Mrs. Parker had fetched for me half eaten.

A direct flight later, and I was outside of Las Vegas and in Centurion's employ, captain of the Legion Program.

"In any case, I was coming in to tell you to leave your stuff," Purdy said, waving toward the open locker at the foot of my bed. "Someone will deliver everything to your new barracks later this morning."

Back under control, I nodded and closed the door behind me.

"Shall we?" Purdy asked, clapping my arm. "Your new team's anxious to meet you."

As we walked down the corridor, I placed the helmet over my head and donned my gloves. The wolf in me didn't like the confinement, but only a limited number of Centurion employees knew about the Legion Program—or me.

We exited the building, passing between a pair of guards. Even with the helmet's polarized visor, I caught myself squinting beneath the bright desert sun. Purdy and I climbed into the backseat of the solar-powered SUV that Rusty had pulled to the front of the building. He sat rigidly in the driver's seat, shooting me wary glances in the rearview mirror.

As the vehicle started forward, I gazed at the enormous campus sweeping across my view out the window. It was Centurion's West Coast operating center: part military base, part research facility. Large dun-colored buildings with black windows rose from trees and heavily-watered lawns. Official-looking solar-powered vehicles navigated between them. Though the campus held a certain aesthetic appeal, the security here was said to be even more stringent than at Area 51—and more deadly. Guards had standing orders to shoot intruders on sight. More valuable than the military secrets were the company's intellectual properties.

Different culture, indeed.

Before long, we were passing through a checkpoint and leaving the main campus behind. To either side of the newly laid road, desert stretched to perimeter fencing. To my right stood distant mountains. We were heading toward a cluster of buildings about a half mile ahead.

"I think you'll like what we've set up out here," Purdy said.

He dabbed his mouth with a folded handkerchief and tucked it back into the front pocket of his suit jacket. Though he possessed the mannerisms of an old-time lawyer, the contract Purdy had presented to me was straightforward enough. In exchange for one year of my service, Centurion's bioengineering division would work on a cure for my condition. If by the end of the year Centurion's engineers had yet to develop a cure, their work would continue, with monthly progress reports. I would be under no further obligations but could remain on the campus free of charge—and would even draw a small salary.

"Don't forget," I said now, my voice low with warning. "I still have right of refusal."

It was an amendment I had added to the contract, basically stipulating that if an assignment placed civilians at risk or seemed generally sketchy, I had the authority to call it off.

"I wouldn't want it any other way," Purdy answered with a smile. "Legion is a segment of Centurion's business model now. A growing one, we hope. Its reputation will mean everything. Why do you think I was so anxious to appoint you its captain? You're a soldier's soldier, a man with a reputation for completing his mission, not to mention a spotless record."

"I thought it was my good looks," I muttered.

Purdy chuckled and slapped my knee. "You let *us* take care of that."

We passed through another security gate and entered the Legion compound. Unlike the main campus, the compound was plain—no grass, trees, or walkways. The various metal buildings, which were the same color as the surrounding sand, looked bereft of people. But as the SUV cruised around a circular drive, a young woman emerged from a large dome-shaped building in the compound's center.

"And here's the lovely Sarah McKinnon," Purdy said as Rusty pulled the SUV to a stop in front of her. "Legion's program manager and one of the sharpest associates in Centurion."

Sarah wore gray slacks, her arms folded tightly around a clipboard pressed to the front of a stiff white blouse. Her brunette hair was in a ponytail, and as she waited for us to emerge, she brushed her bangs from the top of a pair of thick glasses. I tried to read her face but it was as flat as a mannequin's.

"Sarah is going to show you around, get you oriented, and then it'll be time to meet your new team."

"When can I start training them?"

"Everything starts today, Captain Wolfe."

I nodded and opened the car door. When he made no move to get out on his side, I said, "You're not coming?"

"My part in the first act is done. You'll be working with Sarah now. Anything Legion requires from Centurion or vice versa will flow through her—with your input, of course. If you feel you need to talk to someone outside the program, you have my contact info."

"Is she above me?" That was something we needed to be clear on from the get-go. Nothing would complicate the program faster than confusion about who was in charge.

"You'll be reporting to her, yes, but I want the relationship to be collaborative rather than hierarchical. You each have your own sets of expertise."

I cocked my head toward the window. "And she understands this?"

"She does."

When I got out and closed the door, I heard the window power down behind me.

"We must put all preconceptions aside and be flexible," Purdy called. "I told Sarah the same thing."

He dispensed the advice in a way that suggested he was referring to something specific. But when I turned, the SUV was already pulling away, the window sliding back up over his smiling face.

3

The smoothness of Sarah's face contrasted with her rigid bearing, making her age hard to gauge, but she couldn't have been older than thirty. She moved her clipboard to her left hand as I approached, her expression unchanging. "Captain Wolfe," she said, thrusting her right hand forward, "I'm Sarah McKinnon, Program Manager at Legion."

"Good to meet you," I said.

Like her speech, her grip was cold and clipped, lasting for no more than a second. "You can dispense with the helmet. You won't need it here."

I hesitated, remembering Rusty's reaction, but then did as she said. Warm desert air buffeted my sweat-damp hair as I lifted the helmet off. Squinting, I pulled a pair of polarized sports goggles from a pocket and donned them, the elastic band cinching my head.

As the world turned tea colored, I watched for Sarah's reaction to my wolfish appearance. Nothing. No tension around her eyes, no alteration of her breathing, no change in her plain-soaped scent. She simply gave a small nod, as though checking a box, then turned and started into a fast walk toward the building she'd appeared from, ponytail lashing side to side.

I glanced around the dusty compound, which reminded me of some of the bases we'd operated out of in Central Asia. This one had more training elements. Beyond several outbuildings were a long shooting range and a battle-simulation area, complete with mock houses. I nodded, automatically setting up exercises in my mind. The facilities looked more than adequate. Off to the right, several vehicles were parked in a line beside an empty helipad, though none of them appeared military grade.

"I understand we're starting with a tour?" I said, catching up to Sarah.

"There'll be time for that later. The team's waiting in the conference room. We have a lot of material to cover."

Her clipboard was loaded with folders, and she braced it to her front as she reached for the heavy door. But before she could pull it open, I reached forward and pinned it closed.

"Since you and I are going to be working together, I'd like to know a bit about you before meeting the team." I also wanted to get a better gauge of her perception of me. Purdy had given me his assurance that we would be equals, but she wasn't treating me like one. "If you don't mind," I added.

Sarah gave the door another determined tug before turning toward me. I expected a face etched with frustration lines, but her expression remained eerily flat. Beyond her glasses, chestnut-colored eyes appraised me.

"What do you want to know?"

"Your background, for starters. I'm assuming you know mine."

"I'm a medical doctor. MD from Stanford. Internship at UC San Francisco. Trauma and pathology residencies at Johns Hopkins and Harvard, respectively. I enlisted the day after I finished my final residency. Completed my basic at Fort Sill and was deployed a month later.

Military? That was a surprise. "Why enlist instead of going into practice?"

"Because there was a need. I managed the main field hospital for the 915th in Baghlan Province, Waristan."

There was something familiar about that particular hospital. Then it hit me. "You were overrun by the enemy."

"We managed to hold them off until we were exfilled, but yes, they overran the base and hospital." She said it very matter-of-factly, no suggestion that the harrowing event had left a mark. Neither had she cited any accolades, though I knew for a fact the medical team had been officially commended for ensuring the patients made it out safely that night. Several on the team had even manned heavy machine guns. Something told me she'd been one of them.

"So why leave the military?"

"Centurion United made me an offer."

"Better compensation?" I asked, testing her.

If my pointed question perturbed her, she didn't show it. "No more than I could have made in private practice or research. There was a need for someone with my special qualifications."

That pat answer again: *a need*. "To kill monsters?"

For the first time Sarah's eyes shifted slightly as though she had glimpsed something in her mind and then immediately looked away. "To protect the innocent against beings we're only beginning to understand."

I nodded, feeling like I'd finally struck something human. Her words cast me back to the summer morning when I was twelve and Billy and I had gone to fish at Mission Creek. Three teenaged boys showed up. Following an exchange of words, the leader stabbed Billy in the throat. The boys then took turns sucking his blood. I'd sat there, frozen, only moving after they'd left, but I wasn't able to bring help in time. Billy died from blood loss, the boys disappeared, and the police declared them cultists. According to Purdy, though, the boys had been a breed of vampire.

"Was that all?" Sarah asked.

I returned from my memory of Billy's death to find her staring at me. Her credentials were impressive, and her military background assured me we'd be speaking the same language. I even liked her directness. But there was still the matter of our working relationship.

"Purdy says we'll be collaborating in a fifty-fifty partnership," I said.

Her gaze remained fixed on mine, her expression unchanging. It was the look of someone of such high intelligence that her eyes had become instruments for absorbing data rather than conveying emotion or empathy.

"If you have a different understanding," I went on, "it would be better for us to work that out now. I don't want any conflicts over who's in charge cropping up later. Especially mid-mission."

"That's my understanding as well," she replied with a touch of impatience but no apparent bitterness. A promising sign. She adjusted her glasses and seized the door handle again. "Like I said, the team's waiting, and we have a lot of material to cover."

"Right." I released the door so she could open it.

Pushing my goggles up to my brow, I followed her into the dome-shaped building. A short corridor led to a larger circular corridor. Closed doors indicated rooms around the building's periphery, but our destination appeared to be a room in the center.

Sarah crossed the circular corridor and opened another metal door. Maybe to address any lingering concerns I had about the command structure—or maybe just to make sure I wouldn't pin the door closed again—she stepped aside, allowing me to enter first. The round room was brightly lit and more modern-looking than what I'd seen so far. A screen comprising three large LCD panels, currently dark, curved around the wall, while a large table with built-in chairs occupied the room's center. Three of the chairs facing us were occupied.

My new team? I thought in concern as I looked around the table. I had been expecting at least ten members. I'd also been expecting bulky soldiers with square jaws and brush cuts. Not the motley crew looking back at me now.

"How's it going, brother?" Beyond a cloud of smoke, a young black man with braided hair grinned and raised his hand. Maybe it was the darkness of his face, but his teeth and the whites of his eyes looked preternaturally bright, much like the designer sweatshirt he wore. He flicked the ashes from the end of a thick cigar into a tray. "Them's some serious chompers."

I realized my lips had peeled back in reaction to the rank smell of the stogie, and I forced them back over my teeth. "I'm Captain Jason Wolfe," I said stiffly. "And you are?"

"I am Yoofi from the Congo," he responded in a strong accent. "Yoofi Adjaye." For no reason that I could tell, he broke into a fit of giggling. An open metal flask sat near his elbow, and my nose picked up a scent of sweet alcohol—brandy, maybe. What in the hell was this? Didn't Purdy say the training would begin today?

"Were you a member of the Congolese Armed Forces?" I asked.

"Armed Forces?" This made him laugh harder. "I never even held a gun."

"What's your expertise, then?" I felt my hackles rising. "What are you doing here?"

"I am a priest. I come because Centurion ask."

"A priest?"

"That's right, brother. I have a direct line to the big man." He took a sip from his flask followed by several puffs, giggling as a fresh cloud of smoke enveloped his head. "Or one of them, anyways."

I shot Sarah an exasperated look, but she was standing to one side as though giving me space to get to know my team. I turned to the woman two seats over from Yoofi. A head taller than the African, she wore a red turtleneck and sat erect, head poised on a lithe neck. Long black hair matched a pair of narrow eyes that stared at me with an intensity bordering on hostile.

"Are you a priest too?" I asked.

Yoofi giggled, but the woman's mouth remained turned down at the corners as she replied, "No."

"All right, why don't we start with your name and where you're from."

"Takara. Japan."

"Military experience?"

She sneered as though the question was beneath her.

"Takara is an expert in the art of ninjitsu," Sarah answered for her. "Her skills are highly sought after in her country."

Ninjitsu? I thought. *She's a ninja?* "And what brings you here?" I asked.

"That's my business."

My jaw clenched, but she had a point. I was trying to assess whether my teammates were just here for the money or whether they were motivated in ways that could help us cohere as a unit. But would I have disclosed my real reason for signing onto Centurion to someone I'd just met? My burning need to become human again, to begin my life with Daniela?

I gave a small nod and turned to the hulking man sitting at the far end of the table in black fatigues. *Finally,* I thought, *a soldier.* But before I could address him, every muscle in my body stiffened.

Though he was wearing a skull cap, I now recognized the lumpy contours of his head and his dead blue eyes. His name was Olaf. Along with a Centurion associate named Baine, he had been involved in the bombing of the Kabadi's warrior class in Wakhjir Province.

He was the reason I'd been transformed into the Blue Wolf.

4

I stared at Olaf, pulse pounding in my head. The large man looked back at me in complete disinterest. I wondered if he even knew who I was. But I remembered everything about the day we visited the Kabadi's compound: his disappearing to mark the infirmary with infrared lights, the deep shudder of the earth and the cries of the people as the bomb impacted minutes later, the old woman etching the mark of the wolf into my cheek...

A rumbling grew in my chest as I tugged off my gloves. In a jagged flash, I saw myself leaping onto the table and removing Olaf's head with my talons.

"Is something the matter?"

Sarah's voice and cold grip on my arm brought me back. I turned to find her looking up at me with clinical eyes.

"We need to talk," I growled. "Now."

I took a final look at Olaf, who had no idea how close he'd just come to a messy end, before turning and pushing open the door. Sarah joined me in the corridor. "What is it?" she asked.

I paced back and forth, breaths cycling harshly through my muzzle as I tried to talk my beast nature back down. The Blue Wolf was a manifestation of the essential qualities of the Great Wolf, protector of the Kabadi people. And the Blue Wolf had just come face to face with the man who'd aided in eliminating an entire generation of warriors—the Great Wolf's children, basically. It was only by the will of Jason Wolfe that Olaf was still breathing.

"Get rid of him," I said when I could talk.

"Who?"

"Olaf. I'm not asking. Get rid of him."

"But he's a member of the team."

"Not this team." I wheeled on her. "*Never* this team. There's no way in hell I'm working with him. He's a monster, a mass murderer." I wiped my muzzle with a sleeve. Purdy had told me Olaf was being handled internally, but placing him in Legion didn't handle shit. Why in the hell would he do that? And why wouldn't he tell me? Then I remembered his parting words:

Put all preconceptions aside and be flexible.

He'd been smiling when he said that. Was this some kind of a joke to him?

Sarah took a folder from her clipboard, opened it, and began leafing through the pages. "You're referring to the incident in Wakhjir Province," she said, stopping on a page and reading it over. "He was operating under orders."

"So were the Nazi SS," I snarled. "That doesn't change anything. It was his choice to carry them out."

"It wasn't his choice, actually."

"The hell are you talking about?"

"Olaf Kowalski is a nonliving specimen."

"That doesn't mean anything to me."

"Perhaps a brief explanation of his background will—"

"I don't want *any* explanation of his background. I want him the hell out of here!"

But Sarah was already consulting another page in the folder. "Olaf joined Centurion four years ago. While on assignment in Southeast Asia, he stepped on a landmine that dismembered him from the waist down and blew off his left hand and lower jaw. He and his parts were transferred to a Centurion hospital. In addition to surgery, the doctors began him on a tissue-regeneration regimen under development at our bioengineering division. Olaf's condition worsened that night, and he was ultimately pronounced dead. Twenty-four hours later, he recovered fully."

I stopped pacing. "The doctors resuscitated him?"

"No. He awoke in the hospital morgue."

"The morgue?"

"His tissue had fully regenerated. The only evidence of trauma was the network of scars where his parts had been reattached and his wounds stitched closed. He was hypothermic but breathing."

I thought back to the firefight with the Mujahideen when Olaf had been blasted by an RPG round. His left arm was nearly severed at the elbow, but he had fought on. By the next morning all of his wounds had healed, even his dangling arm. Whatever Centurion had given him must have endowed him with regenerative abilities not unlike my own.

"So he's a fast healer," I said. "But I'm still not clear on where the 'nonliving' part comes in. You said he was breathing."

"His vital signs were present, but critically low. An EEG

showed minimal brain activity. An intriguing case. He shouldn't have been alive, and yet he wasn't dead. Hence the term 'nonliving.'"

I snorted. "He was alive enough to direct a bomb strike."

"He was programmed to direct a bomb strike," Sarah corrected me, raising her voice to talk over my next interjection. "Olaf retained the instincts for survival and basic decision-making. He also retained his training as a soldier. Whatever had been drilled into him prior to his stepping on the landmine, he continued to possess. But a section of his parietal cortex was almost entirely devoid of processing power. The parietal cortex of course being the area involved in free will."

"Of course," I said dryly.

"During testing, Centurion found he responded to suggestions. Soon he was able to carry out complex commands—programming, the researchers called it. He was eventually sent to Sigma Base, where he accompanied basic missions. The researchers wanted to know whether he could continue to operate effectively in the field. That's where you encountered him. Baine Maddox asked for, and received, permission to take Olaf on an oversight mission with your Team 5. Centurion didn't know Baine's intentions."

"So what are you saying? He's a zombie?"

"A crude term," she said stiffly, "but if that's how you would prefer to think of him..."

My heart rate had settled back down. If Olaf lacked free will, then maybe he *wasn't* to blame. But there remained other issues—sending someone like him into conflict not the least of them. "Regardless," I said, shaking my head, "if all of this is true, if he was *programmed*, then he's a liability.

What's to stop someone from getting him to work against us?"

"That's been addressed," Sarah replied. "He's been encoded."

"Encoded? I'm going to need a little more to go on than that."

"Humans possess oxytocin, a hormone that enables us to bond with and trust others. The researchers found that by injecting Olaf with a high dose of oxytocin, he responded to instructions from a person whose image was shown to him on an order far greater than anyone else. He imprints on them, like a child to his mother. Right now he'll follow commands from the team and two researchers. That's all. In fact, he's already been instructed to ignore commands from anyone else."

"So if someone like Baine were to come along and tell him to mow us all down with a stream of .50 cal fire...?"

"Baine is dead," she answered.

"I'm aware of that. I'm just using him as an example."

"It wouldn't happen."

"Not even with a shot of oxytocin?"

"The research and compound we use are classified. Someone like Baine wouldn't know what to administer, or even to administer anything in the first place. And the effect wouldn't be instantaneous. We would have sufficient warning that something was amiss. Now if that's all..."

"What does *he* think about all of this?"

Sarah blinked at me from behind her glasses. "What do you mean?"

"Shouldn't Olaf have some sort of say in how he's being used?"

"How can he? He's nonliving."

"My point exactly."

"You're concerned with the ethical issues," she said in understanding. "When Olaf signed on to Centurion he agreed to donate his body to Centurion's research division in the event of death. He asked for this."

The argument was flimsy as hell, no doubt bolstered by a platoon of Centurion lawyers somewhere. "Are there others like him?" I asked. "Is Centurion building an army of zombies?"

In my negotiations with Purdy, I had made it clear that, save to develop a cure, my wolf condition was off-limits to researchers. I didn't want anyone attempting to replicate what I'd become.

Sarah shook her head. "Though other soldiers have responded to the tissue-regeneration regimen, none have done so as dramatically. And none have returned from the dead. The research on Olaf is ongoing. We're still trying to determine why his case is so unique."

"And in the meantime we use him as a soldier," I said bitterly.

"Yes. An injury-resistant soldier. Just think if we could say the same for all of our soldiers one day."

She sounded like she was reading from a script, but it made me think of Parker, my former civil affairs officer. I wondered if an injection of the tissue-regenerating drug would have spared him from the dragon's lethal ice blast.

"We'll see how it goes," I allowed at last. "But at the first sign something's off, I'm pulling him."

Sarah simply nodded. "Was there anything else?"

I gestured toward the closed door to the conference room. "Is this the entire team?"

"There's actually one more. He should be—"

At that moment, the front door to the building clattered open and a figure bisected the flare of sunlight. Combat boots clomped loudly down the corridor. As the door slammed closed, the man who'd come to get me that morning arrived in front of us red-cheeked and puffing, his mutton-chop sideburns shiny with sweat.

"Sorry I'm late," Rusty said as he adjusted his trucker hat. "Had to run Mr. Purdy back to the main campus."

"We haven't gotten started yet," Sarah replied. "Have a seat inside. We'll be there shortly."

Rusty nodded, then glanced over at me. "Captain," he said formally, before pulling the conference room door open and stepping inside.

"He's on the team?"

Sarah nodded.

"Keeps getting better," I muttered.

"Is there a problem?"

"Yeah, there is. When Purdy made his pitch, he said I'd be heading a division of special operatives. I assumed he meant a dozen or so trained soldiers—what I'm used to. But there's only six of us, including you. And we seem a little short on pros. I mean, there's a guy in there who calls himself a priest, smoking like a chimney and sucking down booze."

"I'll be going over everything shortly. As for Yoofi's habits..." She patted the stack of files. "That information is in his profile. You can review all of them following the meeting."

"Why the tease? If he's an alcoholic, just tell me."

"Like I said, you can go over their profiles following the meeting."

"I don't like surprises."

"Me neither, and we're already behind schedule. Why don't we rejoin the team." Her patience apparently spent, she turned and opened the door. I peered past her at my new team.

A priest, a ninja, a zombie, and a guy who looks like he should be working crew on the carny circuit, I thought as I followed Sarah back inside. It sounded like the setup to an awful joke.

And let's not forget the werewolf.

5

"Welcome to day one," Sarah said as I took a seat in the large gap between Rusty and Olaf.

With that bit of preamble, she pulled a small remote control from her pocket and pressed a button. LEGION appeared at the top of the large screen, spaced to cross the seams between the LCD panels, and a series of bullet points dropped into place underneath. A giggle emerged from Yoofi's cloud of smoke.

"There are beings on earth that, for the majority of people, exist only in fiction. The fact is, most of these beings have coexisted with humans since the earliest civilizations, carving out niches for themselves as societies spread and became more complex. In many cases the beings pass for humans; in others, they meld with them. Some, however, prey on them."

In my mind's eye, I saw the three teenaged boys—vampires—draining Billy's blood.

"Centurion classifies those cases as Prodigium IS or Prod IS. Those are the cases we'll be called to put down."

"Hell yeah," Rusty drawled.

Great, a trigger-happy poser, I thought. *Just what we need to round out this "team."*

The screen changed to a map of the world that looked like something from the Centers for Disease Control. The majority of the map was dark, but yellow, orange, and red crosses clustered here and there, and they looked like outbreaks. Most of the clusters appeared to coincide with major cities. The rest were isolated, scattered around with no apparent rhyme or reason.

"For the past decade, Centurion's computers have been scraping and analyzing info on suspected Prod 1 cases, using crime databases and news reports. The crosses represent the frequency of Prod 1 homicides, with the color indicating the degree of certainty that they were, in fact, committed by Prod 1s. Yellow being at the lower end of that spectrum and red in the high-certainty range." A laser dot appeared from Sarah's remote, and she moved it around the map. "Prod 1s appear to operate primarily in dense population centers, but they can turn up anywhere."

As her laser pointer touched some of the isolated crosses, I noticed a few in east Texas, where I'd grown up. One of them might even have represented the vampire attack on Billy.

"Prod 1s are poorly understood by officials, when they're even acknowledged at all. Those homicides often end up as cold cases. There are exceptions, however. Last summer, New York City implemented a program to eradicate Prod 1s that had become embedded in their city."

She clicked the remote and the map changed to shaky footage of a street scene. Screams sounded from off camera as a huge fiery creature, blood spouting from a severed wrist, stalked toward a man on the ground.

"Look at that!" Yoofi exclaimed.

A second man, whom I immediately recognized as Prof Croft, stepped up and swung his sword into the creature's neck. The blade seemed to lodge there. Following a struggle that involved the creature's severed hand seizing Croft's calf, the wizard shouted one of his magic words and nearly blew the creature's head from its shoulders. He then covered the man on the ground as a hail of automatic fire from off camera completed the decapitation of the flaming hulk and dropped its body to the street.

As the footage ended, Yoofi parked his cigar in the corner of his mouth to applaud. "Way to go, brother!"

"That's what I'm talking about," Rusty put in, slapping Yoofi a high five.

Croft's efforts were impressive—damned impressive. It was a shame I'd had to reject his offer of teaming up. But ten years to a cure was simply too long, and New York looked to be in good hands.

"The Prod seen here is known as a ghoul," Sarah said. "You'll be learning about all classes of Prods in the coming weeks. As you see, they can be killed. The problem is cost. New York's program required more than one hundred additional officers and personnel, a special consultant, and equipment. Once property damage was factored in, the total ended up in the hundreds of millions of dollars. That's not sustainable. Indeed, at the start of his second term, the mayor quietly shuttered the program. Legion will offer better results at lower costs."

Though Purdy had tried to sell Legion to me as a humanitarian program, it was a mercenary outfit through and through. With the data Centurion had gathered, their reps were meeting with officials in high-concentration areas to discuss the problem and, of course, the solutions Legion could offer.

We would be battling beings who hurt humans, sure—but the idea of *only* providing those services to those who could afford them bothered me. Purdy had mentioned taking on pro bono cases once the program got its legs, but I didn't see that happening in the first year.

"The other problem is coordination," Sarah continued. "No government or international body has done what Centurion is doing: compiling data with the goal of developing teams and best practices to confront the threats wherever and whenever they appear."

"But aren't non-governmental actors tackling the threat?" I asked, thinking about Prof Croft and his magical Order.

"Such groups exist," Sarah replied. "But they tend to be regional and/or esoteric. And there's little evidence to suggest they've been effective on a global scale. Indeed, we've witnessed a rise of new cases in the last several months."

I remembered what Croft had said about fresh rips around our world making it more susceptible to intrusion from other planes, but that wasn't what I'd been getting at. "No, what I'm asking is whether there will be any efforts to coordinate with them. At the very least we're going to want to avoid friendly fire incidents."

"At this stage, our operations are strictly confidential." She cleared her throat and directed her glowing glasses back toward the screens. "Legion is a pilot program, hence its small size and the recruitment of operatives with unique skills. That would be you five." She pressed the button again, and a column of our headshots appeared on the screens. The laser point squiggled over my wolf face.

"Captain Jason Wolfe is a former special operations soldier and officer with a special knowledge of military weapons and equipment. His recent transformation has endowed him with enhanced strength, speed, and regenerative abilities, as well as wolf-like senses. He and I will be running Legion's day-to-day operations, but he will also be your field commander."

I picked up a scoffing sound from Takara. I turned to find her lips set in a scowl. She wasn't looking at me, but I could feel the challenge radiating from her. My nostrils instinctively flared, pulling in her aroma. It was strong, but not unpleasant, like crushed tea leaves. Beneath that scent was a sharper one that I couldn't put my finger on. I looked away, forcing my shoulders to relax.

On the screen, the laser pointer fell to the next image, which happened to be hers. "A former disciple of the Phoenix Temple in Iga Province, Japan, Takara is an expert in ninjitsu. She excels in stealth, sniper operations, demolitions, and close combat, particularly with blades." Sarah's delivery was matter-of-fact. "Takara can also fly short distances."

Rusty spun toward her. "You can fly?"

Takara ignored him and remained staring straight ahead.

"She will assist in operational planning," Sarah continued. "And though this has yet to be verified, she is said to—"

"Peasant legends," Takara cut in. "Not important."

Though Takara had barely raised her voice, a sudden

tension filled the room. I caught my gaze switching between the two women, anxious to hear the information Takara hadn't wanted shared. But Sarah only nodded and moved the pointer down.

Guess I'll have to wait to read her profile.

"Yoofi Adjaye is a priest of the Gomba tribe in the western Congo. He has a relationship with an entity called Dabu, a god of tricks and the dead. By this relationship Yoofi is able to channel energies that can be used for a variety of operational purposes, including deception."

Yoofi broke into loud laughter, looking around as though we were all in on the joke. When no one joined him, he took a swig from his flask and chuckled some more. I swore under my breath. If I couldn't train that happy shit out of him, it was going to be a long year.

The pointer dropped to Rusty's headshot. "Next up is Russell Hackett, from Maysville, Kentucky. He's been with Centurion for the last six months, working in the security division. Largely self taught, he's an expert in weapons, electronics, and vehicles."

Rusty leaned back and crossed his arms. "Won the Mason County demolition derby four years straight." His self-satisfied smile soured as he added, "Wouldn't let me compete in a fifth, though. Said I was juicing with nitro, but without a lick of proof. Damned politics."

"He also patented a secure wireless motion-detection system that Centurion purchased last year," Sarah continued. "That's how we first learned about him. A medical condition kept him out of the military ... and most other forms of steady employment, for that matter."

"Attention deficit disorder," Rusty announced. "Hell, I just get bored easy."

"He'll be contributing to Legion in a non-combat capacity," she finished.

Thank God, I thought.

"And then there is Olaf Kowalski." I caught Sarah glancing over at me. "Originally from Poland, he is a Centurion soldier with a specialization in light infantry weapons and tactics. He is also a beneficiary of Centurion's tissue-regeneration protocol. He can heal from light wounds instantaneously and more extensive wounds, including bone and organ damage, within twenty-four hours."

Yoofi's eyes glittered as he leaned forward. "Now this I would like to see."

Olaf looked at Sarah, who nodded as if to say that he could go ahead. From beneath the table, a large combat knife appeared in his grip. Turning his right arm over, palm up, he drew a line from his elbow to his wrist. Thick blood welled from the wound and instantly coagulated. Olaf used the edge of the blade to scrape the blood neatly away. Beneath was a thin scab that curled up at both ends and fell to the table. The remaining scar smoothed until it became indistinguishable from his pale skin.

"Pretty cool," Rusty said.

"And you can do this too?" Yoofi asked me.

"Yeah, but you're gonna have to take my word for it."

Yoofi laughed and fell back into his smoke. Even Rusty smirked. But my gaze lingered on Olaf. I was still grappling with the idea he wasn't at fault in the bombing. Hell, I was still grappling with the whole "nonliving" thing.

He replaced his knife in a sheath and raised his eyes to mine. I'd mistaken his bland look earlier for indifference, but now I saw that there was simply nothing there.

"And everyone here has met me," Sarah said, drawing

my gaze back to the screens. "Sarah McKinnon. In addition to running day-to-day operations, I'll be joining you in mission operations as chief investigator and medic. I'll also be conducting research in the field."

As odd-ball as we were, I was starting to see how each member might fit into a traditional Special Ops role. Sarah would act in intelligence and medical capacities; Rusty could handle communications and weapons, with Olaf possibly acting as a junior weapons sergeant; Takara could be used as a sniper and for demolitions; and Yoofi ... I didn't know quite where he fit in yet. Of course all of this was just a mental exercise until I could assess everyone's skills myself.

"The Legion Program is highly classified. You've already signed confidentiality agreements, but before we do anything, it's crucial we go through Centurion's updated policies and procedures for the program." When Sarah clicked the remote, an exhausting display of numbered headings, subheadings, and sub-subheadings appeared on the screen; the paragraphs beneath were thick with legalese. My muscles went jumpy at the idea that this could last the rest of the day.

I took that as my cue and stood. "Can I address the team?"

I could tell by Sarah's rapid blinking that I was upsetting her carefully laid out schedule, but she yielded the front of the room. "Of course," she said.

I took her place and looked over my team members. "Mr. Purdy estimates we have one month before our first assignment. That means I have thirty days to mold us into a functioning unit. Given our varied backgrounds, that's not much time at all. And no offense to Centurion's legal eagles, but this isn't going to help us get there." I gestured toward the screen. "Maybe we can look them over in our own time?" I waited for Sarah's reluctant nod before continuing. "The first thing I need to do is assess your skills, and the best way to do that will be with an exercise. Do we have nonlethal weapons in the armory?"

"A mess of 'em," Rusty said. "You don't see what you want, tell me and I'll get it."

"Good." I consulted my watch. "It's coming on 0900. I want everyone to meet in the armory at 1000 sharp. We're going to play a little game of capture the flag. No holds barred."

Yoofi giggled at that last part. This time I grinned back at him.

Let's see what this team of misfits can do.

6

From my vantage on top of the one-story cement building, I scanned the mock town. It wasn't exactly like being back in Waristan, but it was close. I may have been looking through an ACOG sight, but it was mounted on an M4-styled paintball gun. Olaf was on street level, guarding the one door to our building. He'd chosen a paintball AK-47, which looked right at home in his meaty grip.

I had split us into two teams at the armory—me and Olaf against Sarah, Takara, and Yoofi—and it was game on.

I had already seen Olaf in action in Waristan against the Mujahideen. He had been steady and effective, despite being, for all intents and purposes, a zombie that could take orders. I was more interested in the others right now, particularly Takara and Yoofi. Aside from the brief introductions and what I'd read in their profiles, I knew nothing about their tactical knowledge, combat styles, or ability to work in a unit. Before the exercise was over, I would have a better gauge on all three.

They were playing offense, Olaf and I defense. I'd given them the single objective of grabbing our flag, which was hanging above a wooden table on the first floor of our building.

Now I angled my nose up so it was catching the current coming over the rooftop's retaining wall. The distinct smells of our opponents threaded through those of the compound and the desert around us. We had chosen our respective arsenals in secret—we wouldn't always know what the enemy would be packing. I only mandated that everyone wear Kevlar shirts and vests with ballistic plates for chest and back protection. Though we were using nonlethal weapons, I wanted the team to grow accustomed to the discomfort and extra weight.

Takara had scoffed at the idea—apparently ninjas didn't wear body armor—but I made it clear that it wasn't an option. I was picking up an elitist vibe from her that verged on hostile. Especially toward me. The exercise would be a good opportunity to start reining that in.

"No movement yet," I whispered into my earpiece. "But I can smell them. They're clustered at the north end of the compound." Their team had already had time to strategize, so I wondered what they were doing now.

"Roger that," Olaf answered in his heavy accent.

"Hey, you guys don't mind if I listen in," came Rusty's voice. *"It'll help me work out any kinks in the commo system."* He was in his office attached to the armory.

"Sure," I grunted. "If you keep your mouth shut."

"Roger that, boss."

"Hold your position," I told Olaf.

"Hold position," he echoed.

So far the "nonliving specimen" had operated as Sarah

said he would, carrying out my commands like an automaton. She assured me that when pressure came, Olaf would default to his training and experience; he wouldn't need constant input. Though he seemed to have proven as much in Waristan, I was still anxious to see him tested. What good would he be to us if he shut down in battle?

My nostrils flared, picking up threads of cigar smoke on the wind. A moment later, alcohol joined the rank odor in a dizzying fusion. Using the retaining wall for cover, I peeked toward the smells.

"Be on alert," I said to Olaf. "Yoofi's doing something."

"On alert," he echoed.

A cursory study of Yoofi's profile had explained his constant smoking and drinking. That wasn't for his own consumption—at least not primarily. The tobacco smoke and brandy were offerings to Dabu. They passed straight through Yoofi to the god to whom he was connected. In exchange, he could channel the god's powers. A god who dealt in death and deception.

Deception...

I spun around to find Sarah taking aim at me from a nearby rooftop. I hunkered down as paintballs smacked into the retaining wall and whizzed overhead. "Contact to your nine o'clock," I radioed Olaf. But the rapid chuffing of carbon dioxide from below told me he had heard the shots and was already engaging Sarah.

In a flash, I understood the strategy. Yoofi had employed deceptive magic to get me to believe they were all clustered at one end of the compound while Sarah had been climbing into position to engage me. She didn't need to take me out. That would have been a bonus. She only needed to pin me and draw Olaf's fire so the sniper could take her shot. I peered from behind cover in search of Takara, but it was too late. A distant shot sounded from my two o'clock.

"I'm hit," Olaf said.

"Where?"

"Back of the neck."

Crap. I had declared that shots to a tactical plate or helmet would mean nothing, two shots to an extremity would result in the loss of that extremity, and a shot to the exposed head or neck would spell instant death. Even though Olaf was technically undead, it would have taken him a full day to recover from an actual neck shot from a high-caliber rifle.

"All right, lay there," I told him. "You're out."

"I'm out," he said.

I peered back toward Sarah. Her role in the first exchange completed, she was retreating in a hunker. Her helmeted head bobbed up and down over the retaining wall. We'd have to work on that. And she was about to commit another oversight, this one to my advantage. I fired a suppressive burst in the direction of the sniper fire and then took quick aim at a gap in the retaining wall. When Sarah was even with it, I squeezed twice. She grunted in surprise as blue paint exploded against the side of her neck.

"And then there were three," Rusty said. *"Takara and Yoofi against the Big Bad Wolf."* He was no doubt watching the feeds from the surveillance cameras recording the exercise.

"Thought I told you to shut it," I said.

I ducked, but not before something pegged my helmet in a mist of red paint. A harmless shot, but it didn't matter. If Takara could keep me down, Yoofi had only to step over

Olaf's body to seize the flag and win the exercise. I was determined not to let that happen for several reasons. Mainly, I didn't want Takara believing she had nothing to learn.

A quick peek over the wall showed me a paintball incoming. It grazed the top of my helmet as I ducked again. The shot had come from the upper-story window of a building across the compound. Between a set of heavy drapes, I had glimpsed a rifle and Takara's head poised behind it. She wasn't wearing a helmet, and if I had to guess, she'd foregone body armor too.

Figured.

But that didn't change the fact she was a crack shot. I perched the M4's barrel on the retaining wall and fired from memory. The shots didn't need to strike her; they just needed to come close enough for her to take cover.

Still firing, I reached into a pouch and pulled out a stun grenade. Arming it with my teeth, I stood and winged a line drive. The grenade punched through the curtains and then detonated with a lightening flash and ear-splitting crack.

My hearing picked up Rusty's muted "*Whoa!*" in my earpiece.

I popped up and down to ensure Takara wasn't back in firing position, then scanned the streets around my building. The cigar smoke had thickened into misty currents, but there were no other signs of Yoofi.

I hurdled the wall and landed near where Olaf had removed himself from the exercise, beyond Takara's line of fire. He lay on his back, as straight and stiff as someone in a coffin, but he retained his grip on his weapon. Per the rules, I couldn't ask whether he had seen Yoofi, but a quick peek inside the building showed me our orange flag was still intact.

With my back to the outer wall, I sniffed the air before remembering I couldn't trust my senses. All I could detect were cigar smoke and brandy, their smells more concentrated now—and dank, as though rising from a subterranean cavern. For the first time, I realized Yoofi wasn't actively smoking and drinking. I was picking up a backdraft from the god's realm, a phenomenon that must have accompanied the use of his magic.

A giggle floated from down the street. I looked to ensure Takara wasn't coming from my other side before turning toward the sound. I threw myself flat as a jet of coiling black energy stormed toward me.

Yoofi was a block away, the blade end of his aimed staff smoking from the blast that had ripped overhead. Though he'd missed, I could feel the energy's cold, lingering effect, like a corpse had just wriggled its fingers through my intestines. Yoofi was wearing a brown hooded jacket over his Kevlar shirt, its hem falling behind his knees. The sides of the jacket billowed with each step of his bright white Adidas shoes. He didn't appear to be carrying any weapons besides his staff.

I took aim. I noticed his figure had turned hazy around the edges, but squeezed off two shots anyway. I wasn't surprised when the paint balls passed through him. He ducked and ran toward a side street. *Either he's made himself insubstantial,* I thought, keeping my barrel trained on him until he was safely behind a building. *Or he's not actually where I think he is.*

"This is a fun game!" he called from his cover.

As more cigar smoke gusted past, I noticed my thoughts

blurring slightly as though I'd been hitting Yoofi's flask. He wasn't altering reality; he was altering the *perception* of reality. My main senses were telling me he was around the corner—which meant he wasn't.

What's he trying to get me to do?

I remembered Sarah's attack from the rooftop and looked over my shoulder to see if they were running a similar play. No one behind me. Which meant they wanted to draw me into the next intersection. Once there, I would either be hit by crossfire, or someone would capitalize on my shifted position and make a dash for the flag. Possibly both. The safest move would be to retreat to the building and stand guard inside, but we were down to a three-piece chess match. Their planning had been good so far, and I wanted to see how they would close the match—or attempt to.

I edged along the side of the building, vigilant in all directions, until I reached the intersection. I peered down both streets. No one there. No paintballs incoming. Giggles floated from the next block.

He's trying to draw me farther out, which means they're planning a move from behind.

I took several fast steps forward, as though pursuing the sound, then spun.

Yoofi was almost to the door of the building when I sighted him and squeezed off four shots. This time I wasn't dealing with an apparition. One ball exploded against his chest plate, two hit his shoulder, and the fourth cracked him in the jaw. His smile disappeared as he rubbed his paint-spattered mouth.

"That hurt, man!" he said.

I pointed to the ground beside Olaf to indicate he was out. "No more mojo," I reminded him.

"Nice," came Rusty's voice.

Now it was just me and the ninja. Something told me that was what she wanted. Why else would she have failed to coordinate with Yoofi just now?

As Yoofi lowered himself to the ground, the smoke dissipated along with his deceptive magic. I loaded a fresh mag of paint balls and retreated back toward the target building.

I had spent most of the time before the exercise going over Takara's profile. There were large gaps, including missing dates. She had been born into the country's last samurai family, the Sakumas, in Hiroshima, but for reasons unstated, left them at a young age to join a secretive clan devoted to the practice of ninjitsu. In addition to physical training, she was schooled in survival, stealth, and scouting techniques, as well as how to use poisons and explosives. Takara was formally inducted into the clan when, at fourteen, she succeeded in her first solo mission—lighting a distraction fire to enter the fortress of a wealthy patriarch, whom she then poisoned with strychnine. Had she failed, the clan would have sacrificed her.

She'd gone on to master techniques in hand-to-hand combat, sword play, and sniping. With each successful mission, more esoteric levels of training were opened up to her until she could concentrate considerable energy into her punches and kicks and fly short distances.

Missing from the file was whatever she hadn't wanted Sarah to share during our meeting that morning. Neither did it reveal why she had left Japan to join the Legion Program. Regardless, I had enough info to know that

Takara was one bad babe. The challenge was going to be harnessing her skills.

I was almost to the door of my building when I picked up a fluttering sound overhead. I lifted my face instinctively, exposing my chin to a smashing kick that knocked me back several feet. By the time I set my legs and took aim, a wooden katana was spearing toward me. It struck my carbine with enough force to shear off the barrel and jar the stock end from my grip. The gun clattered to the street in two pieces, with paint balls rolling off in every direction.

Takara descended from her flight and stood between me and the door to the building. Her long black hair lashed quietly around her billowy black attire. As I'd guessed, she wasn't wearing body armor. One hand wielded the katana while the other braced her cocked hip. She had only to beat me to the flag to win, but she made no move toward the building.

"Do you concede?" she asked.

She didn't just want to win. She wanted to make me quit.

When I grunted out a laugh, I tasted blood. "Not a chance."

Because the exercise forbade sharp objects, including talons and teeth, I had declared that pinning an opponent on his or her back for three seconds would constitute a kill. I didn't have Takara's hand-to-hand skills, but I possessed a four-hundred-pound body packed with superhuman strength.

I only had to reach her.

I lunged with animal quickness, but before I could close a hand around her, she drew something from a pocket and blew on it. A cloud of peppery heat burned up my nose and blinded me. My momentum carried me into the sharp thrust of her katana, the blunt tip hammering my gut. Air blew from my lungs in a nauseating grunt. I turned and fell against the wall of the building, tears streaming down my face from the powder.

"No effing way," Rusty muttered in amazement.

I could feel the rest of the team watching me. They had to assume Takara had won, but as long I stood and the flag remained in place, the exercise wasn't over. Through my watery vision, I saw her wrestling Olaf's gun from his grip. Theoretically dead, he shouldn't have been gripping the weapon in the first place. Then again, there were always going to be things our enemies *shouldn't* do.

Springing forward, I drove a foot into Takara's side.

The blow caught her by surprise but also had the unintended effect of wrenching the gun from Olaf's grip. Takara rolled several times before coming to an acrobatic stop on one knee, the gun barrel pivoting toward my face. But I had already drawn my sidearm and squeezed twice.

A pair of thuds sounded.

"Booya!" Rusty shouted over the commo system.

Takara grimaced and looked down at the splashes of blue paint over her chest.

"That's game," I said, reholstering the pistol. "All right, everyone, let's huddle up."

Olaf and Yoofi pushed themselves to their feet, and Sarah descended from the rooftop two buildings away. But Takara only narrowed her eyes at me. I nodded at her to say, *You too.*

But instead of coming, she broke Olaf's gun over her knee and strode away.

7

Takara didn't return following the morning's exercise, instead confining herself to her room. Sarah volunteered to talk to her, but I told her to let it go. I was willing to give Takara the day to process that her old way of operating wasn't going to fly in Legion. But that was all. If she failed to show the following morning, then we'd have a major problem.

I spent the remainder of the day taking the team through the basics of shooting, movement, and communication, and then ended with some physical training. Judging by the weary silence in the chow hall that evening, the others had gotten a good workout. Takara going AWOL notwithstanding, I felt pretty good about our first day. Olaf had performed well, and Sarah and Rusty capably. Yoofi was a babe in the woods, but that was to be expected. Though he giggled through his many mistakes, he listened to my instructions, which was all I could ask.

After dinner, I found him in front of our barracks. A line of wooden chairs had been set out, and he was sitting in the centermost one. His engraved flask dangled from one hand, and he had the end of a cigar pinched in the other. He stared off with a slight smile, eyelids sagging in a way that told me he wasn't seeing the indigo sky or distant mountain range, but something a lot farther away.

"Mind if I join you?" I asked.

Yoofi's eyes sharpened, and his smile spread over his face as he turned toward me. "Of course, Mr. Wolfe."

"You can call me Jason."

"Yes, but I prefer to say 'Mr. Wolfe,' if that is all right. It is how we show respect."

If we'd been in the military, I would have suggested *Captain Wolfe*, but we weren't, so I shrugged and took the chair beside him, upwind from his smoke. "How did you feel out there today?"

His smile broadened. "Very good, brother. Very good."

I didn't doubt Yoofi was naturally cheerful, but I was beginning to suspect the smile and laughter were also defense mechanisms. "The rest of us have had combat training, so I don't want you to get down on yourself. With enough practice and repetition, it will become second nature."

"Thank you for your patience." He took a sip from his flask. "I will keep trying."

"I know you will. Hey, the black energy you shot at me during the exercise this morning. What was that exactly?" I had an idea from his profile, but I wanted him to explain his magic to me.

"Ah, yes. The *Kembo*."

"The *Kembo*? Is that what you call it?"

He giggled. "Yes, it is a force from the underworld of Dabu. Can hurt body, but also spirit. Do not worry, Mr.

Wolfe. The blast I shoot at you this morning"—he shook his head—"not very strong."

I remembered the nausea I'd felt as the black coils had ripped through the air above me. It would make a good ranged attack. "Can the *Kembo* kill?"

"With enough power, yes, I believe it can kill."

"So you've never tested it?"

"No, Mr. Wolfe. Not in that way."

"Not even on an animal?"

"Now why would I want to hurt an animal?" he asked. "What the animal ever do to Yoofi?"

Maybe it was his shocked expression or the perfect innocence of his response, but I began to laugh. That got him laughing too. There was a pureness to the sound that, despite my earlier irritation, was hard not to appreciate. I let the laughter wind down, then turned serious again.

"I respect that, Yoofi. I do. But you understand the purpose of Legion, right? We're going to be hunting dangerous creatures. Creatures that hurt people. And I need to know that you won't hesitate to kill them. Because hesitation on your part—on *any* of our parts—could mean life or death for the rest of the team."

"Oh, yes, I understand. I understand very well. In my village, people come to me from all over when sick or want to talk to ancestors. But sometimes they come when a *nkadi* has ahold of their spirit." When he saw my perplexed look, he said, "A *nkadi* is a demon. Yoofi hate demon, especially demon that hurt people. I use magic to pull demon out and make sure he never come back."

"But aren't you killing the demon then?"

"No, I only throw him down to Dabu." A shadow passed over his face. "Dabu takes care of him there." He took a large swallow from his flask, then puffed fervently for a full minute as if to appease the god whose name he'd just invoked. I grimaced as rank smoke billowed around us.

A Centurion agent had learned about Yoofi while overseeing a contract for a refugee camp near the Congolese border. Yoofi's magic in that region was storied, and refugees were insisting on undertaking dangerous journeys on foot to see him. An evaluation team from Centurion showed up to check him out. Yoofi's abilities impressed them sufficiently that they made him an offer to join Legion. He accepted, fulfilling his dream of coming to the United States, where his favorite hip-hop artist lived, some guy I'd never heard of named Sugar Nice.

But there was no information in his profile on how he had become a vessel for Dabu's magic in the first place. I posed the question to him now.

"In my village, there is a long tradition of worshipping Dabu," he said. "My father and mother were priest and priestess to Dabu. I was their only child, but always in trouble. For tricks on other children, tricks on adults. And I never stopped laughing, even when teachers beat me with the stick. For this, they say Yoofi have a touch of Dabu. But I didn't want to become a priest like my parents. Then one day, Dabu started talking to me. He let me use his magic, and he never took it back."

"So you can heal, create illusions, and cast the *Kembo*. Anything else?"

"With Dabu's blessing, can protect spaces. Sometimes can divine things, but hard to trust Dabu. Always playing tricks."

"Did he give you that?" I nodded at the staff he'd set beside his chair.

Yoofi giggled, then said quickly, "No, no, I found it. Want to see what I can do with blade?"

He took a final series of puffs before setting his cigar and flask down and lifting the staff. The sharp blade protruding from one end had been chiseled from black rock, obsidian maybe. Yoofi held the staff toward one of the wooden chairs, eyes narrowing over his clenching cheeks. He wasn't smiling anymore, and for the first time I perceived something dangerous in his face.

A high-frequency quavering sounded from his blade. I winced and covered my ears. Yoofi lunged forward and swung the staff down. The stone blade cut through the chair like it was paper, and the two halves collapsed to the ground. Yoofi stood back and admired his work. The sound of the blade deepened before falling silent again. As I uncovered my ears, Yoofi's face relaxed around a giggle.

"You like?" he asked.

"Not bad. Not bad at all. Should come in handy when we start practicing decapitations." I stood and clapped his shoulder. "Listen, I have a few things to do before I turn in for the night. Don't stay up too late. Training starts again at 0700, and we've got a lot to cover."

"I'll be there, Mr. Wolfe. Like Sugar Nice say, 'Be ready or be deady, bitches."

"That's ... sound advice."

I entered the building and made my way down the main corridor. What Legion called our barracks was more like a small apartment complex with private suites. I passed Rusty's room en route to mine. His TV was cranked to full volume—a professional wrestling match from the sounds of it. I pounded on the door. Something fell over and broke as he stumbled his way to answer it.

Definitely a good thing he's not involved in combat.

He opened the door a crack and peered up at me. Bits of dried tomato sauce from the lasagna we'd had for dinner ringed his bristly mouth.

"Your volume's turned up pretty high, and I've got some work to do." I pointed to my wolf ears. "Sensitive hearing."

"Oh, shit. Yeah, yeah, sure." He hurried across a living room already littered with clothes and dishware, hopped over the lamp he'd knocked down, and searched for his remote for a full minute before muting the sound.

"Sorry about that," he said, returning to the cracked-open door. Rusty had seemed to relax around me during the day's training, but now that it was just the two of us, I was picking up some discomfort again.

"You did good today," I told him.

"Yeah?" The door opened a little wider.

Part of being a captain was building camaraderie in the unit, and that started at the top. But I wasn't blowing smoke. He had performed well in the day's exercises—his love of guns and his attendance at several survival-type schools no doubt assets. And when Sarah's earpiece had malfunctioned mid-exercise, he had it running again within a minute. We would need that kind of technical expertise in the field.

"You did," I assured him. "And listen, I'm sorry about our little run-in this morning when you came to get me. I was in a bad mood, and I took it out on you. I shouldn't have done that."

Rusty made a *pssh* sound and waved a hand. "Naw, that was my bad. I've never worked in any kind of real military outfit before, and as the missus likes to tell me, the tube between my brain and mouth don't got much of a filter. What I'm thinking just sort of drops out."

"Having a werewolf glaring down on you probably didn't help."

Rusty laughed. "You're not kidding. I came this close to dropping something else. You are one intimidating dude."

"The more you see me, the more you'll get used to it."

He gave me a wary look. "I don't know, boss..."

"You said you have a family?"

"Yeah, back in Kentucky. A big ol' lady and four kids."

"Must be hard on them. You being on the other side of the country."

"For the kids, maybe. The missus?" His lower lip jutted out as he shook his head. "That's been broken for awhile now. Only reason we haven't split is on 'count of the kids. Youngest is six." His face softened. "Little rascal named Hodge. The missus swears she's walking the day Hodge turns eighteen, so we've still got a dozen years to go." He shook his head. "Long ol' time. Especially with the bedroom being a dry county, if you know what I mean."

"Long time to work things out too."

"Maybe," he allowed. "How 'bout you, boss. Got a squeeze box back home?"

"Yeah, a fiancée." My heart pitched a little as I said it. "Daniela."

"Does she know you're..."

"A wolf?" I finished for him. I felt myself bracing against the question, but building camaraderie meant being upfront about certain things. "No. Not yet, anyway. This all just happened."

"Well, you know what they say."

"What's that?"

Rusty looked at me blankly for a second, then shook his head. “Shit, I was hoping there was a saying that sort of went without saying, you know?” His eyes screwed up. “Would something about love being blind work?”

“It could.” But that wasn’t what I worried about with Daniela. She had a saint’s soul; she would love me no matter what I looked like. My concern was for her safety. The Blue Wolf had lost control before—that morning’s encounter with Rusty being the most recent example. It could happen again. Until Centurion restored my humanity, I needed to stay far away from her.

I wasn’t ready to share any of that with him, though. There was camaraderie and then there was fraternization. I wasn’t going to cross that line with Rusty, or with anyone in Legion.

“Hey, do you wanna come in and watch some wrestling?” He opened the door all the way.

“No, thanks. I have my own evening rituals. Don’t stay up too late.”

“Just gonna catch the main event, then I’m turning in. ‘Shrimp Boy’ versus ‘The Anvil.’” Excitement colored his dull brown eyes. “Grudge match, so you know it’s gonna be sweet.”

I grinned before turning away. Rusty was all right.

As I passed Takara’s suite, that grin faded. My hearing picked up a series of deep, meditative breaths. A strange heat pulsed from the door. I raised a knuckle to knock, but then lowered it again. Both my wolf and captain instincts were telling me to leave it until tomorrow.

Just as long as she’s not plotting to kill me in my sleep, I thought as I opened my own door and closed it behind me.

My five-room suite featured a satellite TV, a full kitchen,

and an extra-large bed in a back bedroom. Though basic, it was a big upgrade from the tents and trailers I'd grown used to in my deployments. Unbuttoning my shirt, I grabbed a bottle of water from the fridge and carried it to the small office, where I'd set up my assigned laptop. While the computer started up, I removed my boots and flexed my clawed feet. Much like in the military, we could contact loved ones as long as we weren't in the middle of mission planning. The standard discretion applied.

I accessed the system's video conferencing app but deactivated the camera. A still headshot of my former self appeared above my name. I selected my fiancée from the list and hit CALL.

"I don't get to see your handsome face?" she fake-pouted when she answered.

"Yeah, I'm on a different system," I said, a modulator smoothing out my wolfish voice, "but I can see yours." As I took in her face, I considered the lie I was telling her by hiding mine. "How's my wife-to-be doing?"

"Missing you."

"The feeling is very mutual."

"Otherwise, life goes on in southeast Texas." Her eyes brightened. "Oh, Willis brushed his teeth by himself today."

She was referring to one of the pediatric patients she worked with as an occupational therapist. Whenever she talked about him—or any of them—I could hear her desire to raise kids of her own. I'd promised her three or four, but that was on hold for obvious reasons. I double-checked to make sure the camera was off on my end. "That's fantastic. He still hitting on you?"

Daniela released a wonderful burst of laughter. "That

kid's a hot mess. He says when he's discharged he's going to sell one of his LEGO sets and take me on a date to Chuckee Cheese."

"Pizza and robotic entertainment. Should I be worried?"

"Oh, you've got some competition, mister."

"Damn. I really need to up my game."

"All you need to do is take care of yourself," she said, her lips straightening. "How are things going ... wherever you are?"

I thought about Takara storming off following the morning's exercise and blew out my breath. The others I could manage, but her... "About as well as can be expected at this stage. And don't worry. Where I am is very secure. And routine. We're going to be running exercises for a while."

Even though she couldn't see me, she gave me her skeptical look. That usually made me chuckle, but now I swallowed hard. "Hey, I wouldn't be able to call if there was anything serious going on."

"Any idea of when you might get some leave?"

If the bioengineering division's next phase of testing could buy me hours instead of minutes, I'd be there at the first opportunity. "No, not yet, Dani. I'm sorry."

"Don't be. You're where you need to be right now." As I took a sip of water, I watched her eyes darken. "Hey, um, there's something I need to tell you."

"What is it?" The odd angle of her mouth sped my pulse.

"I debated whether or not to bring it up, but since I'm asking you to be up front with me, I need to do the same."

"What is it?" I repeated, fighting to control my voice.

"My parents saw Kurt in town yesterday."

My breaths turned harsh through my flaring nostrils. Before Dani and I had met, there had been Kurt Hawtin, a nurse from a sister hospital. They'd dated for six months. All softness and smiles on the outside, Kurt turned out to be an abusive asshole. He stalked Dani for weeks after she broke up with him. At one point, he threatened to kill her. All these years later the thought still enraged me. A restraining order had followed. Fortunately, Kurt was already self-destructing. Busted at work for stealing opiates, he lost his license to practice in Texas and eventually left the state. He ended up in Florida, from what Dani had heard. By the time I came into the picture, he was a bad memory.

Lucky for him.

"What's he doing back?" I demanded.

"I have no idea. My parents didn't talk to him or anything. They just happened to see him at a gas station. Look, he's probably just visiting. And I checked this morning; the restraining order's still in effect."

"Listen to me, Dani. If *you* see him out, even if it seems completely accidental, I want you to call the police, and then you call me. Do you understand?"

She nodded. "I will."

I tried to cycle my breathing back down. "I don't mean to raise my voice, but men like Kurt are dangerous. Really dangerous. All of that might have happened five years ago, but it's not like he's forgotten."

"I know. I'm taking every precaution."

"You still have the Glock, right? And your concealed carry is up to date?"

Shortly after we had begun dating, I bought her the Glock 26 as well as a membership to a nearby range, where

I taught her how to shoot. Romantic, I know, but with me being overseas for long deployments, I wanted to be sure she could take care of herself. Thanks to the Crash, crime had been spreading as police budgets contracted. But we weren't talking about random violence now.

"Yes," she replied to my questions.

I squeezed my fists. Why couldn't I be with her?

"I didn't want this hanging over you or your work," she said apologetically. "That's the last thing you need."

"No, I'm glad you told me." I exhaled. "I want to know these things."

"I feel the same way. So whatever you can tell me about what's going on with you..."

"Yeah, I will," I said, watching the monitor where my monstrous reflection was superimposed over her beautiful face. All I had to do was click the camera icon, and she'd know everything. I cleared my throat. "But like I said, life here is pretty routine at the moment."

"Good."

"Yeah, good," I echoed, but without hearing myself.

I was figuring out what to do about Kurt.

8

I arrived at the conference room early the next morning and found Sarah already there, ticking through a pile of notes. We had agreed to divide the day. She would have the first two hours in the morning and the first hour after lunch to educate us on the creatures and situations we would potentially face, which left me the rest of the day to forge us into an effective unit.

"Any word from Takara?" I asked.

She looked up at me, the fluorescent lights turning her thick glasses opaque. "No."

She angled her face back to her notes. I took a seat across the table from her. "I looked over her profile again last night," I said. "At first I thought the issue was a history of operating solo, but she's worked with teams before. I think it's more that she's only faced humans. That kick she nailed me with yesterday..." I moved my jaw around even though the joint had healed within moments of being hammered. "That would have dropped the heavyweight champ. She's not used to someone standing up to her power and then giving it back. Might have thrown her off."

"It was an impressive kick," Sarah agreed distractedly. One thing I'd noticed about my new partner was that she didn't multitask very well.

I looked toward the closed door. "Hey, you started to bring up something about Takara yesterday."

She flipped a page over and began marking its backside.

"Something about her had yet to be verified, you said, but before you could go further, she cut you off. Called it a 'peasant legend.' Whatever it was, I didn't see it mentioned in her profile."

"That's because it was never verified."

"Yeah, you said that yesterday," I growled. "Can you tell me what it was?"

"She asked me not to."

"Look, I'm not prying for shits and grins here. I'm just trying to do the job I signed on for. I need to understand what kind of baggage she's carrying. If it's going to keep her from being effective, she's getting dropped. I don't care how powerful she is."

That got Sarah's attention. She raised her face, but at that moment the door opened and Takara appeared. Her dark eyes moved from Sarah to me, but if they were hostile, I couldn't tell; she wore her expression like a stone. She strode toward the table, her long hair and the same billowy black attire she'd worn during yesterday's exercise fluttering with barely a sound. She took a seat between us. For the first time, I noticed circular tattoos on her palms.

"Morning," I said.

Instead of answering, she laced her fingers on the table and stared straight ahead.

Okay.

Yoofi and Olaf entered shortly. When they took their seats, Sarah handed us each a binder: a catalogue of creatures broken down into classes and subclasses. I was leafing through them when Rusty showed up five minutes late. He gave everyone an apologetic wave. The puffiness around his eyes told me he'd stayed up a lot later than promised. To be fair, so had I.

After finishing the call with Dani, I'd gone online, trying to learn anything I could about Kurt. I found his arrest for the opiate theft when he was still in Texas. As a first time offender, he'd gotten off with six months probation and mandatory drug counseling. When no other court orders or arrests popped up, I pulled up a white pages site and entered his name. I found addresses for him in East Texas and two in Orlando, Florida, where he'd probably settled. I printed them off as well as a couple of listed phone numbers. Next I went to the professional licensing sites for Texas and Florida. His nursing license in Texas was still revoked, but it looked like he was working under a provisional license in Florida. That relaxed my shoulders a little—his turning up in Texas didn't appear to be a permanent move. But I needed to dig deeper, and to do that, I needed someone better connected.

I considered turning to Centurion, but I didn't want to give them any more leverage over me than they already had. Then I remembered Segundo, my team sergeant and second in command on Team 5. One of his brothers was in law enforcement—even better, he worked in Florida. I fired Segundo an email, attaching the information I'd found online, and asked whether he could have his brother take a more thorough look.

"I'll begin with an overview of the material," Sarah said, returning me to the conference room, "and then we'll start on Class Is: undead creatures."

Despite Sarah's bland delivery, the two hours went by quickly, probably because the material was unlike anything I'd ever been taught before. Vampires, vampire spawn, and blood slaves. Yoofi alternately oohed and giggled throughout, while Rusty threw in the odd remark, though I noticed he was having trouble keeping his eyes open. Olaf and Takara remained silent.

As I absorbed the info, I thought frequently of Billy. When it came to vampires, there were fates worse than death, apparently. But the knowledge did little to lessen the horror of that day.

I paid closest attention to how to kill the creatures.

When Sarah finished, she signaled that the team was mine.

Without standing, I said, "All right, we're going to spend the rest of the morning going back over the fundamentals we started yesterday. This afternoon, I'm going to set up some tactical exercises that I'll take you through step by step. Rather than throw a ton at you right now—"

"I want a rematch," Takara said.

I turned toward her, one eyebrow cocked. "I'm sorry?"

"The exercise we did yesterday morning. I want to run it again."

"That wasn't a competition. That was me getting an idea of where everyone was ability wise."

"I didn't show you all I could do."

Was that what she had been upset about? Feeling that she'd underperformed? I didn't know a lot about Japan, but I knew honor was a big part of their culture.

"That's no doubt true of everyone here," I said. "The idea was to throw you into a situation with little to no preparation. I promise that you'll have opportunities in the coming days and weeks to redeem yourself."

Takara's neck stiffened, and for the first time, I noticed narrow crescents of red circling her black irises. "It must be now."

"Repeating the exercise won't help the team."

"Now," she insisted.

I studied her set face. In the military I would never have taken this kind of shit from a subordinate, but I saw an opportunity. I turned to Olaf. "Can you conduct the shooting drills we began yesterday?"

His pale blue eyes didn't so much as flicker. "Yes," he said thickly.

I nodded at Sarah and Yoofi. "Go with Olaf. Takara and I will be there when we finish."

"I'll ready the weapons," Rusty said.

I waited for them to file from the conference room before looking back at Takara. "Okay, here's the deal. We'll run the exercise again, but with just the two of us. You attacking, me defending." Something told me that was what she had wanted, those final moments from yesterday's exercise back. "But here's what I get in exchange. Win or lose, you commit to the team. And that goes beyond never walking away again. I'm talking attitude, receptiveness, everything. Those are the terms. You in?"

The red crescents around her irises began to pulse as she stared back at me.

"I won't lose," she said.

Twenty minutes later, I stood beside the door to the building that held the flag, the same M4 paintball carbine pressed to my shoulder as yesterday, my nose raised to the light wind. Without Yoofi's deceptive magic, Takara couldn't disguise her scent, but I still couldn't smell her nearby. I tuned into my animal hearing, but all I could hear was the rest of the team firing across the compound and the wind raking the desert sand.

And then I did pick up something: a flapping sound, coming from the north side of the building across the street. Her attire?

I listened another moment. No, this was sharper, crisper, like a small tarpaulin.

If she was attempting to draw me out, no dice. I adjusted my grip while keeping watch in all directions. The flapping continued, but now the tenor changed. Something small and orange whipped from behind the north side of the building and crossed the intersection on the wind.

There's no way that was my flag, I thought.

I glanced toward the open door I was guarding. Almost on instinct, I threw a hand to the back of my neck. Two paintballs thumped my knuckles as I lunged into the building for cover. My flag was still on the wall above the wooden table. Takara had released a spare flag as a distraction and then sniped me from the top of the building across the street.

Damn, she was good.

I backed against the wall beside the door and examined my left hand. Red paint matted the fur. She'd hit me twice, which meant I'd just lost the use of my left arm. I lowered the hand from my barrel and let it hang. Sucked, but it was better than being dead.

Takara had moved silently, using the wind to keep her scent from me, and then employed a decoy to expose me for the split second she needed to get off her shots. The question now was how she intended to finish the job. I had no doubt she'd spent her night planning our "rematch"—and so far, it was going her way.

I backed into a corner where I had a good angle on the doorway and flag. I eyed the slanted rectangle of light on the floor. The sun's position was in my favor. Her shadow would forecast any move she attempted through the door. But at that thought, the entire rectangle turned to shadow.

I fired twice, paintballs exploding around the doorway, before realizing no one was coming through. The sunlight had simply disappeared, as if a shade had been pulled. But there hadn't been a cloud in the sky a minute before. Had Takara blocked the damned sun? How?

Doesn't matter how, I told myself as I calmed my breathing and listened. *That she's taken sunlight out as an early-warning system means she's about to make her move.*

Something crashed upstairs. My gaze cut to the corner stairwell, but I kept my aim on the doorway. It was a distraction. Had to be. There were no doors or windows to access the upper story. But now I heard footsteps crossing the room overhead, aiming straight for the stairwell.

Takara didn't possess the mind-warping powers of Yoofi, meaning she really was up there.

I started to train my M4 on the stairwell, then hesitated.

Or was she? I didn't know the extent of her powers. Her profile was sparse, and then there was whatever Sarah wouldn't divulge. Could she throw sounds? Create a duplicate of herself?

The footsteps overhead stopped in the center of the

room. They weren't loud. In fact, I had felt more than heard them: small vibrations through the concrete, like someone trying to exercise stealth. Human ears wouldn't have picked them up. But was that the point? Selling me on the idea she was up there because of the show of stealth? Or was she actually up there?

If Takara's plan is to get into my head, she's doing a damn fine job.

For several minutes nothing happened. The building remained silent. I began to pick up traces of Takara's scent: tea-like and sharp. But were they coming from outside? Upstairs? I was thinking it was more mind-fuckery when the entire building shuddered.

What the...?

Dust and bits of plaster sifted down from cracks spreading over the ceiling. Chunks of concrete began to fall next. I leapt into the doorway an instant before most of the ceiling collapsed.

A wave of dust filled the room and washed past my visor. I took a quick glance outside. I didn't see Takara, but I saw what she'd done to block the sun. Atop the opposite building, she'd raised a free-standing screen—something she must have found in a supply room—to keep the sun's rays from hitting the doorway.

Is there anything she hasn't *planned for?*

I scanned the destroyed room. A shaft of sunlight fell through the dust above, landing on a pile of concrete blocks. Beyond, I could just make out my flag on the wall.

It was still game on.

As I raised my barrel and eyes to the second story, I remembered what I'd read about her ability to focus power. The sunlight was coming in through a hole in the roof.

That's what the meditative breathing I'd heard the night before had been about, I realized. Focusing her power.

With the dust settling, I spotted her across the room. She was facedown among the debris, her black attire still. I checked around me, then stole forward. My mind screamed *trap*, but as her captain, I also had to consider the possibility that she went for broke and got herself hurt. I kept my barrel fixed on her. She'd forgone body armor again, so any shot to her torso would be a kill.

I sniffed. It was her scent. But the closer I got, the more my senses were telling me something was off. The half-buried body looked a little too full in some places, too empty in others. Like it had been stuffed—

I wheeled toward the stairwell, already firing, but Takara had come in low. A leather-booted foot struck the M4's barrel from below. The weapon left my grip in an explosion of plastic and paintballs. As I reared back, a second kick caught me in the chest. The ballistic plate blunted the strike, but not the force. I flew the length of the room and slammed into the far wall. The jarring pain was brief as my healing kicked in, but I was out of position.

As Takara spun toward the flag, I drew my sidearm and fired into her path. She took cover behind a pile of debris that included parts of the wooden table. I covered the pile with my sidearm and rose slowly.

"I'm impressed," I said. "I mean that. You were a second away from winning. How about we call it a draw and join the others?"

"It's not over."

"I caught a glimpse of your getup." I said, referring to the form-fitting black leather suit. "Unless you've got other talents I'm not aware of, there's no way you're carrying a weapon. The moment you move or I get an angle on you, you're going to be covered in paint."

"Try me, *Wolfe*."

"Can I ask you a question? What is it about me you find so distasteful?" When she didn't answer, I gave her some options. "Is it my supernatural strength? That I have rank on you? Or do you just have something against blue-haired freaks?"

"Maybe I have something against Americans."

Okay, that one hadn't occurred to me. "Can I ask why?"

She snorted. "Read your history."

I felt the hair over the back of my neck bristle in frustration. "The only history that matters is that our countries have been allies for the last eighty years. We have a mutual defense agreement that we continue to honor. Did I miss something?"

"You missed *everything*." Then, as though something had detonated, the debris she was crouched behind blasted toward me in a bright red flash. I threw my good arm up—my left was technically incapacitated—and grunted as chunks of brick, mortar, and wood peppered me.

She's making her move.

I dropped my sidearm and bounded blindly through the dust. A second later, I was through and tackling her around the waist, right below the flag. The building shook as we crashed to the floor. Takara was on her back, teeth bared as she struggled to writhe from under my mass. But I had her pinned across the shoulders with my good arm, and was using my legs to keep her from kicking. She wasn't going anywhere.

"You remember the rules?" I said. "One ... two ..."

The same red that flashed in her eyes glowed from her

clenched fists now. I felt a force growing beneath me, and for a moment I was no longer looking at Takara, but a fiery dragon. Then she was Takara again, and the walls of the building were crashing over my back.

Holy shit!

I made a shield over Takara with my bowed body and absorbed the building's collapse. In the sudden darkness, the fire in her eyes thinned to crescents. I waited for everything to settle before holding her to my stomach and standing. The debris was heavy but not deep. It fell from my healing back. I set Takara outside, on top of the collapse.

"You all right?" I asked as I emerged beside her.

One of her hands was clamped to her shoulder where a section of leather had torn away. I glimpsed a patch of her skin. It was warped in a way that suggested intense heat and scarring. I realized that was the second scent I'd been picking up from her. The smell of burned flesh.

When Takara caught me looking, she snapped the shoulder from view and raced nimbly down the collapse. She crossed the street and disappeared, just as she'd done the day before.

I looked after her, then at the destruction around me. Was this the 'peasant legend' Takara had shut down discussion on the day before? That she could channel the power of ... a dragon?

I thought about the dragon shifters I'd faced in Waristan, but Takara's powers had felt different. None of it mattered, though. She had walked away again, in defiance of our agreement.

I dusted myself off and joined the rest of the team at the shooting range. I didn't volunteer what had happened, and they didn't ask. Any discussion was going to be between me and Sarah. We'd have a serious talk about Takara after the exercise, where I planned to recommend her discharge from Legion. She'd proven herself a head case who couldn't be trusted.

But ten minutes later, Takara strode up in a fresh black suit and took her place among the team on the firing line.

Her shooting was damn near perfect.

That evening I opened my laptop and checked my messages. The one I'd been waiting for was at the top—a reply from Segundo. Following Parker's death and my departure, Team 5 had undergone a reorganization. Which was to say the powers that be had disbanded it and used the members to plug holes in other units around the country. It felt like a disservice to the best team I'd ever served with, but that was life in the military. Segundo had ended up on a special-ops unit outside the capital.

As I started to read, I couldn't help but grin a little.

---

wolfe! got your message you flea-ridden bastard. good hearing from you. what can i say? new unit isn't the same without you. got a pompous ass for a captain but at least he's getting us into some action. makes the time till ocs go by faster. and hey could be worse. mauli ended up in balkhar province with team 12. remember the issue they had with food drops last winter? haha! i told him it was karma for rat fucking my care packages.

My grin faded as I thought about how much I missed those guys, then my face straightened altogether.

---

anyway i forwarded your message to my brother and just got word back. said he'll look into this kurt hawtin creep. i'll message you soon as i hear something. dude, i would not want to be him. talk soon bro. love ya

---

I hit Reply and typed:

Glad you're doing well. Just keep your roid rages in check and you'll be fine ;) Thanks for helping me out with this. I owe you. Will tell you everything next time I see you – hopefully over a shrimp boil and a bucket of Bud. If you message me but don't hear back, could you give me a call?

I didn't know how long his brother would take, and there was no telling where I might be. I typed in the number of a secure phone Centurion had distributed to the members of Legion. Like our laptops, the phones were monitored to ensure we didn't disclose anything confidential, but I didn't care. Not when it came to Dani. Anyway, I wasn't doing anything that breached our agreement.

`Thanks, Segundo. Love you too, bro.`

9

By the end of the first week, we had gotten into a good routine. Sarah's creature lectures were informative and actionable; Takara was participating in all of the drills, per our deal; Olaf was absorbing and executing instructions like a well-oiled machine; Rusty was staying on top of the weapons and equipment; and Yoofi was showing more comfort with the basics.

We were far from an elite unit—the tactical exercises remained error-filled—but that was the whole point at this stage: to discover our weaknesses and drill until they became strengths. More and more, I would incorporate Takara's and Yoofi's special abilities into our strategies. I estimated that by week four we would be competent and by week twenty-four ready for just about anything.

I was *not* happy, then, when Sarah asked me to step outside during lunch on day six and dropped her bombshell: "Centurion has a job for us."

"A job?" I said. "When?"

"As soon as we're briefed and outfitted."

"Purdy said nothing before one month. It hasn't even been a goddamned week."

Sarah raised a hand to her squinting eyes, turning slightly so the sun wasn't hitting her full in the face. "They said it's urgent."

"Of course it's urgent," I scoffed. "They don't want to lose whoever the client is."

"The client is a small town in southern Mexico. El Rosario. You asked about pro bono? This is about as close as it gets."

"So it's a résumé builder. Regardless, we're not ready."

"We're all they have. Something down there is abducting children."

I had been preparing to return to the chow hall, but now an ice floe slid into my stomach. I turned back toward her. "Do we know what?"

"No. Some investigation will be involved."

"Are they sure it's not human traffickers?" Sophisticated underground networks spanned the globe, and children fetched especially high prices. The thought roiled my stomach.

"I asked the same question," Sarah replied. "Centurion says no. I read a preliminary report. They're sending over more information now."

I squinted back at her, not saying anything for several moments. I was responsible for the lives of my teammates. No matter how potent some of our powers, or how clear cut the case might be, we weren't a team yet. We were a liability. On-the-job training could get us—and anyone in our vicinity—killed. The prudent course would be to hold off on taking any assignments.

Until I considered the victims. *Children.*

"How did the town know to contact Centurion?" I asked.

"Centurion reached out to them when our algorithm signaled probable Prod 1 activity. A team met with their mayor and police chief yesterday. They signed the contract yesterday evening. Like I said, as close to pro bono as it gets."

Something about the whole thing came off as desperate. Centurion had its competitors in defense contracting, and I wondered if we were witnessing a race into the monster-hunting-for-profit space as well. Whatever Centurion's motives, though, it didn't change the equation.

Children.

I gave a reluctant nod. "I'll tell the others lunch is extended for an hour so you and I can take a look at the info. *Just a look*," I stressed. "I'm not committing to anything yet."

"Meet in my office in ten?"

As Sarah crossed the compound at a fast walk, her boots kicking up dust, I ducked into the chow hall to tell the rest of the team that the afternoon exercise had been postponed, then stopped off at the barracks to check my email. A message from Dani said she was fine, which I took to mean she'd seen no signs of Kurt. Still nothing from Segundo, though.

Dammit.

Either his brother was taking his sweet time, or Segundo was out on a mission. I had no doubt he'd come through, but the last thing I wanted was to head out not knowing Kurt's reason for being back in town and what he'd been up to in the years since he'd left.

I sent a two-word message to Segundo—`Anything yet?`—and shut the laptop.

Sarah's office was in the same building as the conference room, along the outer corridor. I rapped a knuckle on the doorframe. Sarah was sitting at a desk off to the right and waved for me to enter. As I ducked inside, I looked around. Every square inch of desk and shelf space in the small room was filled with books and binders, while still managing to look organized. On a windowsill near the ceiling, I was surprised to see a row of potted plants. Sarah didn't strike me as a plant person. Then again, how well did I know her?

"Have a seat," she said, inching her chair over.

I sat on a folding metal chair behind her so we were both facing her computer.

"Here's the preliminary report," she said, angling the monitor so I could read it.

I stooped low, my eyes moving back and forth across the screen. When I reached the bottom, I turned to Sarah.

"Clowns?"

"We have an assignment," I told the team in the conference room. It had taken two hours of reviewing the information and weighing the need against the risks, but in the end I agreed. "Sarah's going to give us an overview."

The lights dimmed as I took a seat. A map showing Mexico appeared across the LCD screens.

"El Rosario is a small town in the mountains of southern Mexico," she began. "Population twelve thousand, if you include the surrounding villages. The people are mostly indigenous, descended from Mayans. The town is located inside a cold zone—an area that has seen no recent Prodigium I homicides. The closest activity has been in Guatemala City, over five hundred miles to the south. That said, eight children have gone missing from El Rosario in the last month, and there's a high probability the abductors are Prod Is."

Yoofi made an ominous sound as he peered from his smoke.

"The abductions began at the conclusion of a festival that El Rosario hosts each year. The festival coincides with the feast day of St. Paul, the town's patron saint, but it mainly celebrates the people's Mayan origins. Actors dress up in colorful costumes and enact stories from their cosmology: the creation of the sun and moon, the myth of the Corn God, etcetera. But because there are so many children in El Rosario, the festival also features modern-day clowns."

Sarah brought up still shots from the festival, showing the five different clowns. Much like their Barnum and Bailey counterparts, they were men with colorful wigs, face paint, and costumes, but each clown had his own characteristics. One's face was painted to look like a skull, while another had features of a rat. A third's face looked downright homicidal. But the kids who crowded around them were laughing, arms stretched up for balloons and treat bags.

"Never have cared for their type," Rusty said.

"What, Mexicans?" Yoofi asked with a concerned face.

"No, clowns."

"The clowns are known as the Brothers Payaso," Sarah continued. "Their names are Baboso, Calaca, Loco, Rata, and Torpe. They're very popular with the children, as you can see, but when the festival ends, the wigs and costumes go back into storage and the actors playing the clowns retire their roles until the next year. However, in the days following this year's festival, children reported seeing the clowns around town, always at dusk. They appeared to be trying to lure the children into the woods. Adults didn't pay the stories much heed until Miguel Bardoza, age six, disappeared following a clown sighting."

The child's smiling face, two front baby teeth missing, appeared on the screen. The instant I'd seen him on the computer in Sarah's office, I knew I couldn't deny the people of El Rosario our help.

"Miguel and his nine-year-old sister were returning from their grandparents' house after dinner when the sister reported that the clown Baboso appeared at the edge of a field and waved to them," Sarah went on. "In his other hand, he was holding up a bag of chocolates. Though the sister liked Baboso and the other clowns as much as any child in El Rosario, she said something seemed off. 'His eyes looked dead,' she told the police. She tried to steer Miguel away, but he broke free and ran toward the clown, crying out for a chocolate. The clown turned and disappeared into the woods with Miguel following. By the time his sister reached the far edge of the field, Miguel and the clown were gone. A search by the local police and townspeople turned up nothing, and Miguel never returned."

"Were the actors questioned?" Takara asked.

I turned toward Takara. Her interest in the case was a pleasant and welcome surprise.

"Yes," Sarah said. "The five who played the Brothers Payaso were with other people at the time of Miguel's disappearance. The closet in the municipal building where the costumes were stored had been broken into, however, with the face paint, wigs, and outfits cleaned out."

Yoofi shook his head. "Ooh, that's bad."

"So someone stole the disguises to lure the children," Takara said.

Sarah nodded. "It looks that way. The next abduction happened two days later. The victim was an eight-year-old girl named Isabella. No eyewitnesses this time. Her bicycle was found at the edge of a soccer field, close to some woods that climb into the foothills. After that, the town instituted a nighttime curfew. The small police force increased their patrols. Kids were told that the clowns were dangerous and if they saw one, they were to run away and tell the nearest adult. But despite this, the disappearances continued. The remaining victims were three boys and three girls, all between the ages of five and nine."

"Like something out of a damned Stephen King novel," Rusty muttered.

"As of last week, children are forbidden from being out alone at any hour, and that seems to have halted the abductions. The town remains shaken, though. Understandably," she added, as if in afterthought.

She clicked the remote, and the screen changed to a satellite image of the town, red crosses marking the disappearances. The crosses were all on the outskirts of El Rosario where fields and dusty lanes ended and the forested foothills began. The dense green foliage stretched up into a stony ring of mountains.

"How do you know the clowns are supernatural beings?" Takara asked.

"Police patrols sighted clowns on three separate occasions," Sarah said. "On the first, a clown outran a cruiser going forty miles per hour. That's roughly one and a half times the speed of the world's fastest sprinter. On the second occasion, a police officer on foot spotted a clown in an orange grove. He emptied his service pistol into the clown from less than fifty yards away. He claimed he saw the bullets impacting his body, but the clown only hissed and ran away. On the final occasion, a police officer riding shotgun in a cruiser shouted that he saw something and jumped out before his partner could bring the vehicle to a full stop. His partner watched the officer disappear into the woods. He parked the cruiser and ran to catch up. About fifty feet into the woods he found the officer facedown in the leaves, dead. In the ten or so seconds it had taken for him to park and locate his partner, something had snapped his partner's neck. In sum, we have evidence of speed, constitution, and lethality that are far beyond the capacity of normal humans."

"So how many clowns we talking?" Rusty asked with a shudder.

"Based on the descriptions, it sounds like there's a creature for each clown personality, so five."

"And what are we thinking, creature-wise?" he followed up.

"From the scant evidence, Centurion has narrowed it down to something in the undead or lycanthrope class of being. The problem is the MO. Nowhere in its database of cases can Centurion find an example of these classes of creature going to such lengths to disguise themselves."

"That's where the investigation phase of the operation comes in," I said. "After setting up a surveillance perimeter around the town, we'll spend the first few days fact finding. Try to learn as much as we can about what we're facing."

"When do we deploy?" Takara asked.

"2100 hours," I said. "Which means we have a full slate between now and then. We're going to the armory first, where Rusty's been putting together our kits. Then we'll run through several situational exercises in full gear. The rest of the time will be spent packing."

Rusty broke into a clumsy skip as he led the way to his domain. We filed through the armory's front door and into a fluorescent-lit space the size of a small warehouse. To our left stood racks of weapons: all makes and calibers of firearms, with drawers of corresponding attachments and ammo shelved beneath them. One section held nothing but combat knives. In the back corner was a workshop for weapons modifications, and across from us storage for protective suits and body armor with a curtained-off changing area. The other side of the armory was devoted to electronic equipment, with Rusty's computer-crammed office visible through an open door.

Four metal tables for organizing weapons and gear stood in the middle of the armory. They'd been empty following the morning's exercise, but now held open crates. Foam packaging littered the floor as though someone had torn into the crates with a little too much enthusiasm.

I turned to Rusty. "Are those them?"

He nodded as he ran ahead. "They arrived right before the meeting." He peered into a box, angled his head as though reading something, and then announced, "Sarah McKinnon."

She stepped forward. With a proud smile, Rusty lifted out a full-body Kevlar suit. For training we had been using standard wear, but this shipment from Centurion—which I hadn't been expecting until the following week—was tailored to our sizes and was top shelf. Lightweight and highly durable, with extra protection over vital arteries, the suit featured Centurion's patented digital camouflage that changed color and pattern to blend into the wearer's surroundings—some sort of chemical patent. I watched the suit shift now.

"And here's the rest of your getup, ma'am," Rusty said, adding a vest, helmet, gloves, and boots to Sarah's arms. She carried everything to a dressing room. Rusty went down the line of packages, doling out the remaining suits and gear to Olaf, Yoofi, me, and then himself.

"What about Takara?" I asked, looking over the empty boxes.

"I didn't get her measurements until day two," Rusty said. "Centurion must not have had time to put hers together."

"We'll have them ship it to El Rosario," I told Takara. "In the meantime you can grab one of the standard sets." But she made no move toward the protective wear. Instead, she began to undo the ties that fastened her billowing attire. Rusty gawked open-mouthed, while a giggling Yoofi covered his eyes.

But when Takara pulled the one-piece away she was wearing her form-fitting leather suit underneath. I noticed she'd stitched the tear over her right shoulder, bringing to mind the patch of burned skin I'd seen the week before. Her scent suggested the scarring didn't end there.

"I brought my own," Takara said, a hard edge in her voice.

"Whoa," Rusty managed.

Yoofi hurried toward the dressing area. "This is too much."

I shook my head at Takara. "That's no protection against projectiles—much less the teeth or talons of a supernatural creature. We need to get you into something more durable."

"You mean something that will slow me down?" she challenged.

Here we go again, I thought. "Remember our deal? I'm not asking."

"A creature can't bite or claw what it can't catch."

"Wanna bet?" I lunged toward her.

A pair of metallic *snikts* sounded as twin blades popped from the sleeves of her suit. The foot-long stilettos glinted behind her fists and gave off a scent of silver. Her lips quirked slightly as I pulled up, one deadly blade leveled between my eyes, the other at my heart. It was the closest I'd come to seeing her smile.

"I couldn't have done that in one of Centurion's suits," she said.

I didn't care for her backslide into insubordination, especially on the verge of a major mission, but I couldn't *not* admire her speed and cunning. Her skills would no doubt be useful—if they could be integrated into the tactics of the larger unit. "Points taken," I said as she retracted the blades into the suit and stood back. "But go pick out something anyway."

Rusty laughed. "Nice, boss."

Takara looked at me for another moment, eyes hard and black, then strode past the tables toward the suits and body armor, bumping Rusty's shoulder en route.

"Hey, watch the goods!" he protested.

"Why don't you change into your suit with the others," I said.

As Rusty shuffled off, I turned to find Olaf shucking his clothes in the middle of the armory. I joined him—my hair hid everything—and then we took turns adjusting each other's vests. The fit of my new suit was snug but flexible, allowing me to fall to all fours. Even so, the wolf in me didn't like the confinement. Maybe Takara's scarred flesh made her feel the same way.

I sprinted back and forth across the armory several times, returning upright as the others began to emerge from the changing area, the patterns and colors of their camos shifting with their backgrounds. Shunning the Kevlar, Takara appeared with just a tactical vest over her leathers. I decided not to say anything.

When everyone had assembled, Rusty and I inspected their suits. Yoofi's gear needed a lot of adjusting, and he insisted on wearing his long coat over the top to hold his many flasks as well as a wooden idol to Dabu. By the time everyone was fit, we looked impressively like a team.

Which was dangerous.

Sarah, Rusty, and Yoofi lacked field experience, while Takara's background might as well have been in a foreign language. Though elements of ninjitsu overlapped with special ops tactics, too much of it didn't. Strangely, Olaf was the only team member whose skills I came close to trusting at this point. Even so, we hadn't trained as a unit long enough. I would need to manage everyone's strengths and weaknesses in the field, and that began with weapons.

"Since we don't know what we're up against," I said, "we're bringing an assortment of weapons and ammo. We've been training with M4 carbines and M9 pistols, which is what I want Sarah and Takara—and Rusty if it comes to it—to plan on carrying." I turned to Yoofi, who had yet to meet minimal proficiency with either weapon. There was no way I was going to have him waving them around El Rosario. "How do you feel about using your staff?" I asked him.

"Staff very powerful," he said, giving it a spin in his hands. "It's enough for Yoofi."

"All right, good." Maybe I'd give him a low-caliber pistol as a backup in case he lost his staff. But even that thought made me uncomfortable. "As for Olaf and me, we'll be carrying Rusty's new babies, MP88 rifles."

Rusty took his cue and ran to his work bench. The cords in his neck strained as he returned carrying an assembled MP88 and handed it to me with a reverent smile. This was the special delivery he'd been most excited about: Centurion's latest model, fresh from the factory.

The MP88 was basically a high-caliber automatic assault rifle, grenade launcher, and flame thrower bundled into one, the three deadly barrels emerging from a rugged, full-sealed outer casing. I looked over the empty ports for the magazines and fuel tank, worked the charging handles to gauge their slide, then brought the rifle to my shoulder and looked down the sights at the far wall. Felt good. I handed the weapon to Olaf for him to inspect. He'd used weapons like it while a Centurion soldier, and he appeared comfortable wielding the model now.

"They're heavy and complicated, which is why I'm limiting their use to just the two of us for now. As for ammo, we'll be using armor-piercing incendiary rounds. Since we don't know which class of creature we're dealing with, every bullet will be laced with powdered silver. It's deadly to most lycanthropes and hella painful to a lot of the undead out there."

Silver was lethal to me too, but as long as the weapons would be in our hands versus the enemies'...

"When we make contact, we're not taking any chances," I finished. "We're gonna rip those fuckers up."

That got an ardent fist pump from Rusty. He was starting to grow on me. What I'd misinterpreted as macho posturing our first day was simply the man's enthusiasm. He really wanted to be here.

"Go ahead and grab your weapons, then pick up your commo gear," I said. "We've got a lot to cover and not a lot of time."

As I watched the team move toward the racks of weapons, a knot of concern hardened in my gut—probably made worse by the fact that it was still within my power to call off the mission.

Should I? Shouldn't I?

Because once I committed, there could be no second-guessing my decision.

In a flash, I saw my childhood friend Billy Young lying in the leaves, his puckered neck wound leaking blood, ashen face peering up at me. "It's bad, isn't it?" he'd rasped. What if hunters had gotten to those three vampires before they'd found us fishing that morning?

Answer: Billy Young would still be alive.

"Let's go," I called to the team. "Clock's ticking."

10

As the Centurion attack chopper began its descent toward the soccer fields of El Rosario, I gripped my MP88 and looked out over the moonlit town. Set in a river valley, the town had started as a colonial pueblo. In the center, a large white church presided over an empty plaza and marketplace. A grid of cement and dirt roads lined with simple one- and two-story buildings extended out for several blocks.

I peered around the outskirts of town, where the abductions had occurred. At a little past one in the morning, the streets were desolate. All I spotted were a few stray dogs fleeing the thundering sound of our arrival, several of them running through what looked like an abandoned military outpost on the far side of a river. Ruined buildings clustered around a pot-holed parade ground.

At 2100 the night before, a personnel carrier delivered us and our load to the airstrip at Centurion's Vegas base. A cargo plane flew us to another Centurion base outside

Mexico City. There, we transferred to the helos, taking off with three escorts for the two-hour trip to El Rosario.

The preparations back at the Legion compound had been exhausting, even for someone with my stamina, and I was concerned about the rest of the team. Beside me, Rusty was snoring with his mouth open, head bobbing against Takara's shoulder. She didn't seem to notice as she peered out the other side of the helo. Sarah, Olaf, and Yoofi rode in the helo behind us.

I shook Rusty.

"I didn't steal it!" he blurted as he snorted awake.

"Get ready. We're about to land."

Rusty blinked around, then lifted his M4 from between his legs. One of the escorts had already touched down, and soldiers were emerging to establish a security perimeter around our landing site. At the edge of the field, a police cruiser was parked beside a pair of vans. I pointed them out to Rusty so he'd know where we were headed.

When the chopper landed, we disembarked and hunkered in the rotor wash. The other chopper set down behind us. When everyone was out, I led them toward the vans, one a passenger and the other a cargo. Delivered ahead of us, the vans' plain appearances belied their speed and armored durability.

A man in a khaki uniform and a woman in civilian clothes exited the police cruiser as we approached. Though I was wearing my special helmet to hide my face, my seven-foot height drew startled looks from them both. But while the police official shuffled back, the woman stepped forward to meet us.

"You are Legion?" she asked in accented English.

"Yes," Sarah said. *"Podemos hablar en Español si prefiere."*

"No, it's okay," the woman replied. "I understand English very well." The woman was short and stout, no more than five feet tall. Though the town was predominantly indigenous, she was dressed modernly: slacks and a collared shirt. Her one nod to tradition was a woven purse that hung from a strap across her body. She looked the six of us over like a worried mother.

"Are you Mayor Flores?" Sarah asked.

I had wanted Sarah to do most of the talking, not only for her proficiency in Spanish, but because she could establish eye contact. In my work with tribal leaders in Central Asia, I'd learned that what you communicated with your eyes was as important as the words your interpreter translated. It was about establishing trust. And right now Mayor Flores needed as much as we could give her. But Sarah's gaze was cold and formal like her voice.

"Yes," the mayor replied uncertainly. "And this is our chief of police, Juan Pablo."

Understanding he'd been introduced, Juan Pablo nodded his crew-cut head. One of his top front teeth glinted with metal as he uttered a greeting. He remained a safe distance back, however, his gaze flitting over Rusty, Takara, Yoofi, and Olaf, who were arrayed behind us, before returning to me.

Sarah gave a stiff nod. "We're the Legion force. As soon as we load the vans, you'll take us to our compound." It came out more an order than a request. To our right, a line of bulky Centurion soldiers was already loading our equipment and supplies into the cargo van.

"Of course," Mayor Flores replied, "but then it is urgent we talk."

"We have the latest information," Sarah told her. "Once

we've established our headquarters, appropriate security, and a surveillance system for the town, we'll schedule a meeting."

I clenched my jaw. She was missing the obvious: there had been a new development.

"What happened?" I asked, taking care to articulate past the helmet's muffling effect.

"I-I stopped at my office on the way here," Mayor Flores said, "and found this under the door." She reached a trembling hand into her purse, withdrew a piece of paper, and gave it to Sarah. "Juan Pablo already checked it for prints, but there weren't any."

The note was in Spanish, and though I couldn't read it, the spidery script made my skin crawl. Sarah activated her helmet's headlamp, eyes moving quickly behind her glasses as she absorbed the message.

"It's an ultimatum," Sarah said when she finished. "The town is to leave a child at the old military base across the river at midnight tomorrow, or, I quote, 'the town will know death.'"

The police chief muttered and crossed himself. He had already lost one of his officers to the murderous creatures. Meanwhile, Mayor Flores's face looked like it was about to come apart.

"Please help us," she pled. "Please help El Rosario."

We followed the police cruiser toward the center of town. Sarah drove the passenger van, which carried the entire team save Rusty. He was behind us, driving the cargo van. Well beyond him, I could hear the diminishing thump of rotary blades. The helos were leaving, four of them headed to a temporary base forty miles away. There, a small team would remain on standby for evacuation and as a quick reaction force for the duration of our mission.

Otherwise, we'd be on our own.

I kept a close watch on our surroundings as Sarah drove. The adobe homes near the soccer fields gave way to larger cement buildings. Murals advertising Coca-Cola and Orange Fanta colorfully identified several businesses. Up ahead, the church's white bell tower rose high above the rooftops, like a heavenly sentry. But a palpable dread hung over the town. Despite the warm night, doors were closed and windows shuttered; some in the nicer looking part of town featured shiny new sets of security bars.

I turned partway around. From the back row of seats, Olaf stared straight ahead. His thick hands clutched the MP88 to his chest. Takara sat one row in front of him, perfectly erect but with her eyes closed. I'd seen her do this several times prior to exercises. Though I hadn't asked, I guessed it was how she focused her power. Yoofi was on the seat closest to the front. Though he was facing his window, his eyes were glazed over, one hand absently caressing his staff.

"Any impressions?" I asked.

Yoofi's head shook slowly. "Dabu doesn't like this place," he said in a distant voice. "Much evil here. And the evil is growing. Like a shadow, he says."

"Does he know where the evil is coming from?"

"Only that it's not from this world. Dabu never feel such evil before." Yoofi shuddered as his eyes returned to focus. "Usually Dabu laughs when I see him. Not this time."

I straightened as the cruiser approached the public

square and then turned right. We followed the cruiser for another block before it pulled over in front of a two-story building at the block's end. The police chief got out, unlocked a gate, and waved us toward it. Beyond the gate was a roofless carport, large enough for both vans to fit side by side.

"I'll secure the carport," I said. "Olaf, Takara, I want you covering the street."

As the two of them exited the side door, weapons readied, Sarah turned toward me. "I can interview the mayor and police chief while you get set up."

"I want to talk to them too." I said it in a way that wasn't challenging but that wasn't asking permission either. I'd seen enough at the soccer fields to know that, as intelligent as she was, Sarah was blind to emotional cues. And I didn't want us to miss any important info—especially now that we had a midnight deadline to stop whatever was threatening the town.

"Fine," she said.

I got out and sniffed the air. Despite the bulkiness of my helmet, it allowed decent flow. Currents of mountain air, street dust, wood fires, and distant sewage seeped into my nostrils. The scent of the townspeople filled in the spaces, their aroma like strong coffee. No one in the immediate area, though. With the MP88 tucked against my shoulder, I jerked my head, signaling Sarah to pull into the carport. Rusty followed, squeezing his van in beside hers.

I tested a locked door that joined the carport to the main building as Sarah and Rusty dismounted the vehicles. I led them to the front of the building, where the mayor and police chief awaited us. "This is the building your company wanted," Mayor Flores said. "It's very solid, very secure. And it is close to us. You saw the church and square coming in? The municipal building with my office is on the other side of the square, and the police station is beside it."

Behind us, the police chief was unlocking the green-painted metal door to the building. But before he could pull it open, I placed a hand on his arm and turned to Mayor Flores. "Whoever stuck the note under your office door could still be around. We need to clear the building."

She spoke in Spanish to Juan Pablo, who nodded and stood back.

"Olaf, I want you to stay out here on rear security," I said. "The rest of us are going to stack and clear, just like we practiced." I still hadn't assigned Yoofi a loaded weapon, so I told him to use his staff. He nodded and with an uttered word, a ball of dark energy warped the air around his blade.

I breached the door and we filed inside in a rush, taking up positions around a large cement room that held a table, a few chairs, and little else. We made a quick circuit of the bottom floor, calling out the rooms we cleared. A basic kitchen and three rooms with metal bunks stood at one end of the floor, while an office and a large storage space occupied the other. We then moved upstairs into an open area where some cinderblocks and raw planks had been stored.

At the center of the room lay a gray cat. I signaled for the others to hold back as I approached, already smelling the creature's recent death. When I picked it up, its neck lolled to one side. The police chief, arriving behind us, came to a sudden stop. *"No estuvo aquí esta tarde."*

"It wasn't here this afternoon," Sarah translated.

"Could be a warning," I said, holding the cat closer to my nose. Beneath the hair and dead tissue, I detected a peppery smell, bordering on sweet. I peered around. Like the downstairs, thick iron bars fortified the few upstairs windows. "Are there any other keys to the building besides the ones you gave us?" I asked the police chief as I set the cat back down.

Sarah posed the question, then translated his response. "He's pretty sure it's the only set." But I interpreted the nervous activity in Juan Pablo's eyes to mean he wasn't sure.

Great. "Can I see the note the mayor gave you?"

Sarah handed it to me and I held it under the helmet's breathing apparatus. I smelled paper, forensic dust, and the oil of those who had handled it, but no peppery smell. I handed it back, then signaled for everyone to stay put. I performed a sniffing circuit of the compound, but whoever was responsible for the scent on the cat hadn't left a trail.

"All right," I said when I returned. "Takara, I want you to access the roof. Coordinate security with Olaf, who will remain out front. Yoofi, help Rusty unload the cargo van. Let's have that office be our communications center. We'll use the storage space for weapons and equipment. When you finish, get gates up over the two doors leading outside. They're not secure."

I turned to Sarah. "We can meet at the table downstairs."

As the team broke apart to their assignments, Sarah, Mayor Flores, the police chief, and I gathered around the long table. Sarah had retrieved her clipboard, and we watched her sort through the sheaf of papers. The mayor appeared to have composed herself. Having a professional team armed to the teeth in her town no doubt helped—even if there were gaping holes in our preparedness.

At least I'm the only one who can see them. Would hate to

have our first client doubt our capacity before we even get started.

As if in apology for breaking down at the soccer fields, Mayor Flores said, “Nothing like this has ever happened in El Rosario.”

“We understand,” I replied before Sarah could jump into her line of questioning. “And we’ll do everything we can to secure the town and end the threat. To begin, we’re going to need to ask some questions.”

“Yes, of course.”

I turned to Sarah, who was waiting for me to finish, her pen poised.

“Have there been any illnesses in El Rosario recently?” she launched in.

“I can check with the health clinic,” the mayor answered, “but nothing unusual that I’m aware of.”

“People acting rabid or violent or showing unusual strength?” Sarah followed up.

The mayor consulted with the police chief, who shook his head. “No,” she said.

“We passed a large cemetery on the way in,” Sarah said, still jotting down notes from her prior questions. “Have there been any grave robberies recently or any signs that the site has been disturbed?”

Concern creased the mayor’s face as she consulted Juan Pablo again. “No, nothing like that,” she replied. “During the festival, many people go to the cemetery on the third day to celebrate their ancestors. There is food and music, but the burial sites are sacred. They are not disturbed.”

“Have any adults left El Rosario in the past few weeks?”

“Many who can have left with their children, yes, mostly to other cities where they have family. But that was after the disappearances started. Otherwise, no more than usual. Some go to the coast this time of year to work."

"There's been no talk of family members not being able to reach them?" Sarah pressed.

"No."

Though the line of questioning no doubt sounded strange to the mayor, Sarah was being systematic. Centurion's computer algorithm had already eliminated ghouls and wights—they lacked the brains to disguise themselves as clowns and didn't look human enough anyway—as well as several of the more common Prodigium IS. That left a short list of candidates and probabilities. Sarah was eliminating the lowest-probability ones first: lycanthropes, then zombies under the thrall of a necromancer, then humans under the thrall of a vampire or evil sorcerer. It was scary how much I had learned in the last week.

With Sarah's next question, I knew we'd moved on to vampires themselves.

"Have there been any suspicious deaths among the livestock? Cows, horses, pigs?" In the reams of information Centurion's computers had parsed, the algorithms learned that some vampires, especially those newly turned, began with animals before working their way up to humans.

"I don't think so." Mayor Flores posed the question to her police chief anyway. Following a short exchange, he shook his head, then stopped and talked at length, hands in motion.

The mayor turned back to us. "We haven't heard of anything like that, but with all of the cooking and smells of food, the festival attracted a lot of stray dogs. They show up every year. Like pests, they scurry around the market, stealing food. The week after the festival, the police usually have to put out poisoned meat to control the population. But this year, Juan Pablo says they didn't have to. After the festival, a lot of the dogs left on their own."

As Sarah jotted down the information, I mulled the connection. Disappearing dogs, abducted children...

"Have any of the strays acted oddly or attacked people?" Sarah asked.

The mayor shook her head slightly, consulted the police chief, then shook her head with more certainly. An affirmative answer might have raised the probability of vampires. There had been a case in Rome years before where a vampire fed on dogs, but without killing them. The dogs returned as vampire spawn, forming a pack that went after humans. A sorceress in the area eventually put them down and finally staked and decapitated the vampire.

"What do you plan to do?" Mayor Flores ventured.

Since Sarah was running the interview, I gave her a chance to answer—we'd already discussed the plan. But she was making additional marks in her notes, deaf to the mayor's question.

I leaned forward. "We're going to spend the few remaining hours tonight setting up here. Early tomorrow, we'll split into teams. One will set up a surveillance system around the town. No one and nothing will come in or out without our knowledge. The other will conduct a reconnaissance patrol into the foothills. We'll be looking for any evidence of where the children were taken and what took them."

"Oh, here are the things you asked for." Mayor Flores reached into her large woven purse she'd hung over the back of the chair and removed several articles of children's clothing.

"Thank you," I said, already picking up the unique human odors of the disappeared children. That would help during the patrol—as well, I hoped, as the peppery smell I'd detected on the dead cat.

"And tomorrow night...?" the mayor asked tentatively.

She was referring to the ultimatum: surrender another child or the town would know death.

"Let us worry about that," Sarah said.

"What my partner means," I said, looking over at her, "is that we should have more information on what we're facing tomorrow. If we haven't ended the threat by nightfall, we'll regroup. At the very least, we'll have a better idea what we're facing. We'll know how to proceed."

"In the meantime, no one should go out alone," Sarah said. "Not even adults. You need to move up your curfew an hour. Everyone in their homes by six, doors and windows shut and locked."

Though vampires *could* operate during the day, even in direct sunlight, they were much more powerful—and hence active—at night.

"Make it under threat of arrest, if you have to," Sarah went on. "They are not to venture out for anything, and under no circumstances are they to invite anyone unknown inside their homes. If they don't feel secure there, arrange for them to sleep in the church."

"And this will keep them safe?" Mayor Flores asked.

"It will make them safer than they are now," Sarah replied.

But the assurance—if that's what you could call it—did little for the tension across Mayor Flores's face. "We should let you get started, then," she said. Following a round of parting handshakes, I walked the mayor and police chief to the door, while Sarah went into the office, where Rusty had set up her computer.

The mayor paused in the doorway and clutched my hand once more. "These are dark times for El Rosario," she whispered, "but by the grace of God, you have come."

I nodded at her imploring eyes, bid her and the police chief goodnight, and closed the door behind them. As I pulled my helmet from my shaggy head, I caught myself hoping that if God *had* sent us, it was because he thought we were ready. I walked over to the office, where Sarah was all but attacking a keyboard with her fingers, and leaned against the doorframe.

"Sounds like you've reached some conclusions," I said.

"I still need confirmation. I'm entering the query data now."

I waited, watching the glowing reflection of the screen in her glasses. She hit the return key twice hard, then hunched further forward to read. At last she leaned back with a nod and faced me.

"According to the database, the ability to write intelligibly coupled with the existing data suggest vampire. Add the missing dogs, and that probability goes up by fourteen percent. No other creature comes close."

Hence her instructions that the town remain indoors and to not allow anyone inside at night. According to Centurion's data, a vampire required an invitation to enter someone's domicile. That went double for churches. Probably explained the clown disguises. It would be easier for vampires to lure children into the woods than pluck them from their beds. It also explained the note left under the mayor's door. With the restrictions on the children's movement curtailing disappearances, the vampires were demanding the town bring the children to them.

I looked over my massive MP88, remembering Billy's ashen face as he peered up at me and rasped, *It's bad, isn't it.*

"Vampires it is, then," I growled.

11

With the van unloaded and Centurion's patented security gates over the doors, Rusty began setting up the office surveillance system. Sarah configured the computers, and I assembled and organized the weapons. Yoofi left trails of cigar smoke as he paced around, casting what he called *lingos* or protections against evil. Centurion didn't have a lot of intel on magic, but I remembered Prof Croft talking about wards to guard his apartment. I assumed *lingos* were something similar.

Yoofi hollered in surprise.

"What is it?" I called from the downstairs storage room.

He came hustling in, his flasks clinking in the long coat that fell around his legs. "There is already magic here, Mr. Wolfe!"

I set down a drone I'd been arming. "Magic? You sure?"

"Yes, Dabu can feel it."

"What kind of magic?"

Yoofi shook his head. "Dabu cannot tell where it comes from. He just knows it's here."

Whatever its source, I didn't like the idea of someone else's magic moving around our compound. Even at its most harmless, it could be monitoring our actions.

"Can Dabu dispel it?" I asked.

"Don't know 'bout that. When dispel magic, all its power is released."

"But that's the whole idea, isn't it?"

"Ooh, very dangerous to try, Mr. Wolfe. Power could hurt people, hurt equipment. Make weapons explode. And not just in this here building. If powerful magic, could hurt the whole town."

I looked around at our arsenal. "Good to know," I muttered.

Yoofi blinked as though struck with sudden insight. "I know! Dabu will set up the lingos *inside* the other magic, like a fence. That way if bad magic, Dabu's magic will block it."

"That won't set off a reaction or anything? Having two spells so close together?"

Yoofi giggled. "Sometimes, yes. But Dabu promises to be very careful."

Coming from a trickster god, that didn't exactly reassure me. But I decided I'd rather take the risk than be subject to some form of compromising magic. And part of forging us into a team was trusting in my teammates' skills and encouraging their initiative. "Go ahead," I said. "Just be smart about it."

As Yoofi left, I walked over to the office.

"Did you catch that?" I asked Sarah.

She glanced up from her computer. "No, what?"

"Sounds like there might be magic at play. Yoofi's

feeling some strange energy around the building. Could have been left by whoever dropped off the cat."

Sarah frowned at the development. Her fingers hammered the keys as she amended the query she'd made earlier. "A magic-user who is turned retains an ability to cast," she said when the results came up.

"A vampire wizard?"

"Or witch. It's rare, but there are examples."

Damn, I thought, remembering my short battle with Prof Croft. *Human* magic-users were powerful enough. And I was no expert on magic to begin with. "Should that change our planning?"

"Probably, but not yet. Like you said, tomorrow will involve gathering as much information as we can. While you take the teams out, I'll stay and go through the records. I'll also talk to Mayor Flores, find out if there are any practitioners of magic in the area."

"Great," I muttered. "I'll be sure to pack extra ammo."

But would *any* ammo be effective against a vampire wizard?

Following breakfast at 0600, I called the team together downstairs. I had spelled Takara from the rooftop so she and the others could get a few hours of sleep. Since being transformed into the Blue Wolf, my senses were super active at night; as a result, I didn't sleep very well. Fortunately, I no longer required much rest. The last was also true of Olaf, who had stayed on patrol out front.

Now the six of us gathered around a large satellite map of El Rosario that I'd taped to the wall. I'd marked the sites where the children had been abducted. Their photos, with identifying information written on them, were taped beside the map. As impressive as Centurion's technology was, I still thought better with pen and paper.

I took a moment to look over the team. Everyone was attired in their tactical gear. Those of us going out wore packs as well. Takara, not surprisingly, had stuck with only her leather suit and the vest she'd selected back at the Legion compound, and with no helmet in sight. She stood front and center, as though challenging me to say something. Instead, I cleared my throat and addressed the entire team.

"A few words before we head out. Our mission in El Rosario is twofold. One, to find and recover the abducted children. Two, to destroy the creatures that took them. By Centurion's best estimate, we're looking at vampires. At least five. As we learned in training, they're super strong, super fast, and super lethal. Their ability to regenerate also makes them hard as hell to take down. Remember, rounds through the heart can stun a vampire, so that's where you'll want to direct your fire. Decapitation is the only surefire way to kill them."

Though Yoofi had the blade on his staff, Takara had the ones in her sleeves, and the rest of us carried combat knives, we had yet to practice decapitation in training.

"Does anyone think they'll have a problem with that?"

Everyone shook their heads except for Takara, but I wasn't worried about her. I continued.

"Our chances of encountering one during daylight is slim—solar radiation weakens them—but it doesn't mean it can't happen. Especially since half of us are going to be moving through some pretty dense foliage. There's also a chance at least one of them can use magic. Sarah will be staying here to dig deeper into what that might mean. The rest of us will head out in two teams. Rusty and Olaf will take the cargo van to set up Rusty's surveillance system around town."

"I designed her to be installed quick," Rusty said with pride. "Shouldn't take more than four hours. An hour to test, some final tweaking, and we're gold. Right, big man?" He gave Olaf's shoulder a companionable slap. Olaf rolled his deep-set eyes toward him and let out a dull grunt.

The two were going to make an interesting team.

"While they're getting the system up," I said, "Takara, Yoofi, and I will take the passenger van to here, disembark, and patrol the foothills." I indicated an area on the map near where three of the children had disappeared. The scents from their clothing were stored in my olfactory vault. "See if we can pick up a trail. Both teams will remain in radio contact with one another as well as with Sarah. If anyone encounters a vampire, let the rest of us know immediately."

"We have contact," Yoofi said, as though rehearsing.

"We're all carrying GPS locators, so everyone's positions will be on your tablet." I pulled mine from a vest pocket and held it up, a flat gray device a little larger than a standard smartphone. "Rusty sent up two surveillance drones this morning that will coordinate with his perimeter detection system. Both are armed and can be diverted, if needed. Centurion also has a quick reaction force about twenty minutes out, but they're only to be called as a last resort."

Having worked with Centurion soldiers in the field, I was still skeptical about their level of training and effectiveness. I would use them for evac before I counted on them in battle. Especially against vampires.

"One more thing," I said. "Rules of engagement. Though we'll be operating around the edges of town, people are going to be out and about today. If you're carrying a rifle, maintain trigger and muzzle discipline. We are not cleared hot unless and until we're absolutely certain we're dealing with an enemy. Always be aware of your field of fire. The last thing we want is for an innocent to take a bullet. This town has suffered enough. Any questions?"

Takara surprised me by raising her hand.

"Yeah?"

"We're wasting time standing around here."

"Damn," Rusty muttered, blowing out his breath. "That didn't sound harsh or anything."

I narrowed my eyes at her and donned my helmet. Just when I thought we were starting to get along.

"That wasn't a question," I snarled. "Let's roll."

We rode in silence, Yoofi beside me, nodding to the faint beat and string of expletives leaking from his ear buds. Takara was in the back, doing whatever it was she did to prepare herself, eyes closed. Though I tried to swallow it down, her comment back at the compound had left a sour taste in my mouth.

I had puzzled on and off about our exchange the week before, what she'd said about having problems with me as an American, something to do with our history. The only thing I could come up with was the atomic bombing of Hiroshima and Nagasaki, especially since she'd been born in the first, but that had been more than eighty years ago. Our two countries had long since made their peace. And how could she have been there? She wasn't old enough to have experienced Vietnam, much less World War II. I shook my head. There was really no telling with her, and right now I had a mission to worry about.

As we drove through town, I took in the people. The women wore colorful traditional dresses, while the men were decked out in cowboy hats and denim pants, long machetes sheathed at their belts. Worry lines etched their weathered faces. They edged to the sides of the road as our van passed between them. I spotted only a few children, their wrists firmly clutched in an adult's hand.

After several blocks, the people fell away and the road turned to dirt. I rolled to a stop at the end of a weathered cornfield—the site of the first, third, and eighth abductions—and parked at the edge of the tree line. Yoofi removed his ear buds and smoothed his braided hair.

"I'm going to take point," I said. "Yoofi, you'll be flanking me on the left. Takara, I want you on the right and a little behind. You're going to be responsible for rear security. The woods are thick, so no more than five meters spacing. I want us all to stay in visual contact."

Yoofi took a shot from one of his flasks and then clutched his staff in both hands. "I'm ready, Mr. Wolfe."

I turned to Takara, who was still sitting perfectly erect with her eyes closed. "Takara?"

When her lids shot open, narrow red crescents ringed her irises, the same ones I'd seen the morning we'd gone one on one. For a moment, she didn't look quite human, but the effect faded.

"Like we practiced," I told them.

We exited the van. After ensuring the area was secure, we proceeded into the woods, Takara bearing an M4 and me my bulky MP88. The pattern on my camos shifted to blend with the surrounding foliage. The smells of lush leaves and damp soil flooded my nostrils. I wandered around until I picked up a thread of one of the children. The scent was accompanied by the odor of her abductor's face paint. Both were faint, but they gave me a trail.

For the next hour, we followed the scent trail into the foothills. I had to periodically adjust Yoofi's spacing—he was either drifting too close or straying too far—but Takara maintained a perfect five meters as she slipped around trees, ever vigilant to our rear. I may have had little so far to like about her personality, but her skills were undeniable.

Where our first climb leveled off, I signaled a stop. The scent trail had come to a sudden end. I peered around, but there was nothing to see but trees. Far below, bits of El Rosario showed through breaks in the leaves.

Yoofi and Takara kept watch while I removed my helmet and gloves and took a drink of water from my Camelpac. I then consulted the map. I was inspecting the terrain features around our location—where in the hell could the vamp have disappeared to?—when a soft whistle sounded.

I turned to find Takara with her lips pursed, signaling down the hill from us. I dropped the map and raised my weapon. Above the twittering of birds and the gurgling of a nearby creek, I caught a twig snapping. A second twig groaned, as if a foot were easing its weight from it. Not seeing anything, I attuned my lupine hearing toward the site until I picked up a rapid cycling of breaths.

I looked back at Takara and nodded. About thirty

meters downhill from us, behind a thick tree, someone—or something—was hiding.

I listened another moment to ensure there was no one else down there. But there was just one breather, his or her breaths occasionally snagging on a clot of phlegm before starting up again. I signaled to Takara, and she began to move quietly off. I then turned to Yoofi and motioned for him to stay put. He nodded as dark energy warped the air around his blade.

I sidestepped to the left as Takara circled the breather's position. With my enhanced hearing, I could just pick up her movement, but only because I was listening for it. I waited until she was coming around the breather's rear before motioning Yoofi forward. Leaves and branches broke beneath our footfalls, but that was all right. Our target was corralled now.

I kept a steady watch on the tree through the MP88's sights. When we'd approached to within fifteen meters, the brush around the tree's base shook. Yoofi hollered, and a spiraling bolt of black energy shot from his staff. It struck the tree trunk and broke apart in a cloud of rank smoke.

"Hold your fire!" I shouted.

With the smoke providing cover, the breather bolted. I got enough of a glimpse to know what we were dealing with. Swinging my weapon on its strap around my back, I bounded after him on hands and feet. Within seconds, I was behind the sixty pounds of flailing arms and legs. I reached a taloned hand forward and grabbed the boy by the back of his dirty shirt.

"Déjame!" he shouted as I lifted him up. *"Déjame, hijo de puta!"*

I knew enough Spanish to understand he'd just called me a son of a whore.

As his dangling body rotated around the shirt in my grasp, I realized I'd never put my helmet back on. A moment later, we were face to face. The scrawny boy, who couldn't have been older than ten, went slack. His eyes all but stood from his grimy face as they looked over my wolf features.

My teammates arrived on either side of me. "A boy," Takara said in disappointment, sheathing her blades.

Yoofi giggled and shook his head.

I lowered the boy to his bare feet. Thin scratches climbed his legs to a pair of shorts stiff with dirt. His long hair was littered with leaves and twigs, and a cross pendant swung from around his neck. He glanced around at Yoofi and Takara before wiping his running nose and returning his gaze to mine. He looked half-terrified, half-enthralled—and all human.

I pulled out my tablet and scrolled through the photos of the missing children before radioing Sarah. "We encountered a boy on our patrol," I said, "estimated age nine or ten. He doesn't ID as one of the abducted, but he looks like he's been out here for a while. Can you interpret for me?"

"Yes. You can start by asking his name," Sarah said. *"Como se llama?"*

I posed the question. The boy stared for another moment before whispering, "Nicho."

"I want to know where he's from and what he's doing out here," I said.

Sarah provided the translation, which I repeated, trying not to flash my fangs.

"El Sauce," he said, fingering his cross pendant. *"Estoy escondiendo."*

Sarah replied quickly. "He says he's from El Sauce—that's a village one valley over—and that he's hiding."

"Hiding from what?"

When I asked the boy in the Spanish, he whispered, *"El payas—"*

Yoofi let out a yell and collapsed to the ground.

"What is it? What's going on?" I demanded, but Yoofi was babbling in a language I couldn't understand. Had he been shot? He began to writhe, arms and legs kicking like they were possessed.

"El payaso," the boy repeated in a louder voice.

I turned back to him. *Payaso?* Where had I heard that before.

"The clown," Sarah practically yelled into my earpiece. "He said he's hiding from the clown."

I wheeled toward where the boy was staring. In the spot where the trail had ended stood the clown with the skeleton face—Calaca. He watched us with red eyes, his thin lips breaking to form a grin to match the messy one painted around his mouth. His exposed teeth glinted like blades.

"We have contact!" I broadcast to the team.

I shoved the boy behind me with one hand as gunfire exploded from the muzzle of my MP88.

12

Leaves and branches burst as incendiary rounds exploded around the vampire clown Calaca. He was in motion now, his skeletal frame seeming to dance as he flashed in and out of cover. I glanced to my left. Yoofi was still writhing on the ground, his staff beside him.

"Circle to our three!" I called to Takara. Calaca was too damned fast. We needed to box him in. But when I looked over, she was nowhere to be seen. "Takara?" I called into my earpiece.

No response.

Had something happened, or was she freelancing again? Something told me the second. Fantastic. I released another burst of automatic fire. Remembering the boy, I peeked over a shoulder. Nicho was standing stock still, frozen by the sudden appearance of the clown and the ear-splitting explosions. I grabbed him by the shoulder and shoved him flat.

"Stay there!" I shouted, showing him with my hand.

There was too much going on. I peered back up the hill. Calaca's floppy red bow flashed through the dense foliage. Switching triggers, I picked out a narrow thread running between the trees and fired four grenade rounds into his path. Those didn't miss. Calaca released an inhuman shriek as brutal detonations of shrapnel blew flesh from his bones and knocked him from his feet.

I sprinted up the hill until I had a clean line of sight on him. His torn skin was already healing, wounds melding back into waxy brown flesh. Underneath his makeup, he looked like he'd once been a local.

As he leapt to his feet, I switched back to the rifle and poured automatic fire into his emaciated body. More chunks of flesh flew from his bones. The impacts threw him into a tree, his screams more enraged than pained.

"Not so fun when someone fights back, huh?"

His painted face twisting, talons flashing from his fingers, Calaca coiled to launch himself at me. My next burst of rounds blew open his chest and pierced his heart. In a gust of smoke, he flopped face down. A single grenade round fired beneath him flipped him like a pancake.

I arrived above him seconds later. Calaca looked catatonic, blood-red eyes staring past the smoke rising from his body. His shredded skin was closing, but slowly—thanks to the silver powder. I slung my weapon over a shoulder and unsheathed my combat knife. Wrapping Calaca's body with an arm, I sat him up in front of me and placed the knife against his throat. His neck was barely the circumference of my wrist. With my superhuman strength, I had only to flex to take his head off and end him. But first I needed information.

As I waited for him to come to, my skin broke out in gooseflesh. Even through my protective wear I could feel the cold that emanated from him, a greedy chill that sucked the heat of life from anything within its aura.

"I have one of the vamps," I radioed to Sarah. "I want to ask him where they took the children."

"Dónde estan los niños?" Sarah said.

I waited for Calaca's breaths to return in thin gasps, then I embedded the knife blade in his throat until it was sitting atop his narrow larynx. *"Dónde estan los niños?"* I demanded.

I held him from behind, my free arm clenching his bony body. Calaca struggled inside my grasp. His returning strength would soon match mine. I dug the blade in deeper. *"Dónde estan los niños!"*

A giggle rasped from his lips. He drew in his breath as though to answer, but in the next instant the back of his head smashed into my snout. Pain exploding through my nose, I swore and flexed my knife arm. Flesh and bone crunched beneath the blade, but my faltering grasp had given the clown an opening, and now he was twisting free from me. With a final thrust I tried to complete the decapitation, but he was out, and I was falling onto my back.

As he peered down at me, I saw that I had nearly succeeded. One of his gloved hands was holding his head on his nearly hacked-through neck. Half of his face paint had been rubbed away, and I could see a cheap-looking tattoo of a teardrop beneath the corner of his right eye.

I lunged toward him, but a clown shoe caught me in the chest, knocking the wind from me. I lashed out with the other taloned hand, but he was already taking off, head jostling sickly between his hand and healing neck.

Eyes watering from the blow to my nose, I struggled up. I glanced over to make sure the boy was still down—he was—and gave chase. I'd be damned if I was going to let the vampire clown get away.

I brought my weapon around, raised it into firing position—and watched Calaca disappear. One second he had been leaping over a fallen tree, and in the next, he was gone.

"What's going on?" Sarah asked.

I arrived at the spot a second later, but it was as if the earth had swallowed him whole. The clown was nowhere. Heart slamming, I peered wildly around. I then raised my healing nose and sniffed. For an instant I caught an odor of decay, but the smell of the woods rushed over it, and I had nothing.

"Lost him," I growled.

"Is the clown gone?" Yoofi asked.

I turned to find him coming up the hill, leaning on his staff with each limping step.

"Yeah," I grunted, peering around again. "What in the hell happened to you?"

"Ooh." Yoofi shook his head as he arrived beside me. "Dabu was telling me a joke when all of a sudden I heard him scream. The sound like a spike through my head. Something scared Dabu bad. And then just like that"—he snapped his fingers—"the screaming stopped."

I wondered if Calaca had hit him with a spell.

"Did it feel to Dabu like the magic in the compound?"

"Don't know," Yoofi replied. "When it ended, Dabu ran and hid. Won't talk to me."

"So you're defenseless." When he nodded, I sighed and

handed him my loaded Beretta. "Keep the safety on until you need it."

I spotted the boy peeking through the brush and waved for him to join us.

"Where's Takara?" Yoofi asked as he shoved the weapon down the front of his pants like a gangster.

"Good question." I pulled the tablet from my vest and was bringing up the map when something whirred into my hearing. A moment later, the whirring turned to whacking. Shredded leaves fell from the canopy. Yoofi fumbled for the pistol, but I showed a staying hand.

"Sorry I'm late," Rusty said over the commo feed as a drone appeared through the foliage. *"We heard your call, but Olaf and I are a good thirty minutes out. I overrode Drone 1 and sent her over."* The drone hovered overhead, the camera buzzing as it adjusted its aperture to the dim light.

"Just watch where you point the payload," I said, eyeing the missiles I'd armed it with the night before.

"What happened to Takara?" he asked.

"Don't know," I said. "I was just about to pull her up."

"No, that's what I'm saying, boss. She's not showing up in the system."

"Not showing up?" I accessed the map and looked. Sure enough, icons pulsed for the rest of us—I could even see Sarah's back at the compound—but nothing for Takara.

I looked around. The woods were quiet, the smoke from the battle dissipating and drifting off. Aside from some chewed-up trees, there was little to suggest the freak fight that had just gone down.

"Are you seeing anything, Sarah?" I asked.

"Nothing on my system either. Takara, do you copy? Takara, do you copy?"

Once again, no response. Could she have deactivated her GPS and communication? Sure, but why? It didn't make sense. She'd been right beside me just a couple of minutes ago.

"Keep Drone 1 under the foliage and start a radial search of the area," I told Rusty. "I'll see if I can pick up her scent."

"Aye, aye, Captain," Rusty answered as the drone whirred away.

Small crunches sounded in the undergrowth. The boy had gotten up, and now he approached with tentative steps. "It's all right," I said, waving him toward us again. The boy sped up until he was standing beside me. He clutched the side of my pants for security, then peered around wide-eyed.

"El payaso no esta," I assured him. The clown was gone. Then a thought occurred to me. "Hey, Sarah, how do I ask if he saw where Takara went?"

"Dónde se fue el mujer?" she said.

I knelt in front of Nicho and posed the question.

"La sombra," he answered. *"La sombra se la comió."*

"'The shadow,'" Sarah translated. *"He's saying, 'The shadow ate her.'"*

The shadow *ate* her? *"Dónde?"* I asked.

I followed the boy's pointed finger to the spot where the clown had disappeared a minute earlier. Had I missed a cave or something? I left him and searched the area, heaving aside limbs and fallen trees. But the ground was solid. There were no caves, and by the time I had cleared the area, there were barely any shadows. Takara was simply gone.

"I suggest we regroup back at the compound," Sarah said.

"The rest of you could be at risk. There's some new information we should go over as well."

But I was already shaking my head emphatically.

"Not without our teammate," I growled.

13

We searched the area for the rest of the morning, Yoofi and I on foot, Rusty using the drone. Without me having to tell him, Nicho stayed close to my side. When our efforts failed to turn up any signs of Takara, I went against my earlier reservations and called in Centurion's quick reaction force.

By early afternoon, eight men in battle gear joined the search. I organized them into two patrols. From the valley, Rusty made several attempts to reboot Takara's GPS device and reestablish radio contact, but no dice. It was as if Takara had fallen off the face of the earth.

When a hard rain began to hammer the tree canopy in the late afternoon, I suspended the search. We needed to start planning for that night, and with dusk nearing I wasn't going to leave the Centurion force alone in the woods with vampires out and about. Leaving Takara out here was bad enough.

As the soldiers flew back to their base, I drove Yoofi and Nicho to the compound. The van's windshield wipers slashed at the falling rain while the tires crashed through massive brown puddles.

"Is Dabu saying anything yet?" I asked Yoofi.

He shook his head. "I give him much smoke and drink, but whatever happened scare Dabu good. He doesn't want to talk right now."

"Will that change anytime soon?"

Yoofi shrugged his shoulders. "I don't know, Mr. Wolfe."

A god of the dead scared? That didn't bode well.

I looked over at Nicho in the passenger seat. I had given the boy several energy bars over the course of the search, and now, fed, and protected from the elements, he was fast asleep. We would consult the mayor about what to do with him—maybe a family or the church would take him until he could be returned to his village—but in the meantime, I wanted Sarah to talk to him. Find out what he was doing in the foothills and what he knew about the vampire clowns.

I pulled the van into the empty carport. Rusty and Olaf were out, doing final tweaking on the surveillance system. Sarah emerged from her office as Yoofi, Nicho, and I entered the main downstairs room. Though her expression remained flat, I picked up a few strain lines around her eyes. Whether they were out of concern for Takara or from staring at computer monitors all day, I couldn't tell. I removed my helmet and gloves and set them on the table.

"Is anyone hurt?" she asked.

I turned to Yoofi, but he showed his hands. "No, I am fine now. But Dabu needs more drink."

"The vampire and I mixed it up a little," I said as Yoofi went off to refill his flasks, "but he didn't get his teeth or claws into me." I rubbed the place on my nose where Calaca had smashed me with his head. It had healed, but the warrior in me still smarted from not finishing the decapitation.

"Do you believe Takara was taken?" Sarah asked.

"Ultimately, yeah." I walked over to the wall map. "We first made contact with Calaca here." I tapped the spot with a talon. "The boy says he last saw Takara up here. She may have been attempting to climb to a more advantageous position. I don't know because she didn't communicate like we'd trained."

Dammit.

"But that's where Nicho says the shadow 'ate' her." I bracketed the word with hooked fingers and looked over at the boy. He was kicking an empty water bottle around the room like it was a soccer ball.

"The vampire you faced might have been a teleporter," Sarah said.

"A teleporter?" I echoed.

"Like I said, there are accounts of magic-users being turned into vampires. Mayor Flores denied knowing any practitioners of magic in the area, though. And despite an exhaustive search on Centurion's database, I came up with little actionable info, so I looked into ... other sources." She glanced away in evident discomfort. "The internet, namely. The integrity there will always be suspect, of course, but when you described how Takara and the clown disappeared, I began searching for an explanation. It seems some magic-users have the ability to teleport themselves—and others—to remote locations. Allegedly."

"Well, it would explain his and Takara's disappearances into thin air," I said, also thinking about how the scent of the missing child I'd been tracking had just ended. "And Yoofi's confirmed there's magic at play."

"Ooh, very bad magic," he said, rejoining us. He took several gulps from a flask.

"Still, even if we're talking teleportation," I said, "the question remains: Where are they being taken? Any intel on how far these magic-users can teleport? Our search covered a five-mile radius."

"Up for debate," Sarah answered. "I found several forums where fights had broken out over the question. Opinions ranged from only locations the magic-user could see to hundreds of miles."

"So we don't know, in other words."

Sarah shook her head. "I can keep searching."

At that moment, the water bottle skidded past us, Nicho in hot pursuit.

"Let's focus on the boy while we have him," I said. "If he's been in the woods, hiding from clowns, he may have seen other things."

"Nicho," Sarah called. *"Necesitamos hablar."*

The boy left the water bottle spinning on the cement floor and joined us at the table. He chose a seat across from Sarah, then pulled the neighboring chair close to his and waved for me to sit beside him. He'd become attached to me over the course of the day, despite—or maybe because of—my wolf face. Yoofi took a seat at the end of the table and lit a cigar.

"How long were you in the woods?" I asked Nicho.

Following an exchange in Spanish, Sarah said, "Since yesterday."

"Why did you go into the woods? Why did you stay?"

"He says his father grazes their four cattle in the woods around their village. He ties each one to a rope, which is secured to a tree. Their largest cow, a bull with long horns, got off his rope late in the day, so his father sent Nicho in search of him. Nicho could hear the bull lowing high in the hills, so he followed the sound. When he got there, the bull was down on the ground. A clown was kneeling over him, sucking the blood from his neck."

For a jagged instant, my mind replaced the image of a bull with Billy, my childhood friend.

"When the clown looked over at him, Nicho saw a monster," Sarah continued. "The sight scared him so badly he ran. But he became lost, so he hid out that night and for the next day. He said that's when the wolfman found him." Sarah adjusted her glasses. "He means you."

"Yeah, thanks. I got that. Did he see anything else?"

After speaking to him, she said, "Just the shadow that ate Takara."

I dragged a hand through my hair as I got up to pace the room. "Something doesn't add up. If the vampires are preying on children, why is Nicho still with us? There's no way he outran that thing. So either he's lying—and I'm not picking that up—or the vampire let him get away."

"Or he was protected," Sarah said.

I followed her gaze to the cross pendant dangling over the boy's chest. "The other day you told us crosses couldn't protect someone against a vampire," I said. "You called it a myth."

"It is, unless the cross is imbued with power." When I narrowed my eyes at her, she added, "The section on magical artifacts was scheduled for week four. I was going to cover it in detail."

"Yoofi?" I said.

Nicho flinched as Yoofi bent toward his necklace, but I patted the boy's back to assure him it was all right. "Hmm,"

Yoofi said after a moment. "Hard to tell without Dabu, but I don't feel anything in the metal."

I took my turn to inspect the cross. It looked like cheap nickel silver. Embossed on the back of the cross's horizontal beam were the words THE SACRED LAMB. On the vertical beam, MODESTO, CA.

When I read them out loud, Sarah nodded. "The Sacred Lamb is a California-based Pentecostal church that does outreach work down here," she said. "I came across them in my research on the region."

"What's their stance on magic?" I asked.

"Strongly against," Sarah said. "Which would seem to rule out magical protection."

I released the necklace and tapped Nicho's chin lightly with a knuckle, making him smile. "So why else would a vampire leave him alone?"

"Maybe the vampire was too full from bull," Yoofi suggested.

"Yeah, maybe," I said. "Or maybe the vampires have a special taste for the kids in El Rosario. Look at the map—villages dot the region. Strange that none of them have been targeted."

Though Sarah's face remained flat, I could tell she was working out the puzzle.

"All right, let's review what we know," I said. "A group of vampires have appeared in the area. At least one of them is a magic-user. They've lured eight kids from El Rosario—and *only* from El Rosario—into the woods in the last month. And then the vampires are teleporting them ... somewhere. Finding out why they're concentrating on El Rosario could put us one step closer to an answer."

A knock sounded on the front door. “It’s Mayor Flores,” she called from outside.

I put on my helmet and gloves, checked the monitor, and let her and the police chief inside. Both entered wearing rain jackets even though the afternoon monsoon was now spent. The mayor carried a basket, steam leaking from a colorful cloth that covered the basket’s contents.

“I brought tamales for your dinner,” she said, setting the basket on the table. She glanced at Nicho, a question in her eyes, before turning to the rest of us. “How did it go today? We heard the shooting in the mountains this morning, then saw the helicopters come and leave.” Hope lifted her voice.

“The operation is ongoing,” Sarah said stiffly.

I rolled my eyes. For the sake of Centurion’s reputation, she wanted the mayor to believe we were still in control of the situation. But we weren’t, and I knew from experience that there was no quicker way to lose the confidence of a client than for them to find out you’ve been lying to them. If we were going to salvage the mission, we needed to shoot straight with one another.

I stepped forward. “We didn’t find the children or where they had been taken. We did, however, make contact with one of the creatures. A vampire. That was the shooting you heard. We injured the vampire, nearly killed him, but he disappeared. One of our teammates went missing as well. The helicopters were a backup force I called to help search for her. I suspended the search with the coming night so we could focus on the ultimatum.” I had been thinking about that on the ride back here. Knowing the vampires’ next move could be an advantage.

Mayor Flores shared the information with Juan Pablo,

who nodded gravely. Maybe because of their traditional beliefs, they didn't question the notion of vampires. "And this boy?" she asked. "I have seen him in town before, but I don't know him."

"We found him in the woods." I then gave a succinct account of how he'd come to be there. "Is there someone in El Rosario who can take care of him tonight?"

Following another exchange with the police chief, the mayor said, "Juan Pablo's family can take him. They have clean clothes in his size and a spare bed. Juan Pablo will drive him back to his village in the morning."

As Mayor Flores explained to Nicho what was going to happen, the boy looked up at me. I ruffled his hair and nodded that it was all right, that he would be safe. He stood from his chair and followed Juan Pablo. The police chief paused at the door, searching his pockets.

"Over here," I said, lifting the car keys from the table and tossing them to him.

He gave an embarrassed laugh as he caught and pocketed them, and then thanked me in Spanish. Given Juan Pablo's absentmindedness, I hoped the boy would be safe with him.

"It's very lucky he wasn't taken," Mayor Flores said when Nicho and the police chief had left.

"Or maybe there's something more at work besides luck," I said. "Is there any reason you can think of why a boy from the next village would be, I don't know, *passed over* in favor of a child from El Rosario?"

The mayor's brow furrowed as she shook her head. "No. They are indigenous, like us."

"Do the villagers around here have much contact with El Rosario?" I asked.

"Yes, most of them come here on market days to buy and sell."

I racked my brain. There had to be something that differentiated them.

"How about culturally?" Sarah asked. "Do they participate in the festival?"

"Oh, nooo," she said emphatically. "They stay away that week."

Bingo, I thought. "Why?"

"You have seen our church in the town center. It is a Catholic church, built hundreds of years ago. One reason Catholicism became established here was because our people were not made to choose. The first missionaries allowed the people to worship their own gods and ancestors alongside God and the Catholic saints. That is why, during the festival of St. Paul, we reenact the great myths."

"And that's also why the villagers stay away," I said, thinking of the cross around Nicho's neck. "They became Evangelicals."

"Yes, the Sacred Lamb came in the 1950s. They made few inroads in El Rosario, but were able to convince several villagers that the traditional ways were evil. Those villagers became charismatic pastors, and the belief spread throughout the countryside." She paused. "Do you think they are involved in this?"

"Have there been any conflicts between the villages and town?" I asked.

"Some arguments from time to time, but nothing violent. Nothing like this."

"Are any of the pastors especially outspoken?" I followed up.

"There is one," she said. "A man named Salvador

Guzman. He lives in the village of Salamà. He comes here on market days and preaches over a sound system. No one listens to him, though."

Sarah looked over at me, one eyebrow raised in question. The information could explain why El Rosario was being targeted and not the villages, but I couldn't figure out exactly how. Believing strongly enough in the evil of the old ways might have moved someone like Salvador Guzman to violent action, but contracting vampires seemed a dramatic—and suicidal—way to go about it. I thought about taking a trip out to Salvador's village, but I didn't like the idea of traveling at night. Anyway, the clock was ticking on the vampires' ultimatum.

"When's the next market day?" I asked.

"Tomorrow," the mayor replied, "though the crowds have been smaller since the disappearances."

"Do you think Salvador will come?"

"Oh, yes. He has been using the tragedy to strengthen his message. He says we are being punished for our beliefs."

"We'll talk to him then, but first we need to plan for tonight." I checked my watch. "We have just under five hours until the vampires expect El Rosario to leave a child across the river. Don't worry, that's not going to happen. All of El Rosario will be safely indoors."

"We are going to defy them?" Mayor Flores asked worriedly.

"Not exactly." I turned to Yoofi. "Will you be able to cast again by tonight?"

He had been puffing fervently on a thick cigar while we'd been speaking. "Yes, I think so."

"Good. I have a plan."

14

MP88 tight in my grip, I crouched at the edge of a tree line on the outskirts of town and scanned the parade ground. The large moon behind the cloud ceiling cast the old military base in a haunting light. I checked my watch: 23:50, ten minutes until the vampires' midnight deadline.

"Everyone in position?" I whispered.

"Yes," Olaf answered from the tree line two hundred meters away.

"I'm overhead," Rusty said. I had already heard the whirring of the hovering drone. He was controlling it from our compound back in town.

"We are ready," Yoofi said. He, the mayor, and the police chief were in a house across the river from the base.

"You sure?" I pressed him.

"Yes."

"I can see the manifestation through the window," Sarah put in. *"It looks solid."*

Yoofi had spent the rest of the evening giving copious

smoke and alcohol offerings to Dabu, praying that he be allowed to cast through him. At the eleventh hour, when I was on the verge of switching to our fallback plan, Dabu had relented. If Yoofi or Dabu fumbled now, the operation would be a bust.

"Move out," I said.

A door opened across the river. Footsteps sounded on the bridge. Moments later, Mayor Flores and a young girl came into view at the edge of the old base. The girl was wearing a traditional dress and embroidered white blouse, her black hair pulled tightly back in braids. The detail was impressive. My wolf vision even picked up a small heat aura around her.

When they arrived at the center of the parade ground, the mayor said something to the girl in Spanish, showing her hands for the girl to stay. The girl peered around in fear at the thought of being left there alone. She let out a whimper, the whites of her eyes shining large in the night.

"Don't oversell it," I whispered.

Mayor Flores gave the girl a final regretful look, then turned and hurried from the base and back across the bridge. The girl remained on the parade ground as she'd been told. Hands clasped at her chest, she alternately looked into the woods that crowded the edge of the old base and down at her sandaled feet. It was a convincing show, even to someone like me who *knew* the girl was an apparition.

Now we just had to hope the vampires would buy it too.

Seconds ticked by. I listened into the woods. Except for the occasional drip from the day's rain, the trees were silent. I checked my watch again, then took mental stock of our positions. Olaf to my right; Yoofi directly across the river from me; Sarah across the river from Olaf; and Rusty a couple thousand feet overhead. We had the parade ground boxed in with enough firepower to deal serious damage to whatever set foot inside it—living or undead.

I was still kicking myself for allowing the vampire to escape earlier in the day. *Won't make that mistake again,* I thought, glancing down at the line of metal stakes sheathed in my tactical belt. A stake through the heart, and a vamp would go into shock. By the time the stake was pulled, I would have him hog-tied in the razor wire I had packed in a Kevlar pouch. Then we'd get some information—namely where Takara and the children were.

The apparition of the girl blinked in and out.

"What's happening?" I asked, tension deepening my voice.

"Dabu is sensing the evil again," Yoofi said. *"Not as strong as this morning, but still strong."*

"You need to hold it together for just a little bit longer," I said, checking my watch. Two minutes till midnight.

"I will try," Yoofi groaned through the feed.

"I'm seeing movement," Rusty said suddenly. *"The camera can't penetrate the tree cover, but there's some serious rustling going on. Something's coming down the hill and coming fast."*

"Trajectory?" I said.

"Straight for the parade ground."

I listened until I could hear what sounded like a crunching stampede through the woods. The sound was soon accompanied by frothing breaths and snarls. Vampires? I didn't think so. Whatever was coming sounded more animal than human—and they were numerous. Were they here for the child, or was this the promised punishment for *not* delivering the child? Adrenaline dumped into my system as something told me the second.

"We're about to have company and lots of it," I said, checking that my rifle and grenade launcher were both charged. "Rusty, lock on as soon as you have a visual. Olaf, pull in a little. They'll be coming right between us. Sarah and Yoofi, don't let anything cross the bridge."

I stood and peered into the woods where the savage sounds grew by the second.

"They're splitting," Rusty said. *"Got a group heading toward Wolfe and another toward Olaf."*

Crap.

Within another few moments I could see them: dogs. But not the man's-best-friend variety. These had been transformed into undead monsters. Their eyes glowed a sickly green as bits of foam flew from their mouths. I remembered what the police chief had said about the recent drop in the stray dog population. No doubt we were looking at the explanation.

"Undead dogs," I said. "Aim for their heads."

We had learned in training that while killing a vampire required cremation or decapitation in most cases, a vampire spawn could be put down via massive brain trauma. And we definitely had the means.

I took aim at the front of the pack charging through the trees and released a burst of automatic fire. The lead dog fell as incendiary rounds blew chunks of flesh from his chest before taking off half his head. I heard the first shots coming from Olaf's rifle as well. I switched my aim, squeezing off bursts as their sinewy bodies flashed in and out of view. But for every dog that succumbed to one of my explosive assaults, four more seemed to bound into its place. When the pack was less than a hundred meters away, I decided there were too many.

"Olaf, fall back!" I ordered. "Rusty, hit them when they come out!"

The two radioed back their understanding as I took off at a sprint. The girl still stood in the center of the parade ground, but I doubted she was fooling anyone. Yoofi kept up the ruse though, having her flinch away from me as I bounded past her. Off to my right, Olaf moved at a lumbering run. Dogs were just beginning to pour from the woods behind him.

"Missiles incoming," Rusty announced.

A series of explosions shook the ground and lit up the night. Undead dogs yelped and flipped through the air, many of them in parts. But more plunged through the dissipating balls of fire and kept coming. I was nearly to the far side of the parade ground when the dogs bounded past and through the apparition of the girl, reinforcing my theory that no one had been fooled.

Dammit.

More missiles exploded along the tree line. *"I've shot my load,"* Rusty said. *"Sweet Jesus, there are a lot of 'em."*

I stopped long enough to pick off two dogs that were almost to Olaf, but I had my own pack in pursuit. A glance back showed me the slavering mass of at least twenty of them. I turned so that I was running backwards, switched to my flamethrower, and released a sweeping jet of pressurized napalm. The charging dogs went up in plumes of fire. That slowed and confused them, but they kept their feet, making them look like hellhounds.

"Keep going, Olaf!" I called as I cleared the parade ground.

A dog had latched onto the back of his neck, and he was reaching over his shoulder to punch his combat knife into its head. I maintained a steady stream of napalm on the pack coming for me. Another dog got its teeth into Olaf's arm, but like an All-American fullback, Olaf churned on.

The instant he cleared the parade ground, I hit the detonator pinned to my tactical vest. The Claymores we'd placed around the field thudded loudly, blowing shrapnel and silver powder into the pursuing dogs. I swapped for a fresh rifle mag and began lighting up fallen creatures where they kicked and writhed. Having dispatched the two dogs attacking him, Olaf did the same. As the smoke began to drift off, the parade ground looked like a slaughterhouse.

But another wave of dogs were pouring from the woods.

"How many mutts did the vampires drain?" Rusty asked in disbelief.

"Enough to make the town 'know death,'" I said, quoting the vampires' note. I switched my trigger finger to the automatic grenade launcher and fired a volley in the path of the arriving dogs. The explosions blew apart several of them, but the carnage only seemed to excite the ones bounding in behind them.

"It gets better, Boss," Rusty said. *"We've got packs coming in from the north and south now too."*

"Go," Sarah said to me. *"We'll take care of these."*

I looked across the river. Yoofi stood on the rooftop of the house in which he'd created the apparition of the girl. He grimaced, and a coiling black bolt shot from his staff and blew apart an especially large dog. Sarah was on the roof of the house across the street, seated behind a heavy .50 cal machine gun. I nodded. This side of town was in good hands.

"Olaf, head south," I said. "I'll take the pack coming in from the north. Rusty, send the other drone with Olaf."

"What about you?" Rusty asked.

"Rearm the first drone if you have time," I replied. "I may need the support."

I switched my trigger finger back to the rifle and covered Olaf's retreat over the bridge, then followed him at a backward run. When we reached the town side of the river, I turned to Yoofi.

"Blow the bridge!"

He nodded and aimed his staff. A growing ball of black energy swirled around the blade, then cannoned out. The impact didn't so much blow the bridge as dissolve it, the span of wood and earth crumbling into the thrashing river. Several dogs that had started across the bridge plummeted and were swept away. The rest skidded to a stop at the far bank.

"Light 'em up!" I called.

A four-foot flame belched from the barrel of the .50 cal as Sarah worked the thumb trigger. Her aim with the heavy gun was true. I watched long enough to see three dogs explode before I turned and began sprinting to head off the south-bound pack. Above the hammering of the .50, I could hear savage barking ahead—along with the sound of thick nails scratching over wood.

"How are we looking?" I asked Rusty.

"They're in town and spreading out, trying to get inside the houses."

"Hear that, Olaf?" I said. "They're mixed in with civilians now, so careful with your fire."

Between grunted breaths, Olaf answered, *"Yes, sir."*

I'd gone five blocks when I spotted several dogs around

an adobe house. They stood on hind legs, front paws digging at the door and bricks of dried mud, teeth tearing at the wooden frames. Voices screamed inside the house, and now I heard the bawling of a child. When the wood of the front door splintered, the bawling turned to a piercing shriek.

Shit.

I knelt and sighted the dogs throwing their weight into the door. I squeezed off single shots, careful to keep the rounds from impacting the house. The three dogs that represented the most immediate threats went down, skull fragments and brain stuff littering the dirt road. The remaining dogs swung their heads toward me and narrowed their glowing green eyes.

I switched to the flame thrower, igniting them as they launched themselves at me. I then dropped them with short bursts of rifle fire until they were flaming corpses.

I proceeded block by block in this manner, picking off the dogs I could, baiting others into the street and hitting them with napalm before finishing them. Rusty directed me to the most immediate threats. Fortunately, no homes had been breached so far, and I noticed the dogs were staying away from the church, where a number of townspeople had taken refuge earlier in the day.

"How are the others doing?" I asked.

"Yoofi and Sarah are handling the west side," Rusty answered. *"And Olaf ... well, he's still standing. Not sure for how much longer. I've got his dogs in the drone's sight but can't get off a clean shot."*

"Olaf?" I said.

"I am all right," he grunted underneath what sounded like a snarling pile. I could hear his blade crunching into

their bodies. The man had the power to regenerate from bites and scratches, sure. But if the dogs managed to tear an arm off, there would be little to stop them from finishing the job. I doubted Olaf would be able to recover from total dismemberment.

"Call if you need backup," I ordered.

"I will," he managed.

"Boss, you got another pack coming up on your six," Rusty said. *"Like, right now!"*

I'd mistaken the sounds behind me for those coming through my earpiece. Stupid. I wheeled as the first dog plowed into me. The dog wasn't big, but his power surprised me. I fell back several steps. Before I could raise my weapon, half a dozen more dogs piled on until I felt like I was back in Waristan, challenging the Kabadi wolves for control of the pack.

Only this time I was armed and armored.

Jagged teeth dug into my arms and legs but couldn't punch through the Kevlar. Another dog had its jaw around the front of my helmet, foam smearing the visor as the dog's teeth worked madly for purchase.

I dropped my MP88 on its sling and tore my gloves away. My talons freed, I let my wolf take over. In a flurry of slashes, hair and flesh flew everywhere. When a dog went down, I crushed its head beneath my boot. My other boot broke through a rack of ribs. Within moments, I was the only canine still standing.

"Whoa," Rusty said. *"Bad. Ass."*

Panting, I cleaned my face shield off with a sleeve, retrieved my gloves, and brought my weapon back into firing position. "Where are the rest?" I asked.

"A few lone mutts to your east." Rusty directed me to

them, and I finished them off with precise shots to the head.

From there, I sprinted south to help Olaf. Sarah and Yoofi had taken care of the dogs at the river, and I ordered Yoofi to join me. I met him near the town square.

We found Olaf two blocks later. He had fought his way from beneath the pack and was torching more dogs with napalm. With half his shirt ripped away and his left arm soaked in blood, he was a mangled mess, but he insisted he was all right. Together, the three of us put down the remaining undead mutts.

As Olaf and Yoofi peered around, I listened for any more padded footfalls or frothing breaths.

"That's all of 'em," Rusty informed us.

"Nothing more coming from the woods?" I asked.

"That's a negative."

For the first time I let my shoulders relax slightly. "Let's head back to the river. We'll have Sarah take a look at you, Olaf, and then we'll regroup." I couldn't imagine the vampires had spawned any more undead dogs—we had put down more than a hundred. But the canine assault could have been intended to soften up the town's defenses for their own arrival.

"Uh, boss, scratch that," Rusty said. *"We've got something else."*

I looked all around. "Vamps?"

"No, a frigging bull. At first I thought the shooting had spooked it from a nearby field, but the damn thing just buried its horns into a house. And it's backing up for another charge."

"Nicho's bull," I said in realization. "Do you have a clean shot?"

"Not without taking down some infrastructure with people inside."

"Get me there," I said.

Houses blurred past as Rusty steered me through the streets. I had started off a half mile from the attacking creature, though, and Rusty's updates weren't encouraging: *"He's broken inside the home ... Okay, he's back out in the street ... Shit, he's got something in his mouth."*

"A kid?" I panted, trying to push myself harder, faster.

"Yeah, bull's got him by the arm, and he's hightailing it towards the woods."

Streaks of light darted around the edges of my vision as I tried to find another gear. The undead bull was taking the child to the vampires. I couldn't let him. Seconds later, I was passing the breached home. A man and woman had emerged into the street, staring in horror down the dust trail left by the departing bull.

"Mi hijo!" the woman screamed. *"Mi hijo!"*

We'll get your boy back, I thought. *One way or another.*

I struggled to recall my high school Spanish as I jabbed a finger at the neighboring house. *"A dentro!"* Inside!

I was past them before I could see whether they complied.

"Bull's about two blocks from the woods," Rusty said. *"And man, is he moving."*

I skidded around a corner. Ahead I could see the bull's tail lashing back and forth between a massive pair of flanks. Through the dust, I could just make out the child—or his dangling legs, anyway. He was short enough that his feet weren't dragging over the road. Still, I couldn't risk a shot. I'd have to catch the bull and bring him down.

I had closed to fifty meters when the bull broke into the trees and began churning uphill.

No you don't, you son of a bitch.

Headlights flashed from behind me, illuminating the line of trees in pale light. I recognized the sound of the engine: our van. It ground to a skidding stop as I entered the woods. The doors cannoned open and my teammates piled out. I was about to warn them not to fire when Yoofi let out a familiar scream.

And just like that, the bull and the boy seemed to disappear into thin air.

15

"They're winning, dammit," I growled as I paced the room.

Sarah, Yoofi, and I had returned to our compound, where I sent Yoofi to bed. He was still trembling from whatever Dabu had felt before the bull disappeared, and he was in no shape to assist us. Rusty monitored the surveillance system, with orders to report any and all activity. Olaf had recovered fully from his bite wounds and was now patrolling the streets, leaving Sarah and me to strategize. But Sarah was absorbed in her laptop, which she'd set up at what had become our planning table downstairs.

"I wouldn't use the word 'winning,'" she said absently. "They didn't make the town know death as they promised."

"Yeah, because they got their kid." I remembered the horrible image of the boy dangling from the undead bull's mouth.

"It could have been worse."

"And it could have been a hell of a lot better."

I stopped in front of the wall map. Zeroing in on the

parade ground at the old military base, I reviewed the mission in my mind for the umpteenth time. The weaponry, positioning, and communication had been sound. The rest of the team had performed capably, which I had been sure to commend them for. The failure was on me. I had underestimated our opponent. I believed Yoofi's apparition would work because a similar spell cast by Prof Croft had gotten us past a pair of soldiers into a military base a few weeks earlier. But we weren't dealing with humans anymore.

"Maybe we should have used a real child," Sarah said.

I looked at her in disbelief. She was still staring into her laptop screen. "A child isn't bait," I said.

"It would have improved the odds of success."

"So would nuking the entire province."

She glanced up. "We're talking about one child. We had the parade ground covered."

"We're talking about one child with *two parents,*" I said, my voice growing a surly edge. I was thinking of the parents of the just-abducted child, the way the mother had screamed. "Legion could never have guaranteed that child's safety, covered or not. Don't bring it up again."

"I'm just suggesting that at times we need to consider taking calculated risks."

"How can any risk be 'calculated' when we still don't know what in the hell we're up against?" I shouted.

I had rarely lost my temper as a Special Ops Captain, but that was before the Blue Wolf had become my copilot. Prof Croft warned that I could lose control in times of stress, and right now my needle was in the red. I was angry, mostly with myself. Underestimating our opponent, losing another child to the vampires, losing a teammate earlier in the day. Though I'd held deep reservations about joining a mercenary squad, I had believed in my ability to lead them.

That belief was being challenged right now.

"What do you think I'm trying to do?" Sarah replied, her own voice developing an edge. "We need to expand on what we know so we can act accordingly. We need more information."

"From where? The internet?"

The frustrated pinch of her lips told me that was exactly where she had been looking. I took a calming breath, walked up to the table, and closed her laptop. She tensed as though she were going to flip it back open, but then she sat back.

"Centurion has nothing on what we're facing," I said, "and anything you find on the internet is going to be suspect at best. I know someone we can contact, an expert in the field. He may be able to help."

"Who?"

"His name's Everson Croft. He lives in Manhattan and consulted for the mayor's eradication program. He was in the clip you showed us on day one, wizard versus ghoul. I happened to work with him a few weeks ago. I have his contact info."

"No," Sarah said.

"No what?"

"No, you can't contact him."

Anger spread hot over my face. "Why not?"

"Centurion has to vet outside experts, and there isn't time."

"Given the urgency of the situation, I'm sure they'll make an exception."

But Sarah just shook her head again. "Even though

we're on assignment, the Legion Program is technically still in beta testing. The workings of the program remain classified. Even El Rosario's officials had to sign nondisclosure agreements."

"Croft has no interest in stealing Centurion's trade secrets and selling them to the highest bidder."

"The policies and procedures are clear on the matter," she continued. "I'm assuming you've read them?"

I ignored the not-so-subtle dig. "How about we call Purdy then?"

"He'll say the same thing I did. He'll just do it more nicely." She reopened her laptop and leaned forward, her lenses glowing white again.

"And if I call Croft anyway?"

"I'll have no choice but to report you."

I stared at her for a few seconds. "You're a real piece of work, you know that?"

"I'm just doing my job," she replied, hammering the keys. "A job I've worked most of my life to get to. I'm not here to be anyone's friend."

Though I attempted another calming breath, my voice remained thick with emotion. "We're running out of options. By refusing to seek outside help, you're crippling our chances of ever seeing those kids alive again, not to mention Takara. Same with ending the threat. What happened to your talk of calculated risks?"

"I meant risks not covered in Centurion SOP."

I barked out a laugh. "Written by compliance officers who have never been shot at much less had to face down a vampire or a pack of undead dogs. Maybe that's your problem. Maybe you only have an encyclopedic understanding of what these things are, but no firsthand knowledge of their true evil. When I was twelve, three vamps killed my friend. You've read the account—it's in my file. What you didn't read was how they laughed while they were doing it."

Sarah raised her face, eyes hard behind her lenses.

"Maybe *that* should go into the policies and procedures manual," I said. "A requirement that all future members have had at least one encounter with the kind of monsters they'll be facing."

"I do have experience," she said quietly.

I'd been prepared to dismiss whatever she said next, but Sarah's eyes had changed. For the first time they glimmered with emotion. I felt my breathing cycle down. "What happened?" I asked at last.

She averted her eyes and shook her head. "It's not important."

I took the seat across from her, Captain Wolfe again. "I want to hear it."

She stared at the laptop screen until I thought she was tuning me out. "I was fourteen," she said after another moment. "My parents were missionaries, and we were living in a remote village in the Philippines. We had been there for almost a year when we heard rumors of a disease outbreak in a neighboring village. People contracting fevers and dying. My parents didn't seem too concerned for us, or maybe they just hid it well. We had been immunized against most tropical and communicable diseases before arriving. My parents had my younger sister and me wear surgical masks as a precaution, though.

"One night, I was awoken by screaming. I looked out my bedroom window and saw a woman facedown on the dirt road that ran past our house. She looked like she'd fallen. I remember seeing a red high-heeled shoe a few feet behind her. People were crouched over her as she screamed. At first I thought they were trying to help her up, but then I realized they were eating her alive."

"Jesus," I whispered.

"Lights went on in the houses around ours. Villagers began to emerge. They shouted at the people attacking the woman like they knew them, but the people never looked up from her. And more of them were coming, shambling down the dirt road. They didn't look right. Dressed in dirty suits and dresses. Sores on their faces. Some of them carried machetes."

"Zombies," I said.

Sarah gave a small nod. "The Filipino word is *sombi*, and that's what the villagers started to say. My father burst into the room and pulled me from the window and my sister from her bed. As he rushed us to the back of the house, I could hear more people screaming and then the wet hacks of machete blades. My father led us down into a canned food cellar, where he told us to stay. We weren't to turn on the light or make a sound. He said a quick prayer, his voice raw in a way I'd never heard, then kissed our foreheads. When he left, he closed the cellar door and padlocked my sister and me inside."

"Listen, you don't have to go on," I said. "I get the picture. I'm sorry I questioned your experience."

Sarah continued staring at the laptop screen as if the events were playing out in front of her. "The screams went on for a long time. I covered my ears and told my sister to do the same, but I could still hear them. And then windows began to break in our house. Something grabbed the cellar door. I remember the sound of it rattling in the frame. With my ears still plugged, I started chanting, 'Go away. Go away. Go away'—loud enough that I couldn't hear anything else. I must have done that for hours, waiting for the moment a hand would close around my neck, and my sister and I would end up like the woman in the street."

I noticed that Rusty had edged closer to the door of the office to hear better.

"Finally, a light flared over my closed eyes. A hand grabbed my wrist. I knew it was either my father or a zombie. I wished for the first, but expected the second. The hand was wet. When I opened my eyes, I saw a man in an olive green uniform, the front of his shirt spattered with blood. He was shining a flashlight at me and eventually worked my finger from my ear so he could talk to me. He was a member of the Philippine National Army. He was going to take my sister and me someplace safe, but he needed to blindfold us first. He didn't have sores like the zombies, so I trusted him. He covered our eyes with bandanas and knotted them behind our heads. As he led us up the stairs and into the morning light, I realized I could see through a small seam at the bottom of the blindfold. Around our feet was blood and broken glass. I smelled smoke. In the distance I could hear bursts of automatic gunfire.

"Outside, the soldier helped my sister and me into the back of a large truck. We were squeezed in beside other villagers, their eyes covered like ours. As the truck pulled away, I leaned my head back to see better. I knew I shouldn't have, but I couldn't help it. The street was littered with bodies. In an empty lot farther down, there was a huge fire. Soldiers were feeding it with the dead. Every time they heaved another one onto the flames, this awful black smoke would billow up. Right before the truck turned a corner, I saw them throw on my father's body."

"I'm so sorry," I said. "Your mother...?"

Sarah bit her lower lip and shook her head. "She didn't survive the attack either."

"Dude," Rusty said. "I don't mean to eavesdrop, but that is the gnarliest thing I've ever heard."

His voice seemed to snap Sarah from the memory. She looked up from the laptop. "I know your stories," she said, her voice and eyes stiffening. "It's only fair you know mine."

"I'm glad you shared it," I said.

Rusty gave me a look that said, *Speak for yourself, boss,* before disappearing back into the office. As my gaze returned to Sarah, I thought about her medical background—trauma and pathology residencies—and then her military training. When I'd questioned her motivation for joining Centurion, she'd said, *To protect the innocent against beings we're only beginning to understand.* She hadn't been paying lip service. Everything she'd aspired to be went back to the zombie attack. Much like everything for me went back to Billy's murder. But that's where our similarities ended. Sarah had been so focused on attaining—and now preserving—her current position that she'd lost sight of what mattered.

I was searching for something to say, but Sarah spoke first. "We only have a few hours till daylight. What's our next move?" No hint that she'd just relived the most traumatic experience of her life.

I cleared my throat. Now wasn't the time to revisit the debate about consulting Prof Croft. I'd call him later if I had to, and I wouldn't involve Sarah in the decision. If it meant breaching my agreement with Centurion to save those children's lives, so be it. Would that nullify Centurion's obligation to make me human? Would it jeopardize my future with Daniela? Huge questions for Jason Wolfe, but to the Blue Wolf they felt a million miles away.

"Salvador Guzman, the Evangelical pastor," I said. "The mayor thinks he'll be at the marketplace today. I say we get a few hours rest and then talk to him. There has to be a reason the vampires are terrorizing El Rosario and not the surrounding villages. He might know something."

"He might even be the magic-user behind it all," Sarah said.

I nodded. I'd been thinking the same thing.

I checked my email before turning in and found a message from Segundo:

---

sorry for the delay. contacted my bro through an account he doesn't check very often, or so he says. anyway, he did a background check on your boy kurt. it came back pretty clean. no priors except for the drug job in texas. no outstandings. he's been living with the same woman in orlando for the last couple of years. my bro's going to check an arrests database when he goes back in tomorrow, but sounds like your

```
boy is keeping his nose clean.
hope that helps.
```

I thanked him in my response, then closed the laptop with a heavy exhale. That *did* help. Maybe Kurt Hawtin was a reformed man, or maybe he was just doing whatever it took to hold onto his provisional nurse's license. But the knowledge that he'd been behaving, and was in a long-term relationship, seemed to lessen the likelihood that he was back in Texas because of Dani.

Which meant I could return my full attention to the mission.

16

Sarah and I set out for the marketplace on foot the next morning. Other than a sanitation crew loading what remained of the dog carcasses into a pickup truck, there was little to suggest last night's attack. The morning was sunny, the sky a brilliant blue, and the streets surprisingly busy. I guessed some of the people had come from surrounding villages for the market day.

"Do you think we stand out?" Sarah asked as we merged into the foot traffic headed for the plaza. When I looked over, I was surprised to catch one side of her mouth turned up. It was the first time she'd exhibited even the slightest sense of humor. I wondered if opening up about her zombie experience last night had helped lower her defenses.

"Just a little," I said.

We were both wearing our Centurion suits and tactical vests, sidearms at our belts. And then there was my roughly seven-foot, four-hundred-pound frame, which dwarfed the diminutive people of El Rosario. I'd already caught a lot of fearful glances. Good thing they couldn't see my face.

"Next time I'll put in a requisition for suits in the local color," Sarah said.

I chuckled inside my helmet. I liked this side of her.

We turned a corner and entered the market. In front of the Catholic church, tented stalls were arrayed across the plaza, vendors peddling everything from fruits and vegetables to traditional crafts to racks of blue jeans and pirated CDs. There were a good number of vacant stalls, though.

I pointed across the plaza. "I'm guessing that's our guy?"

Sarah followed my finger to where a slender man in a black suit and aviator sunglasses stood on the lower steps of a municipal building. He was shouting into a microphone, broadcasting what sounded like the world's longest run-on sentence through a sound system.

Sarah listened for a moment, then nodded. "It's him."

I radioed Rusty and Olaf as we rounded the marketplace and gave them Guzman's position. Yoofi had recovered somewhat from Dabu's second freak-out, but his god had yet to come out of hiding. He hoped some ritual dancing would change that.

"Can you understand what Guzman is saying?" I asked Sarah.

"Basically that the recent events in El Rosario signify the End Times. The town must reject its false idols and repent or else face eternal damnation. The window for salvation is closing."

I remembered what Mayor Flores had said about the town mostly ignoring the preacher, but this morning a small group was spread around the base of the steps. They remained back a cautious distance, but they were listening.

Two were women in traditional dress. "Looks like he's got at least a few people thinking conversion," I said. "I guess zombie dogs have a way of doing that."

"Maybe that was the point."

"I'm in position," Olaf radioed.

"Okay, we're moving in," I answered.

Sarah and I sped our pace. Guzman continued to rage into his microphone, occasionally mopping his forehead with a white handkerchief. He was younger than I'd first thought, his face smooth and lean, his jet black hair gelled into an Elvis-like pompadour.

Sarah and I mounted the steps on either side of him.

"Necesitamos hablar," Sarah said when the preacher paused for a breath.

Guzman ignored her and thrust himself forward into his next burst of fire and brimstone. He spoke as though entranced. Sarah looked at me, then over at the small generator powering his system. I took the cue, walked over, and shut it off. The voice that boomed over the marketplace died along with the motor. That got his attention.

"How dare you silence an oracle of God!" Guzman cried in accented English.

Without his system, his voice was high and thin. He stormed toward me, his pompadour bobbing on his head. In warning, I held out what was probably the largest hand he'd ever seen. Guzman slowed, regarded my hand and my considerable height, and then came to a stop several paces back.

"My partner asked you a question," I said.

His mouth twitched. "I have a question for you, sinner. Are you ready for what's coming? Are you ready for—"

"You'd be wise to cooperate," Sarah interrupted, coming up behind him.

I stole a glance across the plaza. Olaf was on a rooftop, head bowed behind a sniper rifle. He was our overwatch in case Guzman *was* a magic-user and tried to cast. The preacher didn't see Olaf, though. He was watching his small crowd break apart.

"Esperen!" he called, dropping his microphone to lunge after them. *"Vuelven y arrepentirse!"*

"He's calling for them to come back and repent," Sarah translated.

But Guzman's voice didn't hold the same authority as it did when amplified, and the locals disappeared into the marketplace.

"I bet that makes you happy," he seethed as he returned. "Allowing Satan to claim more souls. Can't you see what's happening? Can't you see what's coming? The signs are everywhere!"

"We just want to talk," Sarah said.

"Who are you?" He parked his sunglasses atop his hair and stepped closer, eyes flicking between us before narrowing in on my visor. His lips slanted into a hard grin. "Why do you hide?" He raised a slender finger and tapped the opaque visor twice. "Is it that you carry the mark of the beast?"

There was no way he could have known about the symbol the old woman had carved into my cheek, but that wasn't the reason for what I did next. Guzman yelled in pain as I grabbed his hand and twisted hard. In the next moment, I had both of his wrists cuffed behind his back. Sarah drew her sidearm and aimed it at his head, but gave me a questioning look.

"That smell on the dead cat?" I said. "Preacher man here is wearing the same on his jacket."

"Are you sure?"

As more of the peppery-sweet smell slipped into my helmet, I nodded.

Guzman was oblivious to our exchange. He seemed to be contracting every muscle as he writhed and bucked against the cuffs. "There's no time for this!" he shouted. "Release me or face God's wrath!"

"The tape," I said.

Sarah pulled a small roll of duct tape from her vest, tore off a length with her teeth, and covered Guzman's mouth. I then jerked him back so that my mouth was beside his ear. I didn't know if he could cast without speaking, but I wasn't going to take any chances. "Listen to me and listen good," I growled. "I have special senses. I feel any magic coming off you, and I'll snap your neck before my partner can put a bullet through your head. Do you understand?"

His eyes flew wide and he screamed something beneath the tape.

I gave him a hard shake. "Shut up. Do you understood? Yes or no?"

His eyes crept up my visor before he gave a slow nod.

"Keep your sidearm on him," I told Sarah as I patted him down. My search turned up a pocket Bible, a billfold, and a set of keys. I took Guzman by the upper arm and led him around the market toward the police station. A much larger crowd than the one that had gathered for his sermon watched us pass.

I called Rusty on the radio. "What's Yoofi doing?"

"Besides chanting and stomping around like a drunk?"

"Tell him to meet us at the police station ASAP."

"You got it, boss. Nice take down, by the way."

The police chief and Mayor Flores, whom we had clued in to our plans, were waiting at the station when we arrived. When Guzman saw them, he began to protest harder behind the tape sealing his mouth. They led us down a corridor to a windowless room with a table and a few chairs. I sat Guzman down on one side of the table and removed his sunglasses. His eyes seethed as Sarah and I took the chairs opposite him, Sarah still covering him with her sidearm.

"Is he behind what's happening?" Mayor Flores asked from beside the closed door.

"We don't know yet," Sarah answered. "But we have reason to believe he was the one who put the dead cat in our compound."

Guzman screamed some more behind his tape.

"We're just waiting on one more," I said. Remembering Nicho, I asked, "Did the boy make it home all right?"

"He did not want to go."

"Probably still in some shock," I said. "Sarah, maybe you should take a look at him."

Sarah nodded, but the mayor was shaking her head. "No one knows where he is now."

My heart missed a beat. "What do you mean?"

"This morning he ate breakfast with Juan Pablo and his family, but when it was time for Juan to drive him back, the boy disappeared. They looked everywhere, but they couldn't find him."

Perfect, I thought. *Someone else missing.*

"Also, Juan Pablo's shotgun is gone," the mayor said.

I frowned in concern, but there was no way to tell whether the two events were connected. The police chief, who struck me as absentminded, had nearly walked off without his keys last night. He could well have misplaced the shotgun. My main concern was for Nicho's disappearance. Even if he hadn't been taken, I still felt responsible for him.

"Have them keep looking," I told the mayor. I then radioed Rusty and instructed him to keep watch for a boy fitting Nicho's description. "Shouldn't be too hard," I said. "He'll be the only kid in El Rosario without an adult attached to him."

I had just completed the order when the door opened, and the police chief showed Yoofi inside. Yoofi stared around the room, as though his eyes were adjusting to the dimness, before finding me. "You wanted to see me?"

"Yeah," I said. "How's it going with Dabu?"

"Yes, yes, going well. He liked my dance. He's still not talking, but he's around."

"Good, take the seat beside Guzman there. If Dabu feels anything like he felt yesterday, tell us immediately." In order to interrogate the preacher, I needed to pull the tape from his mouth. Yoofi would act as our advanced-warning system if Guzman tried to cast or teleport away.

"Tell you?" Yoofi said. "If it happens again, I fall down screaming."

That would work too, I thought, but didn't say it. Instead, I drew my sidearm and with the other hand picked away a corner of the tape on Guzman's face. "You remember what I said earlier? Try to cast and you're a dead man. In fact, don't even talk unless one of us asks you a question. Are we clear?"

I waited for him to nod before ripping the tape off.

He winced, then cried, "Magic? Casting? What is this blasphemy you accuse me of?"

"Hey!" I roared, thrusting my pistol's barrel toward his chest. "What did I just say?"

This wasn't my usual MO for interrogations, but I couldn't take any chances. Guzman looked down at my pistol, then up at my visor. His face screwed up in hatred, but he remained silent.

"Better," I said. "Now, let's cut through the bull. You have strong feelings against El Rosario, right?"

"Not against El Rosario," he said. "Against their evil practices."

"Have those feelings led to action?"

"Yes," he said. "I come to town and I preach. But the words I speak are not my own. They are God's words." He narrowed his eyes at me and Sarah. "When He is not interrupted."

"Anything else?"

"I pray for El Rosario."

"And how do you do that?"

"With my heart, my mind, and my voice."

As he spoke the word *voice*, I glanced over at Yoofi. He was sitting with his staff between his knees, sipping brandy. When he saw me watching, he smiled and tipped the flask in salute.

No signs of distress, apparently.

"Why are children being taken from El Rosario?" Sarah asked.

"They are not just being taken," Guzman replied with a mean grin. "They are being *punished* for the town's sins."

Mayor Flores charged the table, a torrent of Spanish shooting from her mouth. Sarah intercepted her before she could reach the preacher, and convinced her to let us finish the interrogation. But I was fighting to control my own temper. This son of a bitch was acting like he knew something.

"Where are they?" I asked.

"They are beyond the reach of the living."

"Where are they?" I repeated.

"In Hell."

The young preacher wasn't putting us on. I could tell he believed what he was saying. He believed that the children were being punished for El Rosario's sins. But despite what seemed a genuine bias against pagan beliefs, there was no question that the scent on his jacket matched what I'd picked up on the dead cat—and Yoofi's god had sensed magic inside our compound. Could Guzman be rationalizing away his magic as prayers, as acting on God's will?

"Did you *pray* to send them to Hell?" I asked.

"I never pray for people to be hurt," he said. "Only to be saved."

"Not even if the ends justify the means?" Sarah challenged.

"Never."

"Then what were you doing with a dead cat in our building?" I asked.

His brow beetled in confusion as his eyes flicked between us. "Dead cat? What are you talking about?"

I leaned nearer. "You left a dead cat in our building. Why?"

At that moment, the room shuddered. The door rattled in its frame. I peered around, my senses on high alert. Were we under attack? I turned back to Guzman, my weapon hand tense, but his eyes were roaming the ceiling too.

"Just a tremor," Sarah explained as the shuddering died down. "We're not far from a fault line."

Guzman scoffed. "That is no quake. That is the evil moving closer."

"Then why don't you tell us about it?" I challenged. "You can start with the dead cat."

"Are you suggesting I'm involved in witchcraft?"

"Right now I'm only suggesting that you handled a dead cat."

He denied the charge with such a powerful *Pfft* that an aerosol of spit flew from his lips. "You are mistaking me for Chepe. He is the one who handles dead animals and wicked idols."

"Who's Chepe?" Sarah asked.

Mayor Flores answered before the preacher could. "He is the Mayan shaman for the region. He has been performing rituals and ceremonies in and around El Rosario for the last fifty years."

"He is the one you should be talking to," Guzman added with a scowl.

"He is wise and well respected," the mayor countered. "He doesn't have a malicious bone in his body."

Guzman barked out a laugh. "Oh, no? Then explain this." He winced and leaned his head back. When his neck stretched from the collar of his white shirt, rows of angry scratch marks appeared above his collar bone.

"Are you saying Chepe did that?" Sarah asked.

"I was loading my sound equipment into my car this morning," he said. "One minute I was alone, and the next Chepe was standing beside me. He warned me not to go to town to preach. When I ignored him, he grabbed my arm." Guzman's eyes cut to one side. "And then he attacked me."

I was sure more had happened between the shaman grabbing his arm and attacking him, but for now I was thinking about the shaman's sudden appearance and that he had grappled with Guzman.

"Were you wearing your jacket?" I asked.

"Yes," Guzman hissed, looking down at it. "He fouled it with his dirty hands."

I waved Mayor Flores over. Though the smell I'd picked up was stronger than what had been on the cat, I still wasn't sure whether it would register for a human. I asked the mayor to smell the sleeve of his jacket anyway. "I picked up something earlier," I explained. "Peppery and sweet at the same time?"

When she leaned down and gave a few tentative sniffs, the preacher looked around like we were all crazy.

Mayor Flores straightened. "It comes from an incense called *pom*."

"Is that something that can be found at the market?" I asked.

"No, *pom* is very sacred," the mayor said. "It is used in powerful rituals. The Mayan shamans make it themselves."

"How many shamans work in the region?" I asked.

"Just Chepe," she answered.

17

We released Salvador Guzman with instructions to contact the police if he encountered Chepe again. The young preacher scowled as he replaced his sunglasses and strode away with a few final warnings about God's wrath, but I sensed he would call if it meant exacting retribution on his rival.

The rest of us, including the mayor and police chief, regrouped back at our compound. I called Olaf inside. While everyone settled around the table, Rusty leaned against the office door in order to keep one eye on the surveillance monitors. He had the drones on autopilot.

"Chepe is not behind this," Mayor Flores repeated before Sarah or I could start the meeting. "He is a healer. He is the connection to our ancestors, to the gods that watch over us. He would never hurt anyone."

"That's important for us to know," I said. "However, there's a reason he scuffled with Guzman. There's also a reason he left a dead cat in here and cast some sort of magic over the building."

"Dabu felt it," Yoofi said, nodding. "*Very* strong magic."

"Who knows what else he's been up to," Sarah put in.

As Mayor Flores filled in the police chief, I wondered about the magic humming around our space. It hadn't given Yoofi's god the willies like the teleportation magic had done, but according to Yoofi that could have been because they were different spells rather than cast by different practitioners. When the mayor finished, Juan Pablo shook his head. Both wore expressions of doubt that their Mayan shaman, or *sacerdote*, had been involved in anything unseemly.

Sarah pointed an accusing finger at Mayor Flores. "When I asked yesterday, you denied knowing anyone in the area who practiced magic."

"That is because Chepe does not practice magic. He invokes favors."

"Semantics," Sarah said with a dismissive shake of her head. "You understood what I was getting at. From now on, we expect honest answers. By withholding information, you're only making our job more difficult. A job you hired us to do, I should remind you."

"Damn," Rusty muttered from the doorway.

Mayor Flores's cheeks reddened. "Are you calling me a liar?"

"All right, everyone," I said, showing my hands. "Let's all calm down." I waited for the mayor to settle back in her chair before proceeding. "Mayor Flores, Sarah does have a point. Had we known about Chepe's abilities—regardless of whether he's involved in what's happening—we might be further along."

Sarah appeared surprised that I'd come to her defense. So did the mayor. For a moment, she looked like she was going to protest before pressing her lips together and nodding.

"Now, is there anyone else in the area who practices magic or can invoke favors?" I asked her.

"No," the mayor said quietly. "Chepe is the only one."

"Do you know the extent of what he can do?" I asked.

"Like I said, he appeals to the gods and our ancestors to heal and watch over us, to see that we have a good crop and harvest. Everything he does is to ensure our protection and wellbeing."

Thoughts of child sacrifices flashed through my mind.

"I'm going to ask a tough question now," I said. "Is there any reason you can think of—any at all—for why he might have turned from the forces that protect you to forces that would want to hurt you?"

"No!" she cried.

"Any mental changes?" I asked.

When she translated for the police chief, he shook his head emphatically. "No," he echoed.

"You cannot believe what Salvador Guzman said," Mayor Flores insisted. "You saw him. He is brash and aggressive. If they fought, it was because of something Salvador did. Chepe is kind and gentle. He was here for the festival last month, performing the ceremonies as he has for the last fifty years."

"Where can we find him?" Sarah asked.

"Chepe has not been seen in town since the festival," the mayor replied. "He lives alone, outside the mountain village of Concul. There was a telephone at the village store once, but it no longer works."

"How far is the drive?" I asked.

"Not far, but the road is in poor condition."

I found the village of Concul on my tablet and examined the winding route. Even at a conservative speed of twenty to twenty-five miles an hour we could be there in under an hour. "All right," I said. "Sarah, Olaf, Yoofi, and I will head up to his place. Rusty, you're going to stay here and pull double duty: keeping an eye on the town and an eye out for Nicho. We'll radio if we need you."

"No problemo, boss. But that means I'll need both drones in town."

"Fine," I said, then turned to Mayor Flores. "I'd like you and Juan Pablo to stay in town as well. Remind people of the curfew and to keep their doors and windows locked. Rusty will be here if you need him."

I was giving the mayor and police chief busy work, but I didn't know what we were driving into. The vampires had a magic-user on their team, and the Mayan shaman was apparently the only one in the area who practiced magic. I didn't know if he was *their* magic-user, but if my worst suspicions came to pass, I didn't want civilians along for the ride.

"What are you going to do to him?" Mayor Flores asked nervously.

"Depends on what we find," I answered honestly.

Mayor Flores hadn't been kidding about the road. Cut from the hillsides, it was narrow and eroded. Sarah kept the van in four-wheel drive as she climbed collapses and swerved to avoid boulders and washouts. Fortunately, no vehicles came from the other direction. There wouldn't have been room.

"The road should level out shortly," I told Sarah. "Then it's another mile to Chepe's place." I turned to the back seat, where Olaf clutched his MP88 and Yoofi was enshrouded in smoke.

"We don't know Chepe's allegiance," I reminded them. "So what does that mean?"

"We don't shoot unless shot at," Olaf replied in his deadened voice.

"Right. And let's remember that the shot could come in the form of magic."

"Ooh, I hope not," Yoofi said, his eyes large and fearful through the haze.

My jaw tensed. Powerful or not, Yoofi's magic was useless if Dabu ran and hid every time our opponent flexed his muscles. I'd been mulling the problem for the last several miles.

"Have you ever tried talking tough to Dabu?" I asked.

"Talk tough, Mr. Wolfe?"

"Every time Dabu goes into hiding, you have to coax him back out with treats—and this morning, dancing? If the shit goes down, we're not going to have time for that. Dabu is supposed to be a god, right? Well, maybe he should start acting like one and not a kid at his first day of kindergarten."

"Yes, but—"

"You're spoiling him, Yoofi."

Yoofi started to bring his cigar back to his mouth, but then stopped and examined it.

"You are," I insisted. "Look at you. The next time Dabu tries to run away, I want you to do something different. Instead of offering him more, tell him he's cut off unless he stays and fights like a god."

"Ooh, Dabu's not going to like that."

"Which is exactly the point. Maybe it will incentivize him to stop turning tail."

Yoofi frowned in thought, then screwed the cap back on his flask. "Okay," he said. "I try that."

"It's leveling out," Sarah said.

I straightened in my seat as the van heaved over the final feet of our steep climb and arrived onto a road that was basically a pair of rutted tracks through the weeds. It was a huge improvement from the road we'd been on for the last twenty miles, though. Overhead, a dense canopy cast the woods in dusky shadow. Something in my wolf nature didn't like this place.

I consulted the map on my tablet. "The trail to Chepe's place is a couple hundred meters ahead. Olaf, let's get out and walk. I'll take front watch, you take rear." The van was designed to be inconspicuous, but I didn't care for the lack of any kind of mounted gun. It was one on a growing list of requisitions I planned to make when we got back to Vegas.

"Don't you ... run," Yoofi grunted.

For a second I thought he was talking to me, but when I twisted around, I found him stooped forward, one hand clamping his brow, the other seizing his staff. Below his clenched eyelids, his gritting teeth shone white.

"What's going on?" I demanded.

"If you run, no more brandy ... no more smokes..."

Shit, he feels something.

My body jerked against my seatbelt as Sarah slammed the brakes. I straightened to find two clowns standing twenty feet ahead of the van. I immediately recognized the one on the left as Calaca, the skeletal clown we'd encountered the day before. Beside him stood his opposite, a clown with a big head, enormous girth, and clown shoes turned inward: Torpe.

"We're surrounded," Sarah said.

I looked in the rearview mirror. Two more clowns were approaching the van from behind: Rata, the rat-faced clown, and a dumb-looking clown whom I recognized from our briefing as Baboso.

I handed Sarah her M4 and readied my MP88.

"Their hearts!" I reminded everyone. "Drop 'em, and I'll do the rest!" The wolf in me was eager for the match we'd been deprived of the night before.

"Wait," Sarah said. "One of the clowns is missing. Loco."

Orange flashed in my peripheral vision. I turned in time to catch a crazed, cross-eyed clown hitting my side of the van like a mortar. My helmet cracked against the reinforced glass, and I lost my grip on my weapon. When the world went upside down, I realized the van had flipped. I braced my arms against the ceiling as the van tumbled and crashed downhill.

From behind me, Yoofi wailed for his god to come back.

18

The van slammed into something solid, and we came to a violent stop. A foot in front of me, the polycarbonate windshield had been smashed a snowy white. I could only make out a dapple of sunlight and the dark green of leaves beyond. We'd been nailed and nailed hard.

Though my head continued to spin, I had enough directional sense to know my side of the van was aimed skyward. I tore my seatbelt away and pawed the footwell for my lost weapon.

"Everyone all right?" I asked, but it came out a garble. The right side of my jaw had been knocked loose. I pried my helmet off the rest of the way and, using a thumb, snapped the joint back into place. The strained tissue healed immediately. Inhaling, I picked up the coppery scent of fresh blood. Not my own.

Beside me—actually, *below* me—Sarah was slumped over, her body twisted at an odd angle.

"Hey," I said, reaching over to give her a light shake. "Can you hear me?"

She was warm beneath her suit, and breathing, but she didn't respond. Olaf was out in the van's rear. I couldn't even see Yoofi. He must have fallen to the floor. I spotted my weapon by Olaf's feet. I was stretching back for it, my head starting to clear, when a shadow darted past the light through the front windshield. The van rocked as something scaled it.

Crap.

I lunged for my weapon, but before my fingers could close around its stock, my door flew away. A bony hand seized my shoulder and yanked me from the vehicle. I grunted as I landed in the arms of the big vampire clown, Torpe. He drove a knee into my gut, then pinned my arms behind me.

"Think you can hold me?" I snarled, ripping my arms free.

I turned, my talons flashing toward his neck. But before I made contact, Rata darted in and landed a rock-solid blow to my face. My jaw clunked loose again.

Motherfucker.

I spun toward the rat-faced vamp, only to be met by a third vampire, Baboso, who landed a pair of cracking blows to my ribs. I doubled over. Loco jumped onto my back. My fist pistoned back, slamming into the red ball covering his nose. Cartilage burst beneath my knuckles. I knifed my talons into his neck, wrenching and twisting them through tissue and bone. Hissing, the clown managed to tear himself away while he still had a head.

I stood in a hunker, arms spread, talons dripping, breaths cycling hard and fast. The vampire clowns circled me, several of them grinning inside the paint that covered their mouths. Loco straightened his neck with a sick crunch and crazed laugh before replacing the red ball on his healing nose. The vampires may have appeared ridiculous on the surface, but beneath the cheap costumes, they were killers incarnate.

So are you, a wolfish voice reminded me.

"Bring it," I growled.

With a collective shriek, the vampires rushed in. The next minute was a bloody melee of slashing and biting. At first, I gave better than I got. Vampires staggered from my furious, hulking form, faces and torsos gashed, shredded clown paraphernalia littering the forest floor. If not for their regenerative ability, the fight would have been over in seconds.

But the bloodsuckers kept coming back, and it soon became painfully clear that while I could match their speed, I was no match for their numbers. I dropped a hand to my tactical belt.

Need to start staking them. Even the odds.

I pulled out the first in my line of stakes. As the next vampire flashed in—Rata—I met him with a hammering chest blow. The metal tip crunched through sternum and ribs before skewering the shriveled flesh of his heart. His narrow rat eyes flew wide as he stiffened and fell straight back.

As I reached for another stake, two vampires landed superhuman blows to my sides. I staggered, breathing stunned, tears springing from my eyes. By the time I blinked my vision clear, the stake was out of Rata's chest, and he was sitting up, the wound already half closed. He stood and joined the other circling vampires.

Gonna have to hit them harder, faster...

I drew two more stakes, one for each hand. As a vampire flashed in for a frontal assault, I swung with my left, already anticipating the crunch of penetration. But the vampire veered deftly away at the same time my back exploded in pain. With a roar, I whipped around to catch the bloodsucker who had attacked from behind. But he was no longer there. My stake sliced through air. A fresh attack to another blind spot buckled my legs.

"Goddammit!" I bellowed in frustration.

The vampires answered with high laughter.

Panting, I swiped at the next one coming toward me. He slipped the stake as my legs buckled from another attack. Through some unspoken exchange, the vampires had shifted strategies, getting me to commit to one of their numbers, then hitting me hard from behind.

And the attacks were taking their toll. My regenerative abilities couldn't keep up.

I made a weak lunge toward the vampire Baboso. Even had I connected, I wouldn't have done much damage. Boom—another shot to my exposed back. Pain bolted down both legs and dropped me to my knees. Torpe, the big clown, stepped forward and drove a giant shoe against the side of my head.

Dull pain and stars.

I collapsed onto my side, the stakes fallen from my hands. The big clowns, Torpe and Baboso, took turns pounding me. I strained to get up, to fight back, but the repeated bruising to my muscles were turning them to sludge. And the vampires could do this all day. I watched helplessly as the other three vamps scaled the toppled van like venomous reptiles.

Kill them...

The chilling voice swept in from the surrounding forest like dark magic, becoming words in my head. But the message wasn't meant for me. It was meant for the vampires. Was this Chepe's doing?

Kill them all...

"They're coming!" I shouted toward the van.

The vampires working me over redoubled their attack. I grunted and tried to shield my body, but my wincing gaze remained fixed on the van. If I didn't do something, Sarah, Olaf, and Yoofi would be dead within seconds, and the clowns would have weapons loaded with silver ammo. I crawled a hand toward my tactical vest where I'd packed several grenades.

But things were moving too quickly. Loco had already reached the passenger door and begun crawling inside. I watched in dread as his head and torso disappeared—and then reappeared in a hail of automatic gunfire.

Someone's awake! I thought.

Blown back, the vampire fell to the ground with a thud, the top half of him chewed up and smoking. The two vampires behind him, Rata and Calaca, looked at their teammate and retreated.

A helmet emerged from the van door. Expecting to see Olaf, I was surprised to find Sarah using her elbows to muscle herself into better firing position. She sighted on Rata and ripped him with a burst from her M4. He shrieked inside a mist of blood and powdered silver.

The van's side door cannoned open. This time it *was* Olaf, wielding his MP88 like a boss. He wasted no time finding Calaca and blowing his narrow chest open with a burst of incendiary rounds.

Sensing a shift, the vampire Torpe threw my dead weight over his shoulder and took off running. Whatever his plan, it was the respite I needed. My body began to heal in a warm wave. In another few moments I'd be able to waste him and join my teammates. But as gunfire chattered behind me, I realized the vampire was probably only carrying me far enough away so he could safely teleport. The chilling voice returned.

Enter me...

With trees flashing past, I craned my neck around to see where we were going. Up ahead, a narrow black hole was opening in a jungle of dense growth. It pulsed and fluttered like something living. Something evil.

I pounded Torpe's back with my fists. I couldn't let him reach the hole, couldn't let him carry me inside. When a nauseating current of energy passed over me, I felt myself falling.

Too late, I'm going in.

But I didn't fall into an endless nothingness like I'd expected. Instead, I slammed into the ground. Torpe was beside me, face down. Feet from the hole, something had hit him.

The hell?

I scooted backwards—until a hand seized the scruff of my neck and began dragging me back toward the hole. I recognized Baboso by his smell, but I had more fight in me now. I seized his wrist and bent it back until it snapped. He spun toward me, murder in his blood-speckled eyes. I drove a fist into his chin. His head snapped back and forth like a Jack in the Box, but he held on.

When another current of nausea passed over me, I recognized its source.

A coiling black bolt struck Baboso's chest. With a choked cry, the vampire clown released me and staggered backwards. The next bolt drove him into the hole. Sparks erupted from the collision of magic.

"It worked, Mr. Wolfe!" Yoofi called.

The hole shuddered, as though reacting to something bitter, and collapsed in on itself.

I turned to find Yoofi running toward me, smoke drifting from the end of his staff. I relocated my jaw for the second time and pushed myself to my feet. The last of the bruising receded from my muscles and bones until all that remained was a general throbbing, but even that was dissipating.

"I did what you said! I told Dabu that if he run this time, I never give him drink or smokes again. He said 'Fine.' But right before the van crashed, he came back and protected me. Then he helped me heal Olaf and Sarah. I think me and Dabu going to have a big fight later, but for now, he's not running."

I worked as Yoofi talked, plunging a stake through Torpe's chest before the big clown could recover. I then trussed him up with razor wire. I was acutely aware of the gunfire still going off at the crash site. Finishing the job, I lifted Torpe under one of my arms.

"Glad to hear it," I said. "But we've got a fight of our own to get back to." I went to activate my radio before realizing I didn't have my earpiece. Probably fell out when I pulled my helmet off in the van.

Yoofi struggled to keep up as I ran back to the crash site. The shooting had stopped. Sarah and Olaf were no longer there. I peered around. Loco's shriveled corpse lay off to one side, his head severed. The vampire Rata was dead too.

I spotted a scalpel and test tube on the chest of his decapitated body.

Don't tell me Sarah was trying to get a tissue sample.

Sniffing around, I found Olaf on the far side of the van. His throat was torn open and his neck broken, but thanks to the tissue-regeneration treatment, he was still alive—or nonliving. Unresponsive, though. That didn't bode well for Sarah. The chilling voice had given an execution order.

Yoofi arrived, panting, at the crash site. I showed him a staying hand as I listened. A noise reached my pricked ears. I pivoted around until I was staring at a thicket. The noise sounded again: a high-pitched suckling, as though someone was trying to drain his victim very quietly.

I lowered Torpe to the ground and signaled for Yoofi to keep an eye on him. Pulling a stake from my belt, I crept toward the thicket. I could just make out bits of Sarah and the vampire Calaca. His skeletal body was hunched over her, lips pulling greedily from her neck.

You're not to feed, the chilling voice said. *You're to kill...*

"Not this time," I muttered.

I broke into a bounding run. Calaca's face whipped toward me, lips smeared red. When his hands moved, I knew he was positioning them to snap Sarah's neck. Still thirty meters away, I threw the stake like a dagger. It spun end over end at hundreds of miles per hour before implanting in Calaca's chest, pinning him to the tree at his back. Sarah slumped from his grasp.

I reached them a second later, talons tearing through the growth. Calaca snarled and wriggled, one hand clutching the end of the stake, the bony fingers of the other stretching toward Sarah's head.

Kill her! the voice insisted.

The stake hadn't penetrated Calaca's heart. I could fix that.

Slamming a forearm into his neck, I jerked the stake free—"Nice knowing you," I snarled—then plunged it back in, two inches to the left. This time, the stake found its beating mark. Calaca's eyes shot wide as his body locked into a kind of rigor mortis. I eyed his thin neck. With half the team injured, I couldn't handle another hostage. A hard slash of my talons removed his head this time. It fell to the forest floor, eyes staring from their black-painted sockets.

I lifted Sarah and clamped a hand over the ugly gash on her neck. Her eyes were closed, her skin white and waxy. She looked too much like Billy Young had all those years ago. But she still had a pulse. She was breathing. I carried her back to the crash site, where Yoofi remained with a staked and trussed-up Torpe.

"What happened?" he asked in alarm.

"Best I can tell, Sarah tried to cut some material off of rat boy over there. A vamp she and Olaf must've thought was out of action recovered. He took care of Olaf, then grabbed Sarah and started feeding."

I considered how Calaca's greedy appetite may have saved Sarah's life.

"Ooh, does this mean she is a vampire?" Yoofi asked.

"Only if he gave her some of his blood, and I'm pretty sure that didn't happen." I knelt with Sarah, setting her on the forest floor. "She's drained, though. We need Dabu's help."

"Yes, yes, of course." Yoofi knelt beside her. When I moved my hand from Sarah's wound, he drew his breath in sharply through his teeth. "Ooh, that looks bad. And Dabu doesn't like blood."

There was a lot Dabu didn't like, I was discovering. "We don't have much time," I reminded him.

Yoofi closed his eyes and began to mutter in a foreign tongue. Within moments, gray smoke coiled around the end of his staff and began spilling onto the wound like liquid. As I watched I considered that while Sarah might not become a vampire, that didn't rule out a blood slave. We'd learned in her lectures that a slave was created when a vampire drained his or her victim of both blood and psyche. I had stopped Calaca before he could complete the first, and I wasn't sure he'd even begun the second, but we would need to keep a close eye on her.

After several minutes, the smoke from the staff guttered out, and Yoofi opened his eyes.

"Dabu has healed her," he said.

This was the first time I'd seen Yoofi attempt a healing. Anxiously, I waved the smoke clear from Sarah's neck. Dried blood still caked the site, but the gash was closed. I stopped and squinted.

"Is that scar in the shape of a smiley face?"

Yoofi giggled. "Yes, Dabu make joke. You like?"

"No," I growled. "When will she wake up?"

Yoofi worked hard to straighten his lips. "Dabu stopped the bleeding, but cannot put back the blood."

So Sarah was effectively out of commission until she received a transfusion. I blew out a hard breath. I'd have to call Centurion for a medevac. "We've got another in need of healing," I told Yoofi.

He followed me to where Olaf had fallen. "Dabu says will have to wait."

"How long?"

"Hour? Dabu used much energy to make smiley face."

I rounded on him. "He's fucking kidding, right?"

"Dabu always kidding, but not about this."

I pulled the van down onto four wheels and then went into the back for the medical kit. Inside, I found a neck splint. Returning to Olaf, I straightened his broken spine as best I could, slid the splint in place, and secured his head and neck. We would need to medevac him too.

I loaded Olaf and then Sarah into the backseats of the van, where I happened on my MP88. I slung it over a shoulder, then walked to where Torpe's body lay, still paralyzed.

I stuffed him in the cargo space in the very back of the van. It was a tight squeeze for the big vampire clown, making me wish I'd grabbed his scrawny partner, Calaca, instead.

"We going back?" Yoofi asked. "What about the shaman?"

"We have too many casualties. We have to take them down."

"I take them," Yoofi said. "You find the shaman."

"Forget it. I can't let you go down alone."

I *did* hate leaving when we were so close to our best potential lead, but the clown troupe showing up where it did—practically on Chepe's doorstep—probably hadn't been a coincidence. The shaman was involved one way or another. I would have to get our hostage to tell us how.

I climbed into the front seat of the van. The windshield on the driver side wasn't smashed to near-opacity like on the passenger, and the body was in good shape. I reset the transmission and gave the key a crank. I was surprised when the engine turned. It coughed and chugged for half a minute before smoothing out.

"If I push, can you steer her back to the road?" I asked Yoofi, placing the van in neutral and grabbing my helmet. Sure enough, my earpiece was inside. I put them both back on.

Yoofi nodded and took my place. With him working the wheel, I pushed the van up the steep incline, through the broken swath we'd arrived by, until we were back on the road.

"Wolf 2, Wolf 1," I radioed Rusty. "You copy?"

"Loud and clear. What's going on, boss man?"

"I need you to call for a medevac for two."

"Holy shit. What happened?"

"Ambush. One will need blood, and one will need…" What *would* Olaf need. "Hell, just have them meet us down at the fields."

"Copy that." Rusty said.

Yoofi moved to the back to watch over our injured as I climbed in and took over driving. I drove fast. I was conscious of our injured passengers as we jounced down the road, but time was short. I focused on the steep road while scouring our surroundings in my peripheral vision. One of the vampires had gotten away, plus there was that chilling voice I'd heard. I had to assume it belonged to the magic-user—someone who could direct vampires and open holes in reality. Not a person I wanted to encounter on the way down.

Yoofi let out a scream that spiked my hackles.

"Where?" I called, but when I turned a corner, I saw for myself. One of those pulsing black holes was opening in the road ahead of us. I stomped the brakes. The van caught gravel and began slewing sideways.

"Come back here!" Yoofi yelled at his god. "Come back, damn you!"

A figure emerged from the hole and faced us.

It was our missing teammate, Takara.

19

Takara's hair billowed as she strode toward us, eyes red, smoke rising from her leather-clad body. Like the morning she and I had gone toe to toe, she looked terrifying, almost demonic.

But she wasn't my biggest concern right now. The van was heading for a precipice. Grunting, I turned the steering wheel hard into our slide. Inches from the drop, the wheels grabbed ground, and I veered us back onto the gravel road. Speed remained an issue. We were barreling down a steep decline, straight toward Takara and the black hole. I pulsed the brakes.

Fifty meters ahead, Takara stopped and raised an arm. Heat warped the air around her hand tattoo. I braced for a blast. But in the next moment, Takara's hand dimmed, and she collapsed into a heap.

To avoid running her over, I turned hard. One side of the van reared up an embankment before I was past her and able to steer back onto the road. But the black hole was growing, spreading across our path, and we were rushing up on it. I wouldn't be able to avoid it.

Remembering the hole's reaction to Yoofi's magic, I shouted, "Hit the hole with the *Kembo!*"

"Can't," Yoofi grunted. "Dabu ran far away this time!"

I pressed a button that retracted the driver side window, held out my MP88, and fired a burst of grenade rounds. The golf ball-sized projectiles punched through the center of the hole and detonated with dim flashes and muted thuds. I didn't know whether they would be effective—hell, I didn't even know what I was shooting at—and at first nothing happened. Then the edges of the hole began to shake like a jellyfish, and the whole thing collapsed.

The van skidded through the space the hole had occupied a second before and came to a crunching stop. Yoofi's scream tailed off and he peered around. I got out with my weapon and ran back to where Takara had fallen. Though smoke continued to drift from her body, she was cool to the touch. Bits of green jelly clung to her hair. She didn't respond when I shook and spoke to her, but she was breathing. I lifted her behind her knees and arms and ran with her back to the van.

"Make room!" I called to Yoofi. "We've got another casualty!"

Centurion's helos were just landing in the soccer fields when we burst from the woods and onto a dirt road on the outskirts of El Rosario. I bounced the van hard over a small drainage ditch. The rear exhaust gave a harsh cough and a sulfurous odor filled the van as we sped onto the field.

Centurion medics were already hustling toward us with plinths. I parked the van, ran around to the side door, and unloaded Sarah, who was still unconscious.

"She needs blood," I barked as I handed her off.

While I went back into the van for Olaf, one of the medics got a needle catheter into Sarah's arm and hooked up a bag of saline and another of O-negative. When I set Olaf on the plinth beside Sarah's, his eyes popped open. They rolled around a few times before staring at the sky.

"What happened to him?" the medic asked.

"Broken neck and extensive head trauma."

"Holy shit. How is he even awake?"

"He's on Centurion's tissue regeneration protocol," I said. "Be sure to coordinate his care with Biogen. Also, he and Sarah need to be on vampire protocol." Something else we had learned in her lectures the week before. "Secure rooms and twenty-four hour monitoring."

Since our arrival in El Rosario, Sarah had been keeping the support team briefed. The medic swallowed dryly and nodded as he and the others began carrying my teammates toward the helo. Two more medics arrived with a third plinth. "You have one more?" a young woman asked.

"We do." I had radioed the info on Takara to Rusty, who had in turn informed the incoming team. But as I ducked into the van, I found Takara sitting up, both hands holding her head.

Yoofi, who had been helping me unload the casualties, looked from her to me in confusion. "She just get up," he explained.

"How are you feeling?" I asked her carefully. "Do you need help getting out?"

"I don't need treatment," she said in a torn voice. "Take me to the compound."

As the helo carrying Sarah and Olaf lifted off, I turned to the medic. "Can you give us a minute?"

She nodded and stepped back until she was out of earshot.

I ducked my helmeted head back through the van's side door. Takara hadn't moved from her position, elbows on her knees, hands supporting her bowed head. I sniffed to make sure it was her, that she hadn't been changed into something. A veneer of earth and decay hung around her; otherwise, her scent was normal.

"What happened?" I asked. "Where have you been for the last day?"

"Last day?" She shook her head. "Too fragmented right now. Need to rest. Refocus."

"You should get checked out," I said. "At a minimum, you probably need fluids." I was also thinking that she needed to be under vampire protocol for the next twenty-four as well. After all, she'd appeared from the same black hole those creatures had been popping in and out of.

But Takara was still shaking her head. "Take me to the compound," she repeated.

I sniffed toward her again. No open wounds, meaning the vampires hadn't fed on her. Still, she sounded rough. I watched her for another moment. I hadn't been able to get the woman to wear a helmet; there was no way I was going to convince her to be medevacked. Exhaling, I turned to the waiting medics.

"We've got her. Just keep us updated on the others."

At the compound, Rusty met us at the door leading in from the carport. I offered to help Takara, but she climbed out of the van under her own power, walked past Rusty without a word, and entered her room, closing the door behind her.

"No 'Honey, I'm home'?" Rusty lamented.

"She needs to rest," I said, then turned to Yoofi. "What's the status on Dabu?"

He smiled apologetically. "Dabu's still gone. And this time, he won't listen when I talk tough. He says, 'Keep your smokes and drink, Yoofi!' Ooh, he never want to be scared like that again."

"Well, do whatever it takes to get him back," I growled. "We're down to three now, and we need everyone at full power."

"I do my best, Mr. Wolfe." He drew a flask and retired to his room.

I looked at Takara's door, then lowered my voice to Rusty. "Could you get a security gate on this one as well?"

He scratched his right mutton chop and looked back at me uncertainly. "I mean, I *could*—"

"Good. Do it."

"Is there a reason we're locking her in her room?"

"We don't know where she's been for the last day. Or with what."

"Ahh, you think she might be a ..." He hooked two fingers and held them in front of his lips to resemble fangs.

"It's just a precaution."

He winked. "Gotcha."

I wasn't sure how much good a durable gate would do, given the mess Takara had made of the building back at the training compound. But at the very least we'd have some warning.

As Rusty set to work, I went into the office and sent a situation report to Sarah's contact person, William Beam. I had yet to meet our interim director, but something told me he was by the book, just like Sarah. Maybe it was the name. I couldn't imagine he'd respond with anything useful, which meant we were on our own. Good thing I'd grabbed that vampire.

Rusty was finishing the gate as I stalked past him. "So, bad day at the office?" he asked.

"Three casualties and a teammate whose god is hamstrung by fear issues. What do you think?"

"Yeah, bad day," he decided, hustling to catch up to me.

"Might be one bright spot, though. We've got a hostage, someone who knows where the kids are being taken and who's behind it." Without Sarah to interpret, I would need to bring the mayor in to translate. But first I would soften up the vampire with some well-placed silver.

I seized the van's rear door handle, opened it, and stared.

Rusty peered from under my arm. "Hostage? Do you mean that stinking cloud of smoke?"

I waved my arms at the putrid smoke billowing from the cargo hold. If the whole vampires-turning-to-mist thing was another myth, as Sarah claimed, then what in the hell was this? But as the smoke cleared, something began to take shape: a pile of bones in a pool of yellow swill.

"Looks like someone got vaporized," Rusty said.

"And the vaporizer was probably the magic-user controlling him," I muttered before ripping off a string of choice words. The magic-user had just ensured his vampire clown wouldn't talk.

"Then why didn't he just vaporize you guys?" Rusty

asked.

I considered the question. It was a good one. Why sic vampires on us when the magic-user could have reduced us to bones and steaming juice, like he'd obviously done to Torpe? I remembered the harsh cough of exhaust and sulfurous smell as we'd crossed the drainage ditch. The sound hadn't come from the exhaust, though. It had been the vampire going up in flames.

But when I considered *where* that had happened, a different realization hit me. "Torpe wasn't vaporized by a wizard's spell," I said. "There's some sort of ward or protective barrier running around El Rosario. That's why the vampires can only operate outside of town."

"Well, what about those dogs?" Rusty asked. "And the bull?"

"The barrier must not affect them. Maybe because they were animals."

"Well then who left the note? Who stole the clown suits? If the—" Rusty stopped suddenly, eyes wide. Now it was his turn to have an epiphany. "Oh, shit. Follow me." He turned and ran back into the compound.

I followed, closing and securing the door and gate behind us. "What is it?"

Instead of answering, Rusty went into the office and sat in front of the monitor showing the drone feeds. With a few screen taps, he brought up a recording in a second, smaller window. I leaned forward as he clicked for it to play. A drone's camera zoomed in on a boy threading his way through the marketplace. I recognized him immediately.

"You found Nicho."

Rusty nodded. "Only child without an adult escort, just like you said."

"Where's he going?"

"Keep watching."

When Nicho reached the municipal building, he pulled a pair of work gloves from the waist band of his shorts and donned them. Then he retrieved something from his pocket and palmed it. Even with the camera's resolution, I couldn't make out what. He climbed the steps behind a small group of people and disappeared into the building. A half minute later he reappeared, hands empty. He threaded his way back through the market and entered another building.

"Spoiler alert," Rusty said, "he doesn't show up again. But shortly after he ducked in and out of the municipal building, the mayor called. She wanted to talk to you." He cocked an eyebrow. "She sounded upset."

I saw what he was getting at. "You think Nicho's working for the bad guys?"

"Only one way to find out."

I thought back to the boy we'd found in the forest. Other than his shock, I hadn't picked up anything off about him. He'd looked, smelled, and acted the part, all the way up until he'd left with the police chief yesterday evening. But he *had* disappeared this morning.

"There's no way," I muttered, pulling my phone out to call the mayor.

"It's Captain Wolfe," I said when Mayor Flores answered.

"We've received another note, a threat, under the office door," she said quickly.

"What time?"

"Just after ten o'clock."

I signaled for Rusty to rewind the video. He nodded and

brought the video back to the moment Nicho was entering the building. I looked at the feed's digital readout. 10:04. Shit. The timing, the gloves, the thing he had pulled from his pocket...

"What does the note say?" I asked.

"It says that because we defied yesterday's order, we are banished from El Rosario. Everyone must leave town by midnight. If we don't, 'El Rosario will fall into the black pit,' it says. 'And anyone remaining will suffer eternal torture.'" She paused to sniffle. "There aren't enough vehicles to transport everyone, but the nearest town is thirty kilometers away. Those who are able could walk and still reach it by nightfall. But we would have to leave now."

"No," I said. "That's exactly what they want you to do."

I pictured black holes opening up in the road, pulling children inside. It was the whole "if we can't get to them, we'll force them to come to us" thing.

"But what about the black pit?" she asked.

"Everyone will be safer in town," I said, thinking about the barrier.

"Are-are you sure?"

I changed the subject. "The boy who was here yesterday, Nicho. Was anyone able to track him down?"

"The police looked for him on their patrols, but never found him. Something strange happened, though. He told you he left his home two days ago?"

"That's right."

"Well, when one of our deputies drove to his village to tell his parents where he was, they became very emotional. They said that, yes, he went out to find the bull, but that was more than a month ago."

"A month? And they never reported him missing?"

"They thought he'd gone to stay with his uncle's family in another village. He's done that before, when his father became angry with him. But they just learned he never turned up there."

Meaning the magic-user *had* been using him.

"Has anyone seen the shaman?" I asked.

"I thought you were going to talk to him. Chepe wasn't home?"

"We were attacked before we could get there. We suffered a few injuries, but we killed four of the vampires."

"Thank God," she whispered.

"But there's still one remaining, and also a being who commands powerful magic."

"It is not Chepe," she said. "I am telling you."

I grunted. The peppery smell, the ambush on the road to his home ... Too many coincidences for me to doubt his involvement. For a moment, I considered heading back into the mountains to confront him, but that would be stupid. I had no reliable backup, one. And two, the man wielded powers I couldn't begin to understand. I needed to track down Nicho first. If he was working for the shaman, there was a good chance he could tell us something.

The building shook from a tremor like the one that morning.

"All right, listen," I said to the mayor when the tremor passed. "No evacuations. Keep the people of El Rosario in town. We can better protect everyone here. I'll call in a backup force if we need one."

"O-Okay."

"Will you be free later this morning."

"I think so. What for?"

"I'm going to need a translator."

20

The building where Rusty had last seen Nicho was a long colonnade on the south side of the market. I arrived at the colonnade through the thinning marketplace at a run. It had been more than an hour since the feed had captured Nicho going in, which was a long time.

"Just sped through the last thirty minutes of video," Rusty radioed, as if on cue. *"He never came out again."*

"All right, keep an eye on the live feed."

I leaned my head back and opened my nostrils to the air flowing into my helmet. Boom. He *was* here—or had been recently. There were other scents like his, but this one was distinctly Nicho's.

I walked up and down the colonnade, peering into the small ten-by-ten shops lining both sides. *"Un niño?"* I asked the occasional shopkeeper. A boy? To which they shook their heads. With my freakish size, I probably could have asked about an adult and gotten the same response, even though there were a good number of men and women out. Their swirling scents complicated my search.

I considered calling Nicho's name, but a slight sourness to his odor told me he was hiding. I listened for the same rapid breaths I'd heard when we'd first found him in the woods, but there was too much noise. On my next pass, I waited for his scent to grow and then diminish again before stopping. To one side of me was an unoccupied store. On the other, a young woman was selling sandals.

"Un niño?" I asked her.

She shook her head, but not before her eyes made a small, unconscious movement past my legs. The colonnade featured a center thoroughfare and two raised sidewalks. When I turned, I found a grate set in the far curb. Beyond the rusted iron bars, a face ducked away.

He's in the storm drain.

I lunged over, pulled the grate off, and plunged a hand in. I caught the boy by the ankle as he tried to scramble down a narrow tunnel. He shouted as I dragged him back out. Inverted, Nicho swung his fists at me, not coming close. Bits of garbage and rotting vegetable matter fell from his clothes.

"Nicho, *es yo,*" I said. "Captain Wolfe."

Dammit, I don't know enough Spanish to make him understand.

I turned to the young woman selling sandals. *"Alcalde!"* I said. Mayor!

She nodded quickly and ran to retrieve her. Pressure manifested in my palm. I turned back to find that Nicho had swung himself onto my arm and was biting my hand. Though his teeth had no chance of puncturing the glove, the savageness of the bite surprised me. I pulled back his head with my other hand. Cords leapt from his neck as he spit and snarled, but his teeth looked normal. No fangs.

Still, he's nothing like the boy we found yesterday.

Had he been turned into a blood slave? His smell hadn't changed, but maybe that took time. I shoved down all thoughts of having to destroy him. Regardless of what had happened to him, we'd find another way to bring him back. In the meantime I needed to get him someplace safe.

"Give him to me," a voice said.

From the murmuring crowd that had gathered at the far end of the colonnade, an old man stepped forward. He wore dark pants that ended above his calves and a linen shirt with traditional patterns. Wispy gray hair fell from a red bandana knotted around his head. His staff, which featured colorful feathers, suggested who he was. The peppery scent sealed it.

"The shaman," I muttered, adjusting my grip on Nicho.

"Give him to me," the old man repeated. His weathered face was hard to read, his blue eyes cloudy with cataracts. He angled his staff toward us suddenly. I drew my sidearm and aimed it at his head.

"Drop your staff," I ordered.

His lips murmured around strange words as he held tight to his staff.

"Drop it!" I repeated.

I could feel powerful energy building in the enclosed space. Nicho, who had resumed chewing on my hand, now whipped his head toward the shaman. His body went rigid. A gargling sounded in his throat and his eyes rolled back. He looked like he was convulsing.

"This is your last warning!" I said.

It went unheeded. Nicho let out a ragged scream. I narrowed my gaze down the Beretta's iron sights, taking aim at the shaman's chest at such an angle no bystanders would be struck.

Hope the mayor's wrong about you, I thought, and squeezed off two shots.

A commotion erupted as the crowd charged from the colonnade. But as the brass casings clinked to the ground, the shaman remained standing, no blood on his shirt. He set his jaw and thrust his staff toward me. A walloping force knocked the air from my lungs and me from my feet. Sandals flew around me as I crashed through the vendor's table and into the store.

I struggled to sit up, the attack seeming to have stolen my strength. I had managed to hold onto my sidearm, but not to Nicho, who had fallen to the thoroughfare. The shaman pivoted his staff toward the boy as he tried to scramble away. An invisible force snared Nicho.

Wants to eliminate him as a source of intel, I thought.

I found the shaman's head in my sights and fired again. Ear-splitting bangs but no blood. I couldn't tell what was happening—the rounds just weren't finding their marks. Three more shots proved equally futile. Meanwhile, the force suspending Nicho arched the boy's back until it looked like he was going to snap in two. The boy gasped out more screams.

I sprung from the store and toward the shaman. Someone in black reached him first, though. I recognized his smell before I got a clear look at his face. It was Guzman, the preacher.

Grunting, he hit the shaman at full speed. The shaman's staff clattered off as his spiritual rival took him to the ground. Whatever spell had been suspending Nicho cut out, and he fell to his hands and knees.

I grabbed the staff and circled the combatants. They spoke in rapid Spanish as they grappled and threw the occasional punch. Though Salvador Guzman had a good fifty years of youth on Chepe, the Mayan shaman was giving him all he could handle. When Guzman tried to pin Chepe's arms with his knees, the shaman jabbed a thumb into his Adam's apple and wrestled him onto his back.

"Bastardo!" Guzman roared.

But the maneuver had given me the clean blow I needed. Whatever protection the shaman had wielded moments before must have depended on his staff, because my fist landed against the back of his head with a dull thud. I had pulled the punch, sparing the shaman a skull shattering. I needed him alive to tell us where the children were. Guzman wriggled from underneath the shaman as the old man's bandana-wrapped head slumped forward.

"No!" a voice cried.

I spun to find Mayor Flores running toward us. She dropped to her knees beside the old man, one hand stroking the back of his head, before turning her accusing eyes on me.

"What did you do?" she demanded.

"He attacked us," I growled. "And I know you don't want to hear this, but he's involved in the abductions. We'll worry about how later. Right now we need to detain him before he recovers."

"No, you don't understand," the mayor said. "He was looking for help."

"Help?" I said. Guzman, who had sidled up next to me, made a scoffing sound.

"Yes, he came to my office after you and I spoke on the phone," the mayor said. "He says for the past month he has been trying to destroy the evil, but he cannot do it alone. He wants to join forces with you."

Yeah, so he can finish us off.

"Listen," I said between clenched teeth, "everything points to him." I began to tick the evidence off. "The cat in our building—"

"He admitted to leaving it," Mayor Flores said quickly, "to cast a spell of protection. He does not like to use death spells, especially on innocent animals, but they are necessary when the spell must be powerful. He did the same around town, which has kept much of the evil out so far."

Guzman snorted. "Keep out evil by invoking Satan? Ha!"

But I was thinking of Torpe's remains, still smoking in the back of the van.

"What about the vampire ambush this morning?" I challenged. "Did he have an explanation for that?"

"The vampires have been hunting him. It is natural they would stake out his place."

"Yeah, according to him," I said. "He attacked us just now. He tried to kill the boy." I gestured to where Nicho had fallen, but he was no longer there. I looked around. He wasn't anywhere.

"Rusty," I radioed. "Did you catch Nicho leaving?"

"Damn, got sort of caught up in listening to your convo down there. Hold on, let me go back." After a few seconds he said, *"Yep, there he goes, making off like a little mouse."*

I clenched my jaw. Damned ADD. "Where is he now?"

Rusty blew out his breath. *"No telling, boss. I had the camera tight up on the building. He took off north, toward where the trucks and buses are. Might've jumped on one of them. I'll keep looking."*

"Crap," I muttered.

I considered taking off after his scent, but with the mayor still staunchly on Chepe's side, I didn't want her spiriting him away while I was gone. Not when I was still ninety percent certain he was our guy. I walked over and lifted the shaman under an arm. He sagged, his woven purse dangling from his body.

"No," the mayor pled as I started to carry him away. "You don't know what you're doing!"

"He tried to kill the boy," I repeated. "I was right here."

"I saw it too," Guzman said.

The mayor's eyes moved between us. Outnumbered, she appeared ready to accede. But the shaman stirred first. We all looked at him as he began to mumble. Slowly, the mumbles became Spanish words.

"The boy was under a dominion spell," Mayor Flores translated. "Chepe was trying to purge him. The counter-spell was aggressive, yes, but there was no other way."

"More likely he was under *Chepe's* dominion spell," I said. "And Chepe was trying to silence him."

The Mayan shaman spoke again.

"He says the evil is growing stronger. The defenses he set up won't be able to keep it out much longer. And then El Rosario *will* fall into a black pit."

That made me stop. I had assumed the barrier around El Rosario was similar to the protective barriers around its houses and church—an innate feature of the town, maybe. But it made more sense that someone had cast a powerful spell to erect it. Someone like Chepe. The town wouldn't have missed a few stray cats. Also, the mayor had volunteered the info on the barrier. She didn't know the cargo hold of my van contained a vaporized vampire.

I set the shaman on his feet but kept a secure hold on his arm.

"How does he know so much about the evil here?" I asked.

"Because," the shaman rasped, "I created it."

21

The mayor looked at Chepe in shock, her head shaking slowly.

"See?" Guzman said, his eyes gleaming with triumph. "I told you he was behind it!"

I swept the preacher aside with my free arm and drew the shaman in closer. "What do you mean, you created it?"

"I will tell you everything," he said groggily. "Need somewhere to sit."

He and the mayor looked around, but I said, "Not here. Back at the compound."

Still holding to his arm, as much to steady him as make sure he didn't try to break free, I led the way. The mayor kept up at a fast walk, while the preacher ran around us flapping his hands.

"This is exactly what he wants," he all but screamed. "To get you alone so he can twist your mind with his devil's tongue! This very morning, he said that my congregation and I would be safer far away from here. He wanted me to persuade the other pastors to leave with their congregations as well. He knew we were making inroads into El Rosario! He knew the people would soon see his devilry for what it was and come to the light!"

"If El Rosario falls," Chepe said, "your villages will be next."

"If El Rosario falls, it will be because you led them to Satan!" Guzman shot back. "The rest of us are under God's protection."

"That's why you attacked him this morning?" I asked the preacher point blank.

"Yes—well, n-no," he stammered. "It was in self defense. He was trying to poison my mind!"

"Go back to the plaza," I said. "Pack up your things and return to your village."

Guzman looked wildly between me and Chepe. "You're siding with *him?*"

I wasn't siding with anyone at this point, but I needed to get to the bottom of what was going on. For now that meant getting Chepe to the compound where he could talk. Having Salvador Guzman outside, ranting and raving about Satan and the End Times, wasn't going to help.

"If we decide you *do* need to evacuate," I said, "the mayor's office will contact you."

The preacher sputtered for a moment, red blotches spreading across his cheeks. "He's already gotten to you!" he screeched. "He's already warped your thoughts with his black magic!" He pulled out his pocket Bible, opened it to an earmarked page, and began rattling off a passage in Spanish.

"Go!" Mayor Flores ordered him. *"Vaya con Dios, pero ándale!"*

Guzman stalked beside us for several more paces before

snarling and letting us pull away. "You're going to regret this!" he shouted. "He'll take you down a path of evil from which there is no return!"

When we arrived at the compound, Rusty let us in. I seated Chepe at the table and retrieved a bottled water for him as well as an icepack. He nodded as he accepted both, pressing the icepack to the back of his head where I'd struck him. Yoofi wandered in, sized up the Mayan shaman, and took a seat at the far end of the table. As the mayor sat beside Chepe, I pulled Rusty into the office.

"Any sign of Nicho?"

"Not yet, boss. Still looking. But the base just sent an update on Sarah and Olaf. Both are stable but still under monitoring."

That was a relief. "How's Takara doing?"

"Haven't heard a peep. Should we check on her?"

"After we talk to the shaman," I said.

I was as much concerned *for* Takara as *about* her. There was no telling what had happened inside the black hole, but it was something I hoped Chepe would be able to shed light on.

Rusty raised an eyebrow. "We gonna be able to trust anything the old man says?"

I had been wondering the same thing. Though I'd been exposed to plenty of magic in the last month, the mechanics of it still confounded me. I had Yoofi to consult, but his knowledge seemed limited to his own neck of the woods. I needed someone with a broader understanding.

"Hey, can you set up a laptop at that end of the table?" I asked. "I want to try to conference someone in."

"Sure thing, boss. Who?"

"A magic-user I've worked with before. Everson Croft."

"Wait, isn't that the dude Sarah said you couldn't consult?"

"Sarah isn't here."

Rusty showed his hands. "Hey, I was just asking."

What would Sarah say if she were *in the room?* With another midnight deadline—this one for all the marbles—and a Mayan shaman about to tell us what we were up against, would she want to make sure the info was accurate? Or would she still insist on following the policies and procedures, and preserving her position, at the expense of the info's integrity?

Didn't matter, I decided. I knew what *I* would do.

A loud series of beeps sounded from one of the computers. Rusty stumbled over and typed in something. The beeping stopped. "Urgent communication from Interim Director William Beam," he said. "He wants to talk to you."

Probably got my report, I thought.

I peered back at the table where the mayor and shaman were waiting for me. For a moment, I considered ignoring the commo request, but the chain of command was too deeply instilled in me. I may have been in sole charge on the ground now, but Director Beam was above me. I took a seat at the console, logged in, and accepted the request. A private channel opened on the commo system. A moment later, a man's face filled the screen.

"Captain Wolfe," he said.

"Director Beam," I answered cautiously.

He was younger than I'd imagined him, with a slender, aristocratic face and a dimpled chin. What I could see of his blue suit looked expensive. His parted hair shone with gel. I tried not to make a habit of judging people on their looks, but this guy had *douche bag* written all over his face.

"I'll cut right to the point," he said. "We received your report, and after careful review, Centurion has decided to end the mission."

My blood pressure spiked. "What the hell are you talking about?"

"You'll need to arrange with the standby unit for your exfil. We already have a plane ready to go at our Mexico City base. We want you back at the Legion base by 2200 tonight."

I gestured for Rusty to step out and close the office door behind him. "Listen," I said in a low growl, "it's all coming to a head tonight, and we're on the verge of a breakthrough. We need another day."

Beam sighed. "Captain Wolfe, by your own account, half the team is incapacitated. The remaining members, excepting you, lack field experience. It's a formula for disaster."

"I'm not the one who pushed this assignment," I reminded him.

He talked over me. "We run the very real risk of not only failing to fulfill our end of the contract, but of losing assets we can't afford to. We're already operating at a loss. Time to cut."

"And what about the people of El Rosario?"

He looked at me blankly for a moment before nodding in an unconvincing show of sympathy. "It's unfortunate, but we're in no position to help them right now. They're going to have to appeal to their federal authorities. It will be up to the military."

"There's no time to bring in the military," I said. "Anyway, we're not dealing with something that conventional forces can address. I thought that was the whole goddamned reason for the Legion Program."

"Ultimately, yes. But we're still a work in progress."

"So what's this going to say to other potential clients? Why would they work with a program known for pulling out at the first signs of trouble?"

"What's it going to say? Absolutely nothing. That's the reason for our nondisclosure agreement." His expression was so smug that had he been standing in front of me, I would have been tempted to knock it off his face.

"One more day," I said through clenched teeth.

"I admire your dedication, Captain, but our discussion is over. Listen, I have a meeting at the West Coast campus next week. I'll swing by the Legion compound and we'll have a little pow-wow. Discuss how to keep this sort of thing from happening in the future. I'll even see about getting some wagyu steaks. Ever tried one? Delicious. Supposed to be the best in the world."

"There are children missing!" I roared.

Director Beam's lips straightened as he sized up my helmeted head. "Children go missing every day. You were recruited into the Legion Program for your leadership and professionalism. I'm seeing very little of either right now."

"Now you listen to me—"

"And another thing. I'd think twice before defying our orders. As you know, we monitor all communications. We're aware of your fiancée's situation. We have a man shadowing Kurt Hawtin and another keeping an eye on Daniela, to ensure she's safe. If you insist on staying in El Rosario, those men will get recalled. It's not a matter of retribution, Captain, but resources. Like I said, we're already operating at a loss."

Had it not been for Segundo's last email, which had all but assured me Kurt wasn't a threat to Daniela, I might have hesitated. Instead, I said, "Right," and killed the connection.

I stood and paced the room, breaths cycling harshly. I pulled off my helmet and dragged a hand between my ears. There was no way I could end the mission, not with so many people depending on us, not with nine children missing. I slammed a fist into the wall, making the room shake.

Not when we were so close, goddammit!

I pulled out my phone and dialed Purdy. I hadn't wanted to go to him again, didn't want him to have any more leverage over me, but besides being higher up the pole than Beam, he was a negotiator. We would come to terms, even if it meant extending my contract. I was ready to be leveraged.

But I reached Purdy's voicemail.

"It's Captain Wolfe," I said after the tone. "I think you know what this is about. Call me back right away."

A tentative knock sounded on the door. "Sir?" Rusty called from the other side. "Everything all right?"

Everything was pretty fucking far from all right, I thought as I disconnected the call. Maybe Purdy would be able to fix things; maybe he wouldn't. But I wasn't going to sit on my hands while I waited for him to get back to me. I opened the door and pulled Rusty inside.

"Hey, what did Beam want?" he whispered. "What was the shouting and banging about?"

I ignored his questions. "You're good with computers. Can you get me a secure line?"

"I don't know about secure," he said, looking over the laptop. "Centurion's monitoring technology is pretty damned tight. But I can probably bury the call in a bunch of noise."

"Do that, then."

"Why? What's up?"

"We're going ahead with that conference call, and I don't want Centurion eavesdropping."

Rusty grinned. "Bypassing the Man, huh? I like it."

After several minutes of hacking away at the keys, he turned the laptop toward me. "You're buried about as deep as I can get you."

I clapped his shoulder, consulted the slip of paper I'd tucked into my wallet, and dialed. After four rings, and when I was sure it was going to go to another voice mail, someone picked up. But my relief quickly turned to dismay when a female voice demanded, "What?"

It was that damned cat.

"Everson Croft, please."

There was a slight pause during which Tabitha recognized who I was as well. "Is this that blue werewolf? Oh, you sound awful, darling. Just atrocious. You pitiful thing. I thought a witch was going to fix you." Her voice sounded more taunting than sympathetic.

"It's a long story," I growled. "Is he in?"

"What, no time for small talk?"

"No. Can you get him?"

"Oh, I see," she said thinly. "I'm just the help."

The phone clattered down. For a moment I thought she'd hung up, but she'd only dropped the receiver. How she had picked it up in the first place, I had no idea. I listened intently, fully expecting to hear Tabitha settling back onto her perch by the window. But distant voices were soon followed by approaching footsteps. Finally, I heard the receiver being retrieved from the floor.

"This is Everson."

22

I hadn't talked to Prof Croft since we'd collaborated to kill the White Dragon in New York City. It was good to hear his voice. I gave him a quick update on what had happened in the weeks since I'd left, how I was still the Blue Wolf and now working for an organization that tracked and killed monsters. If there had been time, I would have explained why I had elected not to join forces with him, but there wasn't. Instead, I explained the situation in El Rosario.

"That does sound serious," he said when I finished.

"If you've got a few minutes, we could really use your help."

"You actually caught me at a good time. I'm waiting for a potion to cook. Got called to a pixie infestation in Chelsea."

"You *promised* me lunch," Tabitha pouted in the background.

I heard Croft's hand go around the receiver as he

walked into another room. "I have about an hour. Lay it on me."

"Great. I'm going to have you listen in on a meeting with the Mayan shaman I told you about. I don't know much about magic, so I need to know if what he's saying makes sense."

A minute later I had the laptop set up at one end of the table. Croft was plugged in through his landline, so there was no video feed. I took a seat across from Chepe. The mayor was sitting beside him, and Yoofi beside me. Rusty clapped my shoulder as he returned to the office to monitor the surveillance system.

"Can you hear me?" I asked.

"Loud and clear," Croft answered from the laptop.

I nodded at Chepe that we were ready. He took the icepack from the back of his head and set it down. His cloudy eyes moved around the table as he began. He spoke in Spanish mostly, Mayor Flores providing the translation.

"Chepe was called to his work as a *sacerdote* by Maximon himself," she began, "in a dream."

"Who's Maximon?" I asked.

"To the north of El Rosario you have seen a peak that rises above the others?" the mayor asked. "That is Maximon. A descendant of the Corn God, he is the protector of El Rosario."

Chepe nodded and continued.

"When the Catholic missionaries came hundreds of years ago, they made St. Paul the town's patron saint," Mayor Flores said. "Over time, Maximon and St. Paul came to be different names for the same being. Even to those who called him St. Paul, he had the same powers as Maximon, performed the same functions. And he resided in the mountain."

Across the laptop connection, I could hear Croft pulling down books.

"During the Festival of St. Paul, Chepe performs several rituals," the mayor continued as Chepe spoke. "But once every twenty-three years, the Saint's Day coincides with the end of a Short Cycle on the Mayan calendar. A powerful time. Beginning a week before the Saint's Day, Chepe fasts to purify his body, mind, and spirit. When the day arrives, he takes a pilgrimage to a secret place. It is a day's journey. That night, he performs a series of powerful rites to honor Maximon and St. Paul and bring favor to El Rosario for the next cycle."

Croft was flipping pages and muttering to himself now. I couldn't make out what he was saying, but his tone sounded encouraging. In the chair beside mine, Yoofi smiled and puffed a cigar.

"The last time, the ceremony brought seasons of health and good harvests to El Rosario," Mayor Flores translated. Then she interjected, "I am old enough to tell you this is true."

Chepe nodded at her, then picked up his thread, with the mayor translating again.

"But toward the end of the cycle, our good fortune declined. We had seasons of drought. Chepe did everything he could, appealing to Maximon as well as to our ancestors. That kept the situation from becoming worse, but he could only do so much until the next cycle."

The shaman's leathery hands became more animated as he spoke.

"This time he fasted for two weeks," the mayor said.

"And he prepared a special incense, one that would open a stronger channel to Maximon. When the day came, his body shook with energy. He felt more powerful than he ever had before. When he arrived at the site and began the rites, he was sure Maximon would be pleased. But hours into the rites, something happened."

"Oh, crap," Croft muttered through the feed.

The shaman and Mayor Flores seemed not to have heard as she continued the translation. "For the main rite, Chepe built a circle, with colored candles at the cardinal directions. Into the circle he set several offerings. As Chepe chanted and swirled a burner with the smoking incense, the candle flames grew tall. 'This is a good sign,' he thought. 'Maximon can hear my prayers.' Even so, Chepe did not want El Rosario to be forgotten at the end of the cycle, like had happened the last time. So he pushed more of the power that shook through him into the circle. The flames grew taller still. All was going as he'd hoped. But very suddenly, something snapped in the air. More a feeling than a sound. The flames died, and darkness swept over Chepe. Maximon had left him. Chepe didn't know why. He didn't know what he had done. Then an evil voice called from the darkness, 'Enter me.'"

I stiffened, remembering the same chilling command I'd heard in the woods. As though picking up the thought, Chepe's eyes met mine through my visor, and he nodded gravely. He resumed talking.

"Chepe lit a match to see," the mayor said, "and in the place of the circle was a hole. A hungry black hole, its edges moving like lips. Farther down were rings of hooked teeth. Chepe could not say what the monstrosity was, but he knew it was not Maximon. 'Come to me,' it said now. Chepe ran instead. The words followed. Chepe felt them rippling past him, calling the evil beings of the world to the hole."

"That might be what brought the vampires," I said.

"Most likely," Croft agreed.

Mayor Flores nodded as the shaman went on. "Chepe was so weak when he returned to his home that he slept for two days. When he awoke, he tried to return to the site. He was determined to close the hole. But before he could reach it, five vampires met him. Only through a protection spell was he able to survive their attack. He descended to El Rosario that night and cast the death spells that raised the barrier around the town. Protection against the monster and vampires. Shortly after, the children began to disappear. Chepe wanted to help, but he needed more power. He hid in the forest and fasted. After two weeks, he attempted to return to the sacred site, to use the power that had opened the portal to close it again, but the vampires repelled him. They did this several times over the following days. Chepe began to despair until one night he dreamed you were coming."

"Us?" Yoofi said in surprise.

"Yes, the Legion team. And in the same dream, he heard the being that is both Maximon and St. Paul call from a distant place, telling Chepe that you would help him. That same night, he returned to El Rosario to protect the building where you'd be staying. He then went in search of white wormwood."

"Interesting," Croft remarked.

"White wormwood is rare in this area," the mayor explained, "and Chepe had never used it. Maximon told him it would close the hole, which the Legion team would help him to reach." Chepe dug into his purse and surprised me by pulling out a standard Ziploc bag. He gave it a shake to show us the dried leaves inside. My nose wrinkled inside my helmet at the bitter odor.

"And that's what brought him to town today?" I asked.

"Yes," Mayor Flores said.

Chepe's cloudy eyes held both hope and anguish as he nodded and tucked the bag away again.

I turned to the laptop. "Diagnosis, Prof?"

"Um, if you've got ear buds, you might want to plug them in."

I synched my earpiece to the computer. "All right, it's just you and me."

"Sorry about that," he said, his voice suddenly loud in my ear, "but what I'm going to tell you is pretty intense, and I didn't want it to sound to the locals like I was pointing fingers."

"Understood." I signaled to the rest of the table that I'd be back, scooped up the laptop, and carried it into the storage room. "So what's going on?"

"I've been looking up some things while the shaman and interpreter were talking." Croft blew out his breath. "It adds up, but not in a good way. Remember how I told you that our world was more porous now? Well, it sounds like a Chagrath is trying to worm its way in. And succeeding."

"What the hell's a Chagrath?" I asked.

"They're creatures from the Deep Down. Good at sniffing out gods and feeding off the beliefs that sustain them. Nasty things. Picture a hook worm, except a few thousand times larger and with more appendages. In this case the target is Maximon or St. Paul—for the sake of ease, I'll just call him Maximon. Normally, the Chagrath are content to hang back and siphon off the excess."

"But this one went in for the full meal."

"Pretty much. It probably happened when the shaman shot his ceremony with extra juice," Croft said. "Under normal circumstances, that wouldn't have been a problem. But with all the rips out there, the extra energy blew open a hole, allowing the Chagrath into the plane where Maximon resides. The first thing the Chagrath would have done was sunk its hooks into Maximon, making him its host."

"So Maximon is being controlled by this Chagrath now?"

"More or less. And the Chagrath's appetite is huge. Beliefs alone don't cut it anymore. It wants the fleshy packages those beliefs come in. It couldn't enter our world, though, so it needed something to bring the packages to him. The shaman was absolutely right in comparing the voice he heard to a broadcast signal. Being a parasite itself, it's fitting that the Chagrath lured other parasites. In this case vampires. There's an active gang in Mexico City."

I nodded to myself, remembering the teardrop tattoo I'd seen on Calaca.

"They fell under the Chagrath's thrall and are doing its bidding."

"The one remaining vamp, anyway," I said. "But why children?"

"The children's beliefs in Maximon are virgin, unadulterated. That holds an incredible power for a Chagrath. It's like a pure dose of heroin to a junkie. He'll never get the same fix off the old stuff. Probably doesn't even want it."

So the beliefs *had been* key to why the other villages weren't being attacked—just not in the way Sarah and I had thought. It also explained why the Chagrath had no interest in Nicho as sustenance. The boy didn't believe in

Maximon. The parasitic creature had found utility in Nicho as a courier, though.

The muscles across my shoulders bunched at the thought of the creature using innocent children.

Croft went on. “With its line to Maximon—and through him, Chepe—the Chagrath would have known about the clowns.”

“Can we hold out any hope for the missing children?”

“It depends,” he replied, surprising me. “Chagraths can go long periods without food, but that requires rationing. For the last month this Chagrath has only been able to pluck up a child here and there. For purposes of self-preservation, it might have stored them in the equivalent of a slow-digestion chamber until food became more plentiful. It could just as easily have devoured them, though, so we shouldn’t get our hopes up.”

I shielded my mind from the latter thought. “Is that its endgame? More food?”

“Near term, it wants to become strong enough to discard Maximon and break through to our world. Right now, it can only *interface* with our world. Those black holes you’ve been seeing? That’s the Chagrath pushing one of its many mouths against the glass, so to speak.”

So, not teleportation magic, I thought.

“Those holes are also conduits back to the Chagrath’s realm. Children can be carried inside—and have been—beings like the vampires can enter and exit, but the Chagrath can’t come out. Not yet, anyway. With enough children, though, it will be able to break the glass and then it *will* feed, yes. And not just on those who believe in Maximon. It will feed on anyone who believes in anything.”

“That’s the entire human race,” I said.

"Yeah, and Chagraths replicate like viruses."

"We can stop it though, right? What about the dream Chepe had?"

"That sounded like Maximon's last gasp to purge itself of the Chagrath. Interestingly, white wormwood has powerful anti-parasitic properties. The indigenous in the region once used it to treat intestinal worms."

"Will it work on the Chagrath?"

"Infused with the shaman's power, it might."

I didn't like Croft's qualifier, but it was something.

"So it's a matter of—what?—dropping the wormwood into one of its mouths?" I asked.

"The main mouth," Croft corrected me. "The one that first appeared in Chepe's circle. That goes to the core of the creature."

"He said the secret site was a day's walk from here."

"Then you should probably get moving. I didn't care for the wording of the latest threat. Like you guessed, the Chagrath wants to drive enough children out of El Rosario to snatch them up. Failing that, I believe El Rosario *will* fall into a pit, and the creature will claim them that way."

"How, though? I thought you said it needed more children to break into our world."

"Those tremors you mentioned? I don't think those were earthquakes. I have a bad feeling the Chagrath ran up against the shaman's defenses and started burrowing underneath them. That's what you've been feeling. The Chagrath is trying to undermine the town. One way or another it'll get its meal."

"At midnight," I muttered.

"When the veil between worlds is thinnest."

I considered the challenge we faced. Accompanying the

shaman to a remote site defended by at least one vampire, possibly more, arriving there before the midnight deadline, rescuing any surviving children, then throwing the wormwood into the hole and *hoping* it would be effective. And doing all of that with half a team and without Centurion's backing. Didn't exactly sound like a formula for mission accomplished. And if we failed...

"Can your Order spare anyone?" I asked.

"I'm putting a call into them right after I hang up."

"Good." I had the feeling we were going to need backup.

"But I can't make any promises," Croft added. "The higher ups have the power to stop something like a Chagrath, but they're so committed to mending tears right now, there's no telling when they'd get there. Don't worry. I'll make the case. I just don't want you counting on them."

"We'll take whatever we can get."

"I'd go myself, but you're gonna want someone with more experience. I'll keep you posted. Oh, and one more thing. Didn't you say a team member walked out of a black hole this morning?"

"Yeah. She's resting in her room."

"Well, keep a close eye on her. She might not be herself."

"What do you mean?"

"According to the info I was able to dig up, when a Chagrath seeks to control someone, it lays the equivalent of psychic eggs in the person's mind. There's a short incubation period, but very soon the eggs become squirming larvae, and the person's mind is under the Chagrath's control. It's what happened to the vampires and that boy you mentioned."

My hand tingled with the phantom sensation of Nicho biting me. At the same moment, Takara's door began to shake. I turned until I could see it rattling against the gate Rusty had installed. Takara was trying to get out. I snatched a pair of cuffs and pocketed them.

"How do you break a Chagrath's control?" I asked quickly.

"A break dominion spell or one of its variants will usually do the trick."

The same thing Chepe had been attempting on Nicho before Guzman—and yeah, yours truly—had intervened. "Thanks for everything, I'll be in touch," I said quickly, and then ran toward Takara's door. With Sarah and Olaf out of commission and Yoofi's god in hiding, the last thing I needed was for her to be possessed. That would leave just me and Rusty.

Assuming I could restrain her.

"How are you doing in there?" I called carefully.

I waited for a response. It came in the form of the gate blasting from the blown-open door.

I leapt back as the gate ricocheted from the far wall and clanged to the floor. Takara emerged through the dust. Her irises were red, the symbols on her palms glowing through her clenched fists.

Yoofi hollered in fright, and I heard his chair topple over as he scrambled to safety. I kept my eyes fixed on Takara as she stalked toward me. Though the wolf in me relished the idea of a third battle, the captain knew I needed to get control of the situation. And fast.

Holding my ground between Takara and the others, I showed my hands.

"Listen to me," I said. "You're Takara, a member of the

Legion team. You've been in the clutches of a creature who wants to turn you against us. You're not yourself."

She narrowed her eyes at me.

"It is okay," Chepe said, arriving beside me.

I thought he was talking to Takara, but when I glanced over, he was looking up at my visor and nodding. Takara stopped a foot away. Expecting blades to pop from her sleeves, I angled my body in front of Chepe. She jabbed me hard twice in the chest with a finger.

"The next time you lock me in a room," she said, "I'll kill you."

She turned sharply and walked to the kitchen.

"It is okay," the shaman repeated. "No dominion."

"So, she's herself?" I asked him. "You're all right?" I called to Takara.

She grabbed a water bottle, then shouldered past me and strode into the main room, where Yoofi and Rusty watched from the doorway to the office. They were practically hugging one another. She sat at the table across from Mayor Flores, took a swallow of water, and crossed her leather-clad legs.

"I've seen the children," she announced. "They're still alive. But I don't know for how much longer."

23

"Back up just a minute," I said to Takara as I returned to the table. "What happened yesterday? Where did you disappear to?"

"I've been gone since yesterday?"

"Yes," Yoofi said, creeping back to the table. "Right after we found that boy. We looked everywhere, but you were nowhere. You just disappear!"

She took another swallow of water and then nodded slowly. "We found the boy behind the tree," she said, as though retracing her steps, "and then the vampire clown appeared. While you engaged him, I circled to get into a better position. Higher up, I spotted a hole in a bank. I knew that's where the vampire had appeared from. One of us would have heard him, otherwise."

"And so you went in," I said. "Without telling anyone."

"I was just going in to check it out," she shot back. "I thought it could have been the vampire nest, or where the children were being held. But once I passed through the opening ... everything changed." She squinted slightly, her tone becoming less certain. "I wasn't in a tunnel so much as another world. There was mist everywhere, hard to see. When I tried to return through the hole, I couldn't find it. I tried to contact you, but my radio was dead. So I searched for an exit. It felt like I was wandering a system of caverns, sometimes walking, sometimes swimming, but not through water. If you've ever been to the astral realm, it felt like that."

"Can't say I have," I grunted.

She looked me up and down. "I'm not surprised."

Did she just take another dig at me?

I thought up a few retorts but bit my tongue. This was the most that had ever come out of Takara's mouth since I'd met her. Not only that, she had vital intel on the world beyond the holes.

"Travel in the astral realm is a function of thought," she continued. "This realm felt similar, so I stopped and thought of the missing children. The world spun, and moments later I found myself outside of a chamber filled with a green fluid. Inside the fluid, several shapes were suspended. As my senses sharpened, I recognized them as the children. At first I thought they were dead, but the nearest one's leg kicked. Strange-looking tubes ran into his nose, his mouth, both of his ears."

I remembered what Croft had said about a slow-digestion chamber.

"When I reached a hand inside for him, the tubes came to life. They yanked him away from me. The tubes holding the other children did the same, drawing them deeper into the chamber. If I could free the children from the tubes, I thought, I could bring them out. I extended my blades and stepped into the fluid. It was strange, more gel than liquid. I hadn't gone a few feet when the walls shook to life, and more worm-like tubes began attacking me."

I noticed the mayor staring at Takara in a kind of horror-stricken fascination.

"The fighting was intense," she went on. "For every tube I severed, two or three more sprang into their place. I could make no progress toward the children. At last, I was forced from the chamber, where I was confronted by a new threat: batlike creatures with large wings and long tails. I've never seen their kind. They swooped down, intent on wrapping their tails around my throat. I fought them off, but there were too many and no place to retreat. I concentrated my power. When I'd gathered enough, I released it out in all directions. The space around me shuddered, and a hole opened. I stepped through it, and found myself on a road. The van was speeding toward me. And then I ... I must have lost consciousness."

"That was when we found you," I said, wondering if the Chagrath had released her into the path of our speeding van on purpose. Something told me it had.

"Yes, when I came to, we were at the soccer fields. But I could only recall bits of what had happened. I needed to focus." She narrowed her eyes at me. "And then you locked me in my room."

"It was a precaution," I said. "I'm glad you're all right."

She shook her head in irritation and took another swallow of water.

I stood from the table and paced the room. "I spoke further with our consultant," I said. "He thinks we're dealing with an other-worldly creature called a Chagrath. An enormous parasite, basically. It accessed the local god's realm on the night of Chepe's ceremony and is now using children to try to break into our world. Croft believes the written threat is very real. The tremors we've been feeling are the Chagrath undermining the town. If the town doesn't clear out, the Chagrath will sink it."

"Then we need to evacuate right away," the mayor said, shooting to her feet.

"No," I said firmly, motioning for her to sit back down. "The Chagrath will only grab the remaining children it needs."

"What about your helicopters?" she said. "Can't they carry us to safety?"

"There aren't enough to move thousands of people," I replied. "And even if there were, I don't know how safe that would be. If the Chagrath can maneuver underground, it can probably do the same in the air. The only certainty right now is that it can't penetrate Chepe's barrier around El Rosario."

I left out the additional point that Centurion had terminated the mission, meaning I had no authority to call in additional helos.

"But here's the thing," I went on. "We know where the children are now. We know what the creature is. We know where to find it. And we know how to destroy it. Our most limited resource is time. With a midnight deadline, we don't have much. Chepe, can you point out the ceremonial cave on the map?"

I was already planning to use the cargo van to take us at least partway to the site, cutting down on travel time. But as the mayor completed the translation, I watched Chepe shake his head.

"He doesn't know," she said.

"He was just there last month!" I shouted.

"Yes, but he says Maximon guides him to the site."

I looked at the shaman's cloudy eyes and nodded. The old man could barely see. "Will Maximon be able to lead him now?"

"Maximon would not have shown him the dream vision if he could not," the mayor answered.

"All right," I said, calming my breaths. "So we're still looking at a day's journey on foot. Once we arrive, Takara and I can go in for the children." I turned to her. "You know how to navigate that realm?"

"Yes, but..." She scowled at having to admit weakness. "I haven't recovered my strength."

"You'll have the rest of the day," I said, but she continued to look doubtful. "Once we've gotten the children safely out, Chepe will hit the Chagrath with his herb. My consultant believes it will be enough to destroy the Chagrath. He's working on getting a powerful magic-user down here to help us. They may not get here before the deadline, but they'll seal the hole it arrived by."

"And El Rosario will be safe?" the mayor asked.

"Yes," I said, feeling confident in my ability to say that now. Even though we were at half strength—Sarah and Olaf out of commission, Takara without her full powers, and Yoofi without his god—we'd gained a powerful member in Chepe. The rest of us would be armed to the teeth. The Chagrath hadn't liked the taste of grenade very much, and there would be plenty more where those had come from. But most importantly, we knew how to kill it.

"I just need to make a quick call," I said, stepping into the storage room, where I'd most recently spoken with Prof

Croft. This time, though, I tried Reginald Purdy. I wanted to be working with Centurion, not against them.

My jaw tensed when I reached his voice mail again.

"Reginald, it's Wolfe," I said. "You've shot straight with me, so I'm going to do the same with you. I know Centurion wants to pull out, but I'm going ahead with the mission. If you can work it out with the pencil pushers, great. If not, we'll deal with the repercussions when I get back."

I hung up and emerged back into the main room. "Can I meet with the team for a minute?" Yoofi and Takara followed me into the office, while Rusty swiveled in his chair to face me.

"What's up, boss?" he asked.

"I got a call from our interim director today," I told the team, closing the door behind me. "Because of this morning's casualties, Centurion feels the mission is too risky at this stage of the program's development. They want to pull us. I've been trying to get ahold of someone higher up the chain, but no luck so far. Which means going ahead with the mission will put us in violation of our contracts."

"Screw 'em," Rusty said.

"Sort of my thoughts, but I'm not going to pretend to speak for the team. If anyone would prefer to sit this one out, I'll understand."

"I'm in," Takara said without hesitation.

I expected Yoofi to say the same. He had gone along with everything enthusiastically since day one. But instead of nodding, he dropped his gaze to the floor and puffed pensively on his cigar.

"Yoofi?" I prompted.

"I will just be in the way," he mumbled.

"Your god has been an unreliable pain in the ass," I said.

"But even so, you detected the magic in our building that first night, you put a sizeable dent in the undead dog population last night, and just this morning you saved me from being hauled into one of those godforsaken holes and having tubes crammed down my nose and throat. Point is, you've been an important contributor. You're more capable than you realize."

"The boss man's right," Rusty said, clapping Yoofi's shoulder. "We need you."

"I don't know..." Yoofi hedged.

"You dragged your god kicking and screaming back once," I said. "You can do it again."

Though his smile betrayed uncertainty, Yoofi said, "Okay. I come."

Rusty turned to me. "I'd come too, but I'm guessing you want me manning the store?"

"Yes and no. I want a drone going with us."

"You got it, boss," he said, though I could hear his disappointment. He wanted to be with the rest of us for the final assault, not a drone in the sky. "I can help you guys pack and prep in the meantime."

"That would be a big help."

When we emerged from the office, I addressed Mayor Flores. "We'll be moving out shortly. As the deadline draws nearer, there's likely to be more tremors. Keep the town calm. Don't let anyone leave."

"I've never seen your face," she remarked as I walked her to the door. "But I trust you."

"We're going to do our best," I assured her. *With or without Centurion.*

"That is all we can ask. Take care of yourselves."

She said something to Chepe in Spanish that prompted

him to press his hands together and bow toward her: their farewell. I closed the door behind the mayor and turned to the shaman. He seemed to understand enough English that we could get by without an interpreter.

"Will you be ready to go in the next half hour?" I asked him.

"Yes, but first a ceremony."

"I'm not sure there's time."

"To protect," he said. "So the evil does not see us coming. Will not take long."

Given that the Chagrath seemed to know every time we stepped into the woods, stealth *would* improve our odds. "All right," I said, "but after everyone is packed and ready to go."

Twenty minutes later, Yoofi, Takara, and I stood around a circle Chepe had created on the floor of the storage room. The Mayan shaman paced around us, waving his staff in one hand and several lit incense sticks he had produced from his purse in the other. As the familiar peppery-sweet smell rose in the room, subtle currents of energy began to swim around us. It reminded me a little of the magic Prof Croft had performed a few weeks before to create an apparition of me. I listened to Chepe's low chants, which seemed to bend and shape the energy.

I'd had Rusty remain apart from the ceremony, mainly because he wasn't going, but also as a precaution. Prof Croft seemed to believe Chepe was who he claimed to be, but there was no way to be a hundred percent certain. By his own admission, he'd been out in the woods with the vampires and Chagrath for the last month. And we were putting ourselves at his mercy right now.

After several minutes, the shaman stood back. "It is done," he said.

As I stepped from the circle, the protective energy lingered over me like a haze. It distorted my senses, particularly my hearing and smell. The wolf in me felt handicapped. I didn't like it.

"How do you feel?" I asked Takara.

"Like I suddenly have water in my ears and am nearsighted."

It was having the same effect on her. I brought up the concern to Chepe.

"You will get used to it," he said. "Important thing is the evil cannot sense you."

"Would've been nice to have known about the tradeoff before agreeing to this," I grumbled, but he was right. Arriving at the site without detection was more important than being able to hear something a quarter mile away.

Chepe returned the incense sticks to his purse and placed one end of his staff against the ground. He closed his eyes, pivoting one way and then the other. I wasn't sure what he was doing until he stopped suddenly and his eyes popped open. He was divining the way to the sacred site.

"Come," he said, and led the way out of the compound.

Takara shot me a skeptical look. I jerked my head for her to follow. She did so grudgingly, M4 in hand, blades concealed in the forearms of her sleek black leathers. Yoofi followed her in his large, clinking coat, his staff propped over one shoulder. I took up the rear with my MP88 and a loaded tactical vest. We weren't exactly the high-speed unit I'd envisioned a week before, but the only thing that mattered was whether we could finish the job.

"Go kick some Chagrath ass for me," Rusty called.

I gave him a thumbs-up before he closed the door behind us.

As the four of us proceeded down the street, the people of El Rosario watched from doorways and windows. A man and woman approached us, a young girl at their side. Takara tensed, but I recognized them. They were the parents and sister of Miguel Bardoza, the first child abducted. The father spoke to Chepe, before walking up to each of us and clasping our hands in both of his.

"Thank you," he said in broken English, his tortured eyes imploring us to bring back his son. I looked at where his wife held tightly to their daughter, the girl whom Miguel had broken away from the night the vampire Baboso took him. She watched us with pensive eyes.

I held up a hand: my solemn promise that I would do whatever I could to return her brother to her. The girl brushed a strand of hair from her face and raised her own hand. The father backed away with a final "thank you" and joined his family.

As we moved on, I remembered something Nafid had told me shortly before I'd left Waristan. In the moment before her grandmother's death, she said the old woman had declared that the Blue Wolf would protect all. Nafid hadn't known what she meant by that, but now I did. Despite having no connection to the people of El Rosario, I felt a deep and undeniable responsibility for them. They were the victims of a creature who had no business in this world—a creature I could help stop. As long as I remained the Blue Wolf, that would be my role. Not a mercenary, but defending those who couldn't defend themselves.

We were almost to the soccer fields when my hearing picked up the thump of rotary blades. I craned my neck around. Though I couldn't see them, I recognized the sound: the same Centurion helos that had arrived and departed that morning. Only this time, they weren't coming to help us.

Son of a bitch.

They were coming to intercept us.

24

We turned and watched the arriving helos. Four UH-60 Black Hawks. The lead one swooped low and turned, setting down in the dirt road ahead of us in a storm of dust. Another landed behind us, blocking retreat. The other two descended to our right and left, over a soccer field and a fallow cornfield.

Purdy must've gotten my message, I thought bitterly.

Yoofi looked around in alarm as the helos boxed us in, while Takara appraised them coldly. Chepe seemed more concerned with keeping his leather necklaces from flipping around in the roto wash.

"Let me do the talking," I told them.

As the blades wound down, a voice came over my earpiece. It was Sarah's. Though I was glad to hear her recovered enough to be talking, I was not looking forward to our conversation. There was no way in hell Miss Policies and Procedures was going to be cool with this.

"Captain Wolfe," she said stiffly.

"Sarah," I replied, walking a few steps from my team. "How are you feeling?"

"My blood count is back to normal, and I tested negative for vampire. I'm still in the infirmary. Where are you going?"

I imagined her watching our movement on her tablet. "We have the final pieces," I said. "We know where the children are, where the creature is, and how to destroy it. We're finishing the mission."

"There's no longer a mission."

"According to Centurion," I said.

"An assessment team has deemed the risk of continued engagement here too high."

I glanced around at the helos, half-expecting to find rifles aimed from bay doors, but the machines were simply parked like sentries. "What about El Rosario?" I asked. "We leave and everyone dies."

"I read the SITREP you sent Director Beam," she said. "I know about the latest threat."

"A threat that's since been verified."

"By whom?"

Remembering our argument over consulting Prof Croft, I said, "It doesn't matter. The point is that if we don't stop this thing, the town is history."

"Did you find the Mayan shaman?"

"Yeah, turns out he's on our side. We haven't been dealing with a magic-user, but an extraplanar entity. One that was using the vampires and children to gather power. It's trying to break into our world. Chepe protected the town and our building, but that only bought us time. We don't destroy this thing by midnight, and we can kiss El Rosario goodbye."

"Was he vetted?" she asked.

"Like we have that luxury," I growled. "At this point it's Chepe or nothing. He knows where to find the creature, and he knows its weakness. If he's bullshitting us, we're no worse off."

The silence that followed sounded thick in my earpiece. When Sarah spoke again, she said, "That doesn't change the fact there's no longer a mission. The helos are there to take you out."

"Then they're wasting fuel." I signaled to my team that we were continuing.

"Hold on," Sarah said, after we'd gone a few steps.

From the helo parked in front of us, a figure jumped out and hustled toward us, a huge gun in his arms. Bandages covered half his head while a thick brace bracketed his neck. As Chepe and my teammates gathered around me, I could only stare. I didn't fucking believe this.

"You're using *Olaf* to enforce our evac?" I said to Sarah.

"He requested to be included."

"What do you mean, 'requested to be included'?"

"He's almost recovered from his injuries—the brace is a precaution. That will increase your fighting force to four."

"Wait a minute," I said, shaking my head. "Are you saying...?"

"I'm not saying anything. But unless and until the backup team hears directly from Director Beam, the chain of command goes through me. By then you should have a good head start."

Our connection cut out for several moments during which the helos' blades started up and their big bodies began to lift off. They were leaving. I didn't think it was possible, but Sarah McKinnon had surprised me. I wondered how much of her decision had to do with the vampire attack, or the fact I had saved her.

Olaf arrived in front of me. "I come," he said.

I extended a hand. "Good to have you back."

But instead of shaking, Olaf dug into his vest and pressed several test tubes into my palm.

The connection with Sarah returned. "Any material you can collect from the creatures you encounter, including the extraplanar entity, will help us combat Prodigium IS in the future," she said. "Just don't forget to label them."

I snorted and slid the tubes into a vest pocket. That *hadn't* surprised me.

"Thanks," I said as the helos thumped away. "But what are you going to tell Centurion?"

We were both jeopardizing a lot.

"Beam's going to have a shit fit when he finds out, but if you succeed, it won't matter."

"Is that an order?" I asked with a smile.

"Yes. Now go succeed."

For several hours we climbed a torturous path through the woods, pausing occasionally so Chepe could consult Maximon. I stayed close to the shaman while the rest of the team moved behind us in a column, Takara at the rear.

I'd given Yoofi my M9 again, and as I'd feared, he whipped the Beretta toward every sound. But there weren't many sounds to begin with. Trees that would normally have been full of birdsongs and the rustlings of small animals were eerily quiet. We seemed to be the only things moving.

"Take it easy," I told Yoofi. "Remember your training."

At one point I signaled a stop so I could listen, but with my wolf's hearing largely muted, it was a pointless exercise. For good and ill, Chepe's magic seemed to be doing its job of concealing our presence.

It couldn't protect us from the rain that began to fall in the late afternoon, though. Camouflage ponchos appeared from packs, while Yoofi pulled the hood of his coat over his head. The shaman covered himself with a sheet of plastic that should have made a racket with the rain striking it, but the magic he'd cast absorbed the sound. We trudged on as a deep rumble sounded.

"Ooh, I don't like thunder," Yoofi remarked.

"Not thunder," I said. "That was another tremor."

A second one, even stronger, rocked the ground underfoot.

Yoofi clamped a hand over his mouth to keep from screaming.

I radioed Rusty. "How's it going down there?"

"Whole lotta shaking," he answered. *"You close?"*

When I posed the question to Chepe, he turned testy. "It is ahead, just ahead."

Seeing as how our destination had always been ahead, that didn't tell me anything. "How *far* ahead?"

"Yes, it is ahead," he repeated, speeding his pace.

"I'm not sure," I told Rusty. "But we still have six hours."

Another tremor, the most violent one yet, made the five of us come to a stop.

"Well, don't go all commercial fiction on me and cut it to the

last second," Rusty said. *"We're fixing to lose buildings down here—"* He grunted as though trying to keep all of his computer equipment from rattling off their perches. A crash sounded. *"Well, dadgummit."*

"What was that?" I asked.

"The monitor for the compound's surveillance system. At least it's not one of the drone feeds."

I could just hear the small machine whirring high overhead.

"All right, keep us posted on conditions down there," I said, waving the team onward.

As I caught up to Chepe, he turned his face partway toward me. Water dripped from the eaves of the hood he'd fashioned from the sheet of plastic. "It is ahead, yes," he said in a milder voice. "But I cannot say how far. Maximon still leads me. I feel his pull. But I feel other things too."

"You mean the tremors?"

"Tremors out there. But tremors in here too." He tapped his chest.

A strange foreboding crept over me. "What kind of tremors?"

"When life becomes death, I feel them," he said. "Because my magic now surrounds the group, I feel them very strong." He was referring to the ceremony he'd performed on us. He had done the same for Olaf before we stepped into the woods. "Tremors tell me someone dies tonight."

I looked from Chepe to my teammates. "Someone in our group?" I asked in a lowered voice.

"Someone in group," he affirmed.

"But from what? The Chagrath?"

"From he who comes behind."

I turned, my weapon in firing position. My teammates reacted in kind, but there was no one and nothing in the foliage at our backs. When I turned back, Chepe had forged ahead. I radioed Takara.

"Keep a close watch on our six," I said. "Could be someone following us."

"I'll try, but I'm still recovering from the spell. You sure we can trust this man?"

I watched Chepe use his staff as a walking stick to step deftly through the thick growth. The truth was, I *wasn't* sure. But it was like I'd told Sarah: we didn't have much choice at this point.

"I'll keep an eye on him," I radioed back.

The rained had tapered under a darkening sky when my satellite phone buzzed. I pulled it from my vest. I could have let it go, but it was either going to be William Beam or Reginald Purdy, and it wasn't fair to make Sarah run interference from a sick bed. When I answered, though, it was neither one.

"Captain," a macho voice boomed, "how the fuck are you?"

"Segundo," I said in a lowered voice. "Good to hear you, buddy, and thanks for getting me that intel, but I'm mid-mission. I'll have to call you back."

"Unless you're getting shot at, you need to hear this. I'll keep it short. I told you my brother was gonna check some other databases?"

"Yeah?" I said, a knot already forming in my gut.

"Turns out this Kurt Hawtin was arrested twice in the last month for suspected abuse. He was never charged, though, 'cause his girlfriend denied he did anything to her. Last time was about a week ago. She ended up in the hospital with a broken jaw and some nasty bruising."

That would have been right before Daniela's parents saw him in our hometown.

"Something else you should know," Segundo continued. "He applied for and received a gun permit about a month ago. The guy's packing."

For a moment the slick green foliage and steady march of my teammates faded out. A man who once swore he would kill Daniela was armed, dangerous, and way too fucking close to her.

You need to be home, I thought. *You need to be protecting her.*

"All right, thanks," I said as my surroundings rushed back in. "I've gotta go."

"Good luck, bro."

I hung up and dialed Daniela. The call went straight to voicemail.

"Dani, it's Jason. Listen, I want you to take your dogs and gun and go to your parents'. You're not safe at your house. Stay there until you hear from me. Kurt is armed, and he might be looking for you."

I was about to sign off when Chepe waved to the rest of us and then pointed ahead. We were approaching a massive wall of stone—the top of the mountain that looked over El Rosario.

"It is on the other side," Chepe said.

"Your parents' house," I repeated into the phone. "Right away. I'm going to try to get down there as soon as I can.

Love you, Dani. Be safe." I ended the call and put the phone away. As we emerged from the trees, I leaned my head back and took in the impressive yellow-stoned peak. The earth let out a low rumble, sending a small slide of scree down its tall face.

We had arrived at Maximon.

It was another hour of following Chepe in the growing dark, the old man's sandaled feet picking their way nimbly through a maze of boulders, until we arrived at a large crevice in the backside of the mountain. A foul odor of earth and decay leaked from the opening.

"Is the site in there?" I asked Chepe.

He nodded. "I could not get this close before. Vampires always waiting."

I peered around and took several sniffs. Four of the vampires were dead, but one remained. I wasn't picking up anything—either outside or coming from the cave. As Takara rounded into view, she signaled that our six was clear.

"How we looking, Rusty?" I radioed.

"You're clear down to the tree line," he replied.

Beneath Drone 1's watchful eye, I waved the team forward. "Takara and I are going to scout the cave," I told them. "Olaf and Yoofi, I want you to stay outside with Chepe. Wait till you hear an all clear before bringing him in." I paused before turning from them. "Anything yet?" I asked Yoofi.

"Sorry, no," he replied. "Dabu is still hiding."

Then hopefully we won't need him, I thought.

I readied my MP88 and took the lead through the opening. Beyond the crevice, a cave stretched ahead. Its stone walls glistened with moisture and moss. Takara entered behind me. We proceeded carefully down a long corridor that made several turns, lizards and spiders scurrying from our path. When I peered back, I caught the red crescents of my teammate's eyes glinting in the darkness.

With every step forward, the smell of decay grew stronger.

The cave ended in a chapel-sized room. My gaze immediately fell to the floor. I could see the implements Chepe had used in his ceremony the month before—candles, cocoa beans, balls of resin, an incense burner—but they were scattered everywhere. In the floor's center, about ten feet across, was the black portal he had spoken of. But I couldn't see it as anything other than a giant mouth, pressed to the glass of our world, as Croft had put it.

Beyond the Chagrath's writhing lips, a gelatinous range of humps stretched to a blackness not even my wolf vision could penetrate. The descent was ringed with rows of hook-like teeth. Takara made a sound of disgust.

"Can't believe we're going down there," she whispered.

I couldn't either, but if that's where she said the children were...

"We have the Chagrath in sight and we're clear," I radioed. "Bring Chepe in."

"All of us come?" Yoofi asked.

"Yes. Rusty will keep watch outside."

As my voice echoed off the stone, the Chagrath stopped pulsating, as if trying to listen. Takara's gaze crept up my visor. Without warning, the giant creature began to shake. We braced ourselves as the cavern vibrated. I imagined the

Chagrath shrieking beyond the glass, but the only sound I could hear was the dull boom of falling rocks outside.

After several moments, the creature's body relaxed and resumed pulsating.

"What the hell did you just do?" Rusty asked. *"I thought the compound was gonna fall down on my head!"*

"It senses someone's here," I whispered.

Meaning we needed to get a move on. I turned toward the entrance. Moments later Chepe stepped into view, holding aloft a small torch made from resinous sticks. Yoofi and Olaf flanked him. As they arrived in the sacred site, I signaled for them to remain as quiet as possible.

While Yoofi and Olaf stared at the Chagrath, Chepe closed his eyes. After several moments, he nodded and opened them again. A low resonance seemed to hum around him.

"Maximon says it is time," he whispered.

"How long will you need to prepare the wormwood?" I asked.

"Not much."

"All right, while you're doing that, Takara and I are going to find the children." I pointed to Olaf and Yoofi. "Your job is to protect Chepe." Not least of all because he was our ticket back out of the portal. "Rusty, let them know if anything's coming up the mountain."

"Will do, boss."

I turned to Takara. "Ready?"

Her lips wrinkled as she stepped to the edge of the portal. "Let's get this over with." Her hair billowed up as she dropped in. The interface between our worlds rippled, and Takara disappeared. The Chagrath's throat convulsed like it was choking on something. I eyed the rings of teeth.

"Here," Chepe said, giving me a small handful of wormwood as the mountain rumbled. "You can use it on anything down there. When you are ready to come back, magic will show the way."

It better, I thought, and dropped in after Takara.

25

A powerful wave of nausea passed through me as I dropped. I expected to launch down the long chute of the creature's throat. Instead, I was suddenly standing in a tunnel, mist swirling around me. The ground squelched as I took my first steps, MP88 poised to unleash hell.

I raised my head. Even with my suppressed sense of smell, the odor of decay was overpowering. Made sense. According to Croft, a Chagrath was the equivalent of an underworld bottom feeder.

"Takara?" I called.

"Over here," she whispered.

I turned to find her stepping from the mist.

"To reach the children, you said it's just a matter of thinking about them?"

Her leathers glistened as she slid her free arm through the crook of my elbow. "Close your eyes."

I sniffed to make sure it was really her and then did as she said. A moment later, everything began to spin. When we stopped, I opened my eyes. We were standing in a misty cavern.

"Dammit," Takara muttered. "They were in there."

I turned to where she was looking. A chamber about the size of a large living room stood empty, but I could imagine the greenish liquid Takara had described as well as the suspended children. Gone now. The thought that the Chagrath had consumed them made me queasy all over again.

"Cover me," I said, and stepped into the chamber.

I eyed the walls, wary of the attacking tubes Takara had told us about. Nothing moved from the walls now. I sniffed the air. The scents of the missing children were still in my olfactory vault, and I was searching for matches beneath the prevalent odor of decay. I was picking up another odor now too, slightly acidic, like bile. I didn't like what that suggested.

"Anything?" Takara asked.

"My sense of smell isn't at peak strength, but..." I turned my head. "Hold on. I'm getting traces of the children." I followed the scent trail until I was stepping from the chamber again. "They were moved," I said in profound relief. "They were taken this way."

Takara followed me through the mist. We hadn't gone far when shrieks sounded from above. Takara and I angled our weapons up. "Crap," she said. "It's those bats I told you about."

A section of mist swirled as one of them dove toward me. In a glance, I saw leathery albino wings, a writhing tail, and an eyeless head. Either Chepe's concealing magic was wearing off, or it wasn't effective down here.

I flipped the switch for the flamethrower. As the tail

reared to lash around my throat, I unleashed a blazing jet of napalm. The creature burst into shrieking flames and thudded to the ground. I swept more fire across the mist that formed a ceiling. To my side, Takara squeezed off precise shots with her M4.

"Keep moving!" I called.

We fought back to back as I led us along the scent trail. More of the bat creatures fell around us, some in fireballs, others in spattered messes. Whatever Takara's and my personal problems, there were very few others I would've wanted down here with me.

As the bats thinned, we sped our pace. The trail led to the far end of the cavern, where the mist thinned. A sudden proliferation of stalagmites and stalactites jutted from the floor and ceiling. They reminded me a little of the back of the White Dragon's palace in Waristan. I switched to my rifle, and Takara and I picked off the remaining bats.

"Trail leads to the far wall," I said.

"There's nothing there," Takara pointed out. "Just wall."

"My nose isn't lying." I began to thread my way through the stalagmites.

"Watch out!" Takara called.

Something wrapped my right arm and both legs. A looked down to find several ropelike tendrils tightening around me. They were coming from a large stalagmite to my right, only it was no longer a stalagmite. A dozen amber eyes had opened over its rocky body. And now a goopy mouth of teeth yawned into view.

The hell?

I tried to rip myself from the tendrils, but they only stretched. Then, without warning, they contracted, yanking me toward the giant mouth. I struggled to angle my weapon toward it, but several tendrils had wrapped the barrels. A guttural rumble sounded from the creature's throat.

Takara's blades slashed through the tendrils, releasing me.

"Thanks," I grunted, pivoting my weapon toward the creature's mouth.

I fired a single grenade round past its teeth and ducked away. The detonation was muted—the creature must have tried to eat it. When I looked back, green fluid seeped from its blown eyes, and it toppled over. But the other stalagmites had come to life. They were sliding toward us like slugs, tendrils writhing from their craggy bodies.

"They're trying to get between us and the wall," I said, suggesting my nose had been right.

Takara got the message. "I'll check it out. Can you take care of these things?"

"Yeah," I grunted, already firing off more grenades. The creatures must have been operating under some kind of bite reflex, because to the last, their mouths snapped closed around the grenades. And to the last, the explosions blew out their eyes and knocked them over.

Irises blazing, Takara rose into flight. Seeing her move through the air was pretty damned impressive, but I didn't look for long. Another wave of creatures was coming in. Fortunately, they were just as dumb as the others. As long as I stayed clear of their tendrils, I could pop grenades into their mouths all day long.

As I paused to switch mags, I glanced up. Takara had reached the wall and was feeling over it. Slinging her M4 across her body, she popped the blade from her right sleeve and drove it into what had looked like stone. The wall rippled beneath the impact. She sawed down a short distance, then retracted the blade. A piece of the wall sagged like a loose corner of wallpaper. She seized it and pulled. Beyond the façade was a fluid-filled chamber.

Inside, the shadow of a suspended child came into view.

Movement overhead caught my eye. "Above you!" I called.

The creatures were on the ceiling too. Concealed by the mist, one of them had inched into position above Takara and then dropped. She shoved herself from the wall, but not in time. The pointed head of the massive creature slammed into her thigh. She grunted and fell.

If that thing lands on her, she'll be crushed.

Switching my trigger finger to the rifle, I took aim and released a tight burst of fire. The incendiary rounds burst over the creature's body, taking out a couple of its eyes. More importantly, the attack knocked the creature off its trajectory. Takara landed hard, but not underneath the thing. It crashed down behind her. As it righted itself, the creature whipped several cords around Takara's neck and began dragging her toward its gaping mouth.

Hurdling the creatures I'd taken down, I arrived above Takara and slashed through the cords with my talons. I then scooped her up and jumped back as another of the creatures crashed down. More of them were converging above us. I found a recess in the wall to set Takara.

"You all right?" I asked.

She peered around groggily. "Just need a couple of minutes."

"Wait here."

Flipping the rifle to automatic, I sprayed the creatures

sliding across the ceiling. The explosive impacts knocked them loose, and they plummeted like wrecking balls. Upon landing, the dozen or so creatures lurched onto their slimy bases and began sliding toward us. I swapped fuel tanks, switched back to the flamethrower, and coated them in fire.

Choked cries went up. Ropey tendrils writhed blindly from torched bodies. The cavern shook. I didn't know how the creatures were related to the Chagrath—whether they were from its realm or parts of the Chagrath itself—and I didn't care. I just wanted the disgusting things dead.

Within another few moments, they were.

I scanned the ceiling to make sure there were no more before turning back to Takara. She was already back on her feet, but her first several steps were staggers. The leather had torn away where the creature had struck her thigh, and blood welled from the already-scarred skin.

"Stay there," I said. "I'll get the kids."

Her response was to rise into flight again. Seizing the peeling corner of wall, she pulled until she'd returned to the floor and a large section of the chamber was exposed. I counted the suspended figures. Nine of them, all with tubes running into their nostrils, mouths, and ears. More of the tubes squirmed along the walls. When Takara started to enter, I grabbed her arm.

"The Chagrath will try to snag whoever goes in," I said, setting down my weapon and stripping off my vest. "You're a better shot than me. I need you out here to pick off the tubes before they get to me."

For a moment she looked like she was going to argue, but then she nodded and moved her M4 into firing position. I removed my helmet and boots so that I was only wearing the Kevlar suit. Finally, I donned my sun goggles and tightened them. They were protection against the sun, but I hoped they'd also help me to see through the green suspension.

"Go," Takara said.

I took a deep breath and plunged in. The medium was just as Takara had described it—less liquid and more like a gel. I swam through it in powerful strokes, the goggles doing their job of keeping the stuff out of my eyes. I fixed my sights on the child in the very back, a young girl I recognized as Julia, the fifth child taken. Tubes began to wriggle from the walls. Muted cracks sounded as Takara shot through them, allowing me to focus on the child.

When I reached her, I looked over the tubes running into her face. Were they draining her life? Keeping her alive? Both?

Only one way to find out.

I took the wormwood Chepe had given me, and rubbed it along the tube entering her left ear. The segmented tube contracted and spasmed as though trying to shrink from something noxious, then withdrew from her ear. The other tubes followed suit. Before they could recover, I wrapped an arm around Julia's waist. She jerked, as though from a cough reflex, and her eyes shot open.

I turned and swam hard for the opening. Moments later, we were out. Julia gagged until a gout of greenish fluid poured from her mouth. She spit several times and began to cry. A good sign. I set her on her side and plunged back in.

This time, I recovered two kids.

"Keep it up," I told Takara as I set down the gagging, crying children.

She nodded as she changed mags, oblivious to the

blood flowing from her thigh and pooling around her right boot.

Two more trips netted me five more children, including the boy who had been grabbed by the undead bull. Just had one to go. The final child was Miguel Bardoza, the first child taken, and belonging to the family who had seen us off earlier in the day. As I swam toward him, I thought of his parents' desperate eyes and his sister, who had acknowledged my wave with one of her own. The boy's curly hair fluttered gently in the suspension.

When I arrived beside him, I repeated the ceremony with the wormwood. The tube writhed from the contact, but instead of releasing Miguel, it worked in coordination with the others to tug him deeper into the chamber.

Was the wormwood losing its strength?

I surged after Miguel as rounds zinged past me, severing the tubes reaching from the walls. I squinted past the boy to see where the tubes were taking him. In the back wall, a mouth was opening. But it was less like the ones on the stalagmite creatures and more like a fleshy sphincter.

The tubes are pulling him too fast, I thought as I struggled to find a higher gear. *Not going to reach him in time.*

And the angle of the tubes doing the pulling was such that Takara wasn't going to get any clean shots.

I stretched an arm back and gave her the cease-fire sign. When shots continued to rip through the tubes reaching for me, I repeated the sign with more emphasis. Takara had to be wondering what in the hell I was doing, but the shots stopped. As tubes wrapped me, I made sure to keep them off my right arm. They began pulling me after Miguel, pulling me toward the mouth.

I let them, even straightening my body so I would move through the suspension more cleanly.

It's working. I'm gaining on him.

We were almost to the mouth when I drew even with Miguel. With a gurgling roar, I slashed my talons through the tubes binding my legs. They fell away in pieces. I planted a foot above the mouth's muscular lips and slashed again, this time through the tubes wrapping my body. Freed, I reached over, grabbed Miguel as he was about to enter, and sliced through the tubes around his head.

Drawing him to my side, I thrust us from the wall. But something was happening—a force from the mouth was pulling us toward it.

Its draining the room, I realized, *sucking all the suspension out.*

I signaled wildly to Takara, my lungs beginning to burn from lack of oxygen. I prayed she understood my message. Seconds later, grenade rounds punched past us and into the sphincter.

I covered Miguel as the detonations went off. Several shards of shrapnel hit my Kevlar. One knifed through the side of my neck, but that was all right. I could heal. More importantly, the suction force had stopped. I looked back to find the sphincter sagging like the mouth of someone who had suffered a major stroke.

Takara switched back to the automatic rifle as I stroked toward her, blood from my closing wound trailing behind me. I emerged from the chamber with a gasp and looked down at Miguel. His eyes remained closed. Worse, he wasn't trying to breath. Around us, the eight other children were coughing and crying, but Miguel only lay limp in my arms. I held his chest to my ear until I picked up the barest pulse. I flipped him over and began a modified Heimlich, using the large knuckle of my thumb.

"C'mon," I urged.

I thought again of his parents and sister as he jerked with the thrusts. Finally, he ripped one of the loudest belches I'd ever heard, and a torrent of the green stuff splashed over the floor. Miguel spit a few times, then rubbed his eyes. I turned him back over, and he blinked up at me.

"Un lobo?" he rasped. A wolf?

"That's right," I laughed in relief. *"Un lobo."*

I set him down and keyed my earpiece. "We've got 'em," I said, before realizing we didn't have a connection down here. What had Chepe said? When we were ready to come back, magic would show the way?

"Over there," Takara said.

I followed her finger to where a line of purple light was glimmering into view: the way out.

"My arms are big enough for six or seven if you can handle two," I said, putting my gear back on. "How's your leg?"

"It will be fine," she said, even as she limped on it.

Hopefully Yoofi or Chepe would be able to heal her once we were out. I pulled on my helmet last, then began gathering the kids. Some accepted being scooped up, others struggled and screamed. I left the two who were standing for Takara. She took one in each hand and cocked her head for me to lead.

I followed the trail of purple light, vigilant for anything else that might fly or drop down on us. But the Chagrath seemed to have amassed his forces in front of the hidden chamber that had held the children. Our way was clear. I didn't like the rumbling around us, though. Something told me it was the Chagrath redoubling its efforts to undermine El Rosario.

I moved at what was about quarter speed for me, glancing back to make sure my teammate was keeping up. She was, even though she winced every time she planted her right foot.

"Come on, Takara. You can do this."

She narrowed her eyes as though I'd just insulted her. "I'm fine."

After what felt like a mile, we turned a corner and an opening appeared ahead. Beyond, I could make out Chepe. He was sitting cross-legged at the edge of the portal, his face aglow in candlelight.

"We're almost there," I called back.

When I turned to face the hole again, a force hit me in the side, and the kids went flying. I landed on my back and looked up. The clown Baboso was standing over me. Only he was much bigger down here. I couldn't remember seeing him smile before, but now his red-painted mouth stretched into a grin revealing a pair of metallic fangs. Their scent was unmistakable.

Silver.

26

I leapt up and spread my arms so that I was between Baboso and the children. None of the little ones seemed to have been hurt—the floor of the cavern was soft and wet. I listened to them crawl to the wall behind me, where they gathered in a sobbing huddle. Takara had shoved her two children to the ground and was advancing with both wrist blades extended.

As precise a shot as she was, the corridor was too crowded for a firefight. I slung my MP88 around to my back, then yanked my gloves off. Baboso's blood-speckled eyes moved from me to Takara and back.

Then they shifted to the children.

"Forget it," I snarled. "You're never touching them again."

I eyed his fangs warily. I wondered briefly if the gang to which this vampire had belonged was at war with werewolves, hence the silver-plated teeth. Regardless, he'd never faced a wolf like me before.

I lunged in low and pistoned a hand up. The black

blades of my talons tore through cold, bloated flesh. By the time the vampire clown's entrails spilled out, the talons of my other hand were arcing toward his throat. Blood jetted up, but not from the clown.

A sensation like molten fire exploded through my hand and down my arm. Without me even seeing him move, his silver-plated fangs had punched through my palm. The pain boiled my blood.

With a roar, I drove my free fist into his forehead. The impact dented his skull and drove him, stumbling, into the far wall. But he was still grinning, only now with a hairy slab of my hand dangling from his teeth. I staggered back, holding my wounded hand to my stomach. The tissue was regenerating, but not as fast as the clown's. His stomach closed at the same time his forehead popped back out.

He swallowed my piece of hand and came forward.

Takara met him this time, blades flashing. But in another faster-than-the-eye-can-see move, Baboso pummeled her with a backhand. The blow knocked Takara to the ground, where she rolled several times.

Need to slow him down, I thought, *which is going to mean a stake through the heart.*

As Baboso tracked Takara, who was laboring up to a knee, I drew a stake from my belt with my good hand and lunged forward. Catching the hand, Baboso buried his fangs back into my flesh.

I staggered from the fresh torrent of pain. I'd almost forgotten how much silver hurt.

The stake fell to the ground. The clown giggled around my hand between slurps of blood. He was draining me—and way too fast. I tried to muscle him back, but I was too weak. I brought my weapon around on its sling. When he giggled again, I jammed the rifle barrel into his mouth.

"Suck on this," I grunted.

The burst of automatic fire blew out the back of his head. The big clown fell ass down and stared at me in a daze, his eyes jittering in different directions. On instinct, I dropped the barrel to his chest, but I'd heard a couple of the rounds carom off a moment before. I was lucky none had struck the children. With a blood-caked hand, I recovered the stake from the ground and made another lunge for the clown's heart. He clubbed my hand away. On my next attempt he hit me even harder.

His eyes straightened as he rose to his feet.

"The Chagrath is tapped into him somehow," Takara said. "We can't defeat him this way."

No wonder the clown was moving so damned fast. The Chagrath's realm, the Chagrath's rules. I glanced at Takara, then at the back wall, where all nine children were huddled now.

"Take them," she said.

"I'm not leaving you here alone."

"Take them!"

Her voice was changing, becoming more piercing. When I glanced at her again, *she* was changing. The red light blazing from her eyes and palms was radiating around her, creating the same feathered dragon I'd glimpsed during our one-on-one exercise a week earlier.

Only now the dragon was growing to fill the corridor.

"Go!" she shrieked. But her lips hadn't moved. The word had come from the dragon's beaked mouth. "And don't return, unless you wish to die."

I backed away and then turned toward the children. "*Vamose!*" I said. "This way."

I herded them toward the portal and the end of the purple trail that still glimmered along the floor. The children complied, anxious to escape what must have seemed like a never-ending nightmare.

The portal rippled with the first child's passage. Beyond, I saw Yoofi startle back before understanding what was happening. He took the child by the hand and ushered her over to the blanket against the wall. Olaf moved into a position to stand guard over her.

When the rest of the children peered back at me, I made a brushing motion with my hand, telling them to join Olaf and the girl. They did, plunking through the portal like pebbles into a well.

I noticed one child standing frozen beside me. It was Miguel. The bits of jelly over his face glistened red as he stared back down the corridor. When I followed his gaze, I understood why.

The vampire clown Baboso, the one who had abducted him, was thrashing inside a firestorm. Takara hovered above him, no longer my teammate, but another being entirely, the fire seeming to radiate from her feathery form. Flesh blew from the vampire clown's screaming body. I swallowed, finding the show of power both beautiful and terrifying.

"Go!" the dragon shrieked again.

I wrenched my gaze away, lifted Miguel into an arm, and carried him through the portal.

"Mr. Wolfe!" Yoofi exclaimed. "You are all right!"

I nodded and handed Miguel to him. As he took the child and sat him on the blanket with the others, I noticed the shaking around us wasn't just the vertigo of having returned from the Chagrath's realm. The entire mountain felt like it was about to come crashing down.

Amid the chaos, Chepe continued to sit cross-legged at the edge of the portal. Light from dozens of candles wavered over his closed eyes. The bag with the wormwood rested in the palms of his upturned hands.

"We're just waiting on one more," I told him.

When he didn't answer, I turned to Yoofi. "How close is he to being ready?"

"How close?" he said. "He's been ready for hours!"

"Hours? But we were only down there for..." I trailed off as I remembered Takara's last experience in the realm. What had felt like a few hours to her had, in fact, been an entire day and night.

"Yes, yes!" Yoofi said "It is almost midnight! Where is Takara?"

"She's coming," I said, peering into the portal. But I still couldn't see anything beyond the ridges and teeth that dropped into blackness. They shuddered in violent quakes.

Almost midnight? I checked my watch. *Fucking hell.*

"C'mon, Takara," I whispered toward the portal.

I keyed my earpiece, which was working again. "How's it going down there, Rusty?"

"Not good, boss. We're talking non-stop seismic activity for the last hour. I'm losing equipment left and right. My monitor for Drone 1 crash-landed right before you called. Trying to reroute the feed..." He grunted. *"Reroute the feed to one of the few computers still standing."*

"Hang in there. We got the kids out."

"*Well, hot damn!*" Rusty said in relief.

"A few more minutes and Chepe will hit it with the wormwood." I continued to watch the portal for Takara. "And we're still clear up here?"

"*Last I checked. Like I said, the monitor took a swan dive. Shit. Someone's pounding on the door.*"

"See who it is first," I said.

"*Lost that monitor too, but it's gonna be the mayor. She called a little bit ago and we got cut off.*"

"No, you need to—" I started to say, but was drowned out by the unmistakable sound of a shotgun blast through the feed. "Rusty!" I shouted. The children who were crying stopped long enough to stare up at me.

"*Son of a bitch,*" Rusty seethed.

"What happened?" I demanded. "Are you all right?"

Sounds of scuffing and struggle took hold with Rusty swearing between grunts. My first thought was that Nicho, the possessed boy, had shown up with the stolen shotgun. But Rusty had too big a fight on his hands, and the boy didn't weigh more than sixty pounds soaking wet. If Rusty was up against something undead, I hoped to hell he was putting his training to use.

Finally, the sounds of struggle stopped.

"Rusty?"

"*Yeah,*" he panted. "*Still here.*"

"What in the hell was all of that?"

"*Son of a gun surprised me with a chest full of shot. Good thing I was suited up.*"

"*What* surprised you?"

"*What was the kid's name? Nacho?*"

"You've been fighting a ten-year-old this whole time?"

"Hey, he was out of his mind. Scrapping like a wired dog." Rusty paused to catch his breath. *"Finally managed to cuff him, but it took a dose of chloroform to put him down. Jesus, Joseph, and Mary."*

"If we get out of this, we're going to need to work on your hand-to-hand skills."

"If we get out of this, I'll be spending the next month at the Bunny Ranch in Vegas."

"Get those monitors up," I ordered.

The portal rippled, and Takara staggered through. I lunged forward and caught her before she collapsed. The red light was waning from her eyes as smoke drifted from her body.

"The clown is destroyed," she murmured.

I helped her down and then turned to Chepe, but he was already on his feet. Power hummed around him and the bag of wormwood as he chanted in a low, resonant voice. Beyond the portal, bright green and orange spots were breaking out over the Chagrath, while the shaking around us intensified, seeming to rise to another pitch.

"Let's get everyone out!" I shouted to Yoofi.

"No. Chepe says we're protected in here. Not protected out there."

He was probably referring to some sort of magic the shaman had cast over the space. I peered around, not convinced the walls were going to withstand much more shaking. But there were avalanches outside, and we were a good half mile from the tree line. I looked at my watch—bare minutes to midnight—then back at Chepe, who was reaching into the bag of wormwood.

One way or another, this was going to be over soon.

"Boss!" came Rusty's urgent voice. *"I restored Drone 1's feed*

and was going back over the footage—you've got someone coming up!"

The next sound I heard was a shot. Not from Rusty's end this time, and not from a shotgun. The explosion had originated from a .38 caliber. The bullet ripped through Chepe's side and dropped the shaman. Dried wormwood fluttered from his outstretched hand and fell harmlessly over the cavern floor.

I turned toward the figure emerging into the light of the cavern. Amid the confusion and my suppressed senses, I hadn't heard or smelled him.

"I told you he was a devil!" Salvador Guzman screamed. "I told you he would bring the end upon us!"

27

Olaf swung his MP88 toward the preacher.

"Stop!" I shouted, already bounding toward him. "He's possessed!"

"The *beast* cometh," Guzman snarled, jerking his revolver toward me. Bullets clanged off my helmet and slammed into my shoulders, but my protective gear kept them from going any further.

I leapt and smashed the gun from his grip. When I landed, it was with one hand palming his head. I took him to the ground. He struggled under my weight, but without the superhuman strength Rusty had described in his battle with Nicho. Between my fingers, Salvador Guzman's eyes remained red-rimmed, but now they looked more horror-struck than hate-filled.

"How did you know where to find us?" I demanded. There was no way he'd tailed us up here undetected. The Chagrath had to have guided him. *"How?"*

"I followed him," Guzman grunted.

"Bullshit. We would have seen you."

"No, not this time. Last month, during the festival. I followed him up and I watched. I listened. I heard him calling to Satan. When I saw him leading you from town earlier, I knew where he was taking you. Now look!" he shouted above the rumbling. "Look what he's done!"

I glanced over a shoulder to find Chepe still lying where he'd fallen. Yoofi was kneeling beside him.

"It's not Satan," I growled. "And Chepe didn't call it up. That's an underworld creature he was trying to stop." Whatever doubts I'd harbored against the shaman earlier, I was fully convinced now of his good intentions.

"Oh, he's manipulative," Guzman said with a sneer. "But you know that already. Don't you, *beast*?"

We didn't have time for this. The preacher wasn't possessed by anything except his own violent zealotry. I patted him down, then flipped him over hard. From my pack, I pulled a length of cable and secured him. I then stuffed a towel in his mouth to shut him up.

Pulling off my helmet, I glared down at him. "Don't move."

As Guzman's eyes met mine, they flew wide, and the preacher released a muffled shriek. *Beast enough for you?* I thought, replacing my helmet. I signaled for Olaf to keep an eye on the preacher and rushed over to Chepe with a medical kit.

"He doesn't look good," Yoofi said.

With each straining breath, blood bubbled from the old man's lips. His chest hitched and rattled. I pulled his blood-drenched shirt up enough to see the entrance and exit wounds. They were bad.

"Can you heal him?" I asked Yoofi.

"Not without Dabu," he replied apologetically.

I swore and opened the kit. Chepe reached a trembling hand toward mine and shook his head. "No time," he rasped.

My watch showed three minutes till midnight. I looked at the portal, where the shaking Chagrath had turned even more toxic-looking colors of green and orange, then down at the scattered wormwood.

Could Chepe complete the ceremony?

As though hearing the thought, the old man shook his head again.

"No power," he said. His cloudy eyes moved to Yoofi. "Must be him."

"Me?" Yoofi leaned back on his staff. "No, I am sorry, but Dabu is a thousand miles away. He wants nothing to do with this place."

"You heard the man," I said, raking up the wormwood. "It's you or no one."

Yoofi swallowed hard and looked at the handful of dried herb I held toward him.

"Listen," I said, "you've called Dabu back before, you *have* to do it again."

Yoofi accepted the wormwood, but with a shaking hand. "He will not listen."

Amid the quaking, the cavern lurched to one side. Olaf stumbled to keep his footing, while the children clung to one another. Balls of resin rolled around. "Then *make* him listen!" I shouted.

"How?"

"You know him better than anyone."

"Parts of town are starting to sink," Rusty radioed. *"And I'm seeing some pretty scary shit on Drone 2. Crevices are opening. A couple of houses have already gone in. And something's*

moving around at the bottom of those cracks. Some kind of giant worm."

Shit, I thought, *it's getting its food supply.*

"That's an appendage of the Chagrath," I said. "If you get a clean shot, nail it."

"I've got the drone locked on. How's it going up there?" he asked nervously.

"If you lose communication with us, have Drone 2 give you a lift out of there."

"That swell, huh?"

I was watching Yoofi, who still appeared to be mulling over what I'd said about making his god listen. A sudden light came over his face. He clenched his hand around the wormwood and wheeled toward the portal.

As Yoofi began to speak, I carried Chepe a short distance away and started to treat his wounds. It was the only activity I felt I had an ounce of control over at the moment. I worked methodically, falling back into my field training and experience. To my left, Olaf stood over the screaming children. To my right, Takara had curled onto her side, her powers spent. Both of their gazes were on Yoofi.

He spoke sternly, the hand with the wormwood held over the portal, the other clutching his staff straight overhead. His coat trembled around him. He looked convincing, anyway. But when I searched the staff's black blade for something—anything—to suggest Dabu's return, there was no warping force or black smoke. There was nothing.

I checked my watch again. Two till midnight.

The portal began to ripple and then rise. The interface was stretching, the Chagrath pushing its way into our world. Its bloated lips pulsated above the concentric rows of hooked teeth.

How big is this fucking thing that it's also under the town, miles away? I thought.

As the interface began to peel from the Chagrath, I stood with my MP88—a weapon that suddenly felt puny.

"I take them outside!" Olaf called, flipping on his weapon's tactical light. He was referring to the children. I hesitated before nodding. Despite my early, violent mistrust of the man, Sarah had been right. We'd given him the mission parameters, and he had followed them to a *T*. Right now that meant keeping the children safe. Plus, with the Chagrath emerging, it couldn't possibly be more dangerous out there than in here. Especially if I started shooting.

"Be careful," I told him.

Olaf helped the children up and began shepherding them from the cavern.

"You should go too," I told Takara. But she shook her head and struggled to her feet. Threads of smoke still drifted from her body, and she winced like she was in incredible pain. Regardless, she worked her M4 around into firing position.

Yoofi continued to talk and shout as the Chagrath rose above him. The African priest, with his braided hair and bulky coat, looked like a child. The Chagrath broke through and angled its wormlike head toward him. Its mouth opened and closed, as though tasting the air.

Stupid mortals, came its chilling voice. *You have no idea my power...*

Takara and I opened fire. The hideous being recoiled as rounds exploded in and around its mouth. The cavern lurched again, this time to the other side. Rocks crashed down. Yoofi stumbled to keep his balance, but he maintained his stance, the hand clutching the wormwood held straight forward.

The Chagrath recovered from our initial assault, more surprised than hurt. Its body bulked as it rose higher.

I have arrived, it whispered. *And I will only grow more powerful as I feed...*

Takara and I released more bursts of gunfire. We might as well have been blowing bubbles for all the good they did. I considered calling for everyone's evacuation, even Yoofi's, but I couldn't.

Not with so much at stake.

"C'mon, Yoofi," I whispered. "I believe in you, man."

Without warning, the air seemed to leave the room. A thunderous black bolt shot from Yoofi's staff and into his hand holding the wormwood. A moment later a purple and white aura burst around Yoofi's fist, lighting up the cavern. As the Chagrath dove for him, Yoofi hurled the wormwood, which had coalesced into a crackling ball of energy. The Chagrath released a horrid scream as the potent energy ball disappeared down its gullet.

I bounded in, seized Yoofi around the waist, and pulled him from the descending path of the Chagrath. More rocks crashed around us. I shoved Yoofi ahead of me and shouted for him and Takara to flee the cavern. Yoofi picked up Chepe, while I lifted Guzman by an arm.

The twenty or so feet of the Chagrath that had emerged was flipping around like a giant leech coated in salt. Where the wormwood had gone down stood a vein-like network of purple trails, pulsating and beginning to ooze black pus.

Had Yoofi's power been enough? Would the thing retreat to its realm?

As though to answer my questions, more of the Chagrath squeezed forth.

I switched to the grenade launcher and, running backwards, pumped bursts into its mouth. But the detonations seemed to do little more than remind the Chagrath we were here. It straightened and lunged toward us. I turned and sprinted, shouting Takara and Yoofi onward.

We emerged to an apocalyptic scene of flashing skies, crashing rain, and boulders cascading down the mountainside. Below, branch lightening made jagged arcs over the thrashing trees. Olaf had taken the children a short distance from the cavern, probably as far as they *could* go, given the chaos. Now he was huddled with them under a stone shelf. I handed the preacher off to Takara, who appeared to have recovered some, and pointed to the others.

"Go!" I shouted. "Try to get them out of here!"

As they made their way down, Yoofi still carrying Chepe, I backed from the cavern entrance and pulled the electronic tablet from my vest. I accessed a laser feature for calculating positions.

"You still there, Rusty?" I asked as I took the cavern's coordinates.

"Still here, boss man," I could hear destruction all around him. *"But I don't know for how much longer."*

"I'm going to give you some coordinates. Hit it with Drone 1's entire payload. Then take Drone 2 and get the hell out of there." I read the coordinates off the tablet. "You're cleared hot."

I bounded behind cover. The missiles weren't going to

hurt the Chagrath, but if we could collapse the cavern, it might buy us enough time to get out of the being's range. A peek showed the mouth of the cavern glowing orange and green through the downpour.

It's emerging.

Rusty's voice returned a second later. *"Incoming in three ... two ... one ..."*

I ducked low. The mountain shook as the drone's missiles slammed home. More boulders smashed down. In the dissipating smoke and dust, I saw that the entrance had been buried. I hurried over to the others.

"I don't know how much time we have," I shouted above the rain, taking Guzman back from Takara, "so we're gonna have to move. There's a valley on the other side of the mountain from El Rosario. Should be stable—"

I felt more than heard Guzman scream as the mountain above us shook. I turned to find the rocks over the just-collapsed cavern trembling. The Chagrath burst forth. It crackled orange and green, but pus was pouring from its body now. The psychic words it issued were little more than gibbering shrieks. It reared up, lightening flashing around it, then threw itself toward us.

I crouched back and made sure everyone was behind me. One way or another, we were going to escape this thing, get the children to safety, and then figure out a new strategy for El Rosario.

But it wasn't looking good.

I tensed as the enormous being neared, its twisting lips reaching, straining. I fired a burst of incendiary rounds, already knowing they couldn't do anything. The Chagrath landed ten feet from us—and burst apart over the boulder field. Black pus sloshed off to both sides in thick waves.

The mountain trembled for another moment, as though settling back into place, then went still. The sky stopped flashing. The rain thinned to a drizzle. Behind me everyone had gone silent, even the children.

I stared in disbelief. Where the Chagrath had been was ... gunk.

Finally, someone spoke, his voice faint and rasping: "Thank you."

I turned to find Chepe clasping Yoofi's hand in both of his. His face was pale, his body limp where Yoofi had set him, but his cloudy eyes shone above his smile. Yoofi looked from Chepe to the steaming remnants of the Chagrath and back.

"Did I do that?" he asked.

Chepe nodded and patted his hand. "You have a powerful god."

Yoofi giggled in disbelief, then shook his head. "I will have to make him an extra big cigar, then."

I wanted to hug Yoofi and ask what in the hell he'd done to get Dabu to come back, but there wasn't time. Chepe was critical. "We passed a clearing on our way up," I said. "I'll run him down and arrange for a lift. Can the rest of you bring Guzman and the children?"

My teammates nodded, but as I stooped for Chepe, he shoved my arm back.

"No," he rasped. "I will be buried here."

"What are you talking about?"

He tapped his chest. "I told you about tremors here. I told you one of us will die, from he who comes behind. Remember this?" I looked over at Guzman. "I want to be buried here. On the mountain of Maximon."

"Nothing's preordained," I told him, even as I thought

about the old Kabadi sorceress declaring that the Blue Wolf would protect all. "We have medics who can help you."

"They are safe now." Chepe looked past me to the children and smiled. "Evil gone."

His lids slid to half mast as he breathed for the final time.

"Evil gone..."

28

I buried Chepe under a cairn of stones, then went off to perform a final task as Yoofi spoke a few words, one priest to another. He set his favorite flask at the head of the cairn, which was touching.

When Yoofi indicated he was done, I lifted him onto my back and began bounding down the mountain. Takara and Olaf had already started down with Guzman and the children. I'd arranged for Centurion to pick us up at the clearing. That they agreed told me Sarah's assessment had been on the mark: with this company, success trumped everything.

I craned my neck around. "So how did you make Dabu see the light?" I asked.

"I thought about what you said," he shouted against the wind. "How I know Dabu better than anyone. And it's true. I know his good, and I know his bad. He's very funny, but also very jealous. I so much mention another god, and he want to explode. One god especially." Yoofi giggled. "Even now Dabu don't want me to talk about her. Udu is her name. She's Dabu's sister, god of the earth. So I tell Dabu, if you don't come, I give all smokes and drink to Udu. He still say nothing. Too scared. So I start the prayer to Udu. I almost finish, and *that's* when Dabu come. And brother, did he come. I never feel that much power before."

"You did great, Yoofi. I couldn't be prouder of you."

"It's like Sugar Nice say, 'After all the bullshit I been dealt, I got no qualms 'bout hitting 'neath the belt.' And Dabu deal me a lot of bullshit this trip, man."

I laughed in agreement.

The helos arrived at the clearing shortly after we did. When everyone boarded, they lifted off and swung toward El Rosario. Within minutes, the town came into view in my natural night vision. It was pretty much what Rusty had described. The outskirts were a wreck. Several homes had fallen into the crevices that stretched toward the town center, while others lay in ruin, but still above ground.

As a nearly full moon emerged from the clouds, I thought about the dead, the ones the Chagrath had consumed in order to emerge. Although the soldier in me knew collateral damage was an unfortunate corollary of combat, the Blue Wolf swore to do better next time.

My gaze ranged over the center of the town—blessedly intact. The Chagrath hadn't made it that far. And the luminous white church, where many in the town had taken shelter, remained standing.

Still, I thought, *we can do better.*

By the time we touched down, a crowd had gathered around the soccer fields. We disembarked and lifted the children down. The Centurion medics had checked them out during the ride. Apart from shock, they were in good health. A couple of the older children had taken on parental roles and they now carried the smallest ones. Olaf, Yoofi, and Takara held the hands of the other children, while I grabbed Guzman and hauled him out.

The parents of the missing had already begun to separate from the crowd and run toward us. Amid laughter and crying, they found their children, lifted them into their arms, and smothered them with hugs and kisses.

When Mayor Flores approached me, there were tears in her eyes as well.

"El Rosario will never forget this," she said. "We thank you so much."

I accepted her hug, expressed condolences for those they had lost that night, and then explained what had happened to Chepe. For several moments, she was too overcome to speak.

I handed Guzman over to Juan Pablo, who jerked him to his police cruiser. Eyes fixed on my visor, Guzman screamed behind his gag—no doubt about beasts and damnation. The people of El Rosario didn't spare him a second of their attention. Maybe he would convince his fellow prisoners.

Mayor Flores wiped her eyes as she watched the police cruiser pull away. "The other pastors said Salvador was becoming too zealous. I should have kept a closer eye on him." She turned back to me. "So it is all over?"

"It is," I said, remembering Chepe's final words. "The evil is gone."

"Can we call on you if we need you again?"

I met her gaze from inside my helmet. "Legion's here for you. Before we take off, we'll give you a direct number."

She thanked me again before leaving to check on the reunited families. Off to my right, Miguel Bardoza was back with his family. Wrapped in his father's and mother's arms, I had to identify him by smell. The only part of him I could actually see was one of his hands. His sister was right there, clasping his wrist like she would never let go again.

When she caught me looking, she smiled.

Still concealed inside my helmet, the Blue Wolf and I smiled back.

At that moment Rusty radioed. We had been in contact on the way down. With the Chagrath's disappearance, not only had the quakes ended, but Nicho returned to a sane version of himself. Rusty placed him in police care and then took stock of the office. He estimated the equipment damage to be in the tens of thousands of dollars. Director Beam was going to love that.

"Got a call from Croft while you were handing off the children," he said. *"Turns out the Chagrath wasn't just sent back to its realm, it was blown from freaking existence. There's still a gaping hole, but a couple of wizards are en route to stitch it up. Should be there by morning, before anything else tries to crawl through. They'll take a look at Nicho and the children too. Clean any remaining Chagrath gunk from their systems. You did a helluva job, he wanted me to tell you."*

I glanced over at my bloodied and haggard team, remembering my first assessment of them and Rusty: a priest, a ninja, a zombie, and a guy who looked like he should be working crew on the carny circuit. But damned if my group of misfits hadn't gotten the job done.

"It was a team effort," I said. "Way to hang in there tonight."

"Anything's better than hanging from the end of your claws."

His reference to our first encounter made me chuckle. "Any word on Sarah?"

"She not there yet? She was supposed to be coming in."

I turned to where the helicopters had landed and spotted her emerging from one of the newly-arrived. I waved her over. "I'll send some Centurion guys to help you load the van," I told Rusty. "I want us out of here inside the hour."

"You got it, boss."

With the mission accomplished, my thoughts were already back on Daniela. I couldn't ignore the burning concern I felt.

"Good to see you up and about," I called as Sarah arrived in front of me. "How are you feeling?" Her face was still a little pale, but her eyes were back in the business of absorbing info.

"I'm fine. Well done tonight."

Though she spoke stiffly, I caught her gaze going to the family reunions still happening around us. I didn't have to ask to know she was thinking about the Philippines and how things might have gone differently had there been a team like Legion around. She'd been right to defy Centurion's evacuation order—policies and procedures be damned—and I sensed she knew this now.

"Have you talked to Director Beam?" I asked.

"No, not yet. Do you have my samples?"

I snorted as I reached into my vest, pulled out a filled tube, and handed it to her. Though I knew now that there was a human buried somewhere inside her, Sarah's clinical detachment remained remarkable. She held the tube up to the moonlight, turning it one way and the other.

"It's not labeled."

"'Chagrath Goop,'" I said. "There."

I'd remembered to scoop up some of the black gunk while Yoofi took care of Chepe's final rites. Sarah pulled out a pen, wrote something on the label—probably not "Chagrath Goop"—and placed the tube in her pocket.

"Was that the only sample?" she asked.

"Yes." My satellite phone began to ring. "Excuse me."

I turned and looked down at the number. Not one I recognized. Was this Segundo calling with an update? My heart pounded the back of my sternum as I answered and brought the phone to my ear.

"Yes?"

"Captain Wolfe," a genteel voice said.

"Reginald Purdy," I replied, my heart cycling back down. "You received my message?"

"I did."

In the silence that followed, I braced for the rebuke. Instead, he broke into hoarse laughter.

"I'm calling to congratulate you."

"So you're all right with what I did?"

"Listen to me, Captain. What you did is what the Legion Program is supposed to stand for."

"Good," I cut in. "Then I need a favor."

29

Four hours later

Two Centurion agents were standing beside a sleek sedan on the tarmac of the Houston Airport when my private flight touched down. They looked like spooks in their black suits. Or pall bearers.

I ran over to meet them.

"The shooting happened about forty-five minutes ago," one of the agents said.

"How fast can you get me there?"

"Climb in," the other agent said and took his place behind the wheel.

It was Saturday morning and still dark. That factor plus the car's speed cut a normally hour-and-a-half trip to just over forty minutes. It felt like ten times that.

When I started hyperventilating, I removed my helmet even though the agents hadn't been briefed on what I was. There had been no time to get another experimental injection to me, either. I was still the Blue Wolf. The agents exchanged looks, but didn't say anything.

I made several calls. None were answered.

"It's this right," I said, even though the driver was already turning.

My voice was more guttural than usual, the words seeming to tear my throat.

She didn't get my message last night, I thought numbly. *She stayed home.*

As the agent navigated the streets of Daniela's neighborhood, I was jumping out of my skin. I had to restrain myself from throwing the door open, bailing out, and sprinting to her house myself.

At last the driver turned onto her street. A squad of police cars came into view. Her driveway was cordoned off with yellow tape, an officer controlling access. Beyond, her red front door was open. Officials went in and out. My heart pounded sickly as I stared from the tinted window.

"We have no jurisdiction here," the driver reminded me. "What do you want to do?"

The question draped me like a massive weight. I'd tried to get here in time, but I hadn't.

"Pull over," I said.

The driver eased to the curb across the street from her house. The sky was just beginning to pale, and Daniela's neighbors had emerged in bathrobes and bed-stiff hair to see what was going on. They stood in small groups consulting one another, sharing suburban intel. My hearing picked up bits of what they said.

"...two shots, one right after the other..."

"...ambulance left about twenty minutes ago..."

When my phone rang, I nearly fumbled it to answer.

"Jason," Daniela said, her voice shaking badly. She added quickly, "First, I want you to know that I-I'm fine."

"What happened?"

"I shot him," she said. "I shot Kurt."

I'd known that, of course. What I didn't know was how it had happened.

"You're all right, though?" I asked. "You're not hurt?"

"No. I'm fine."

"All right. Just take a deep breath, then tell me what happened."

"I just told the police everything. They're still here. Where are you?"

"I'm in the states. What happened, Dani? Please, tell me."

She paused to blow out a shaky breath. I did the same, forcing my shoulders down. "He showed up early this morning and started banging on the front door. The dogs went crazy and I woke up. I got out of bed and checked from the kitchen window. It was Kurt. He must have seen the blinds move because he demanded I come out and talk to him. When I wouldn't, he—"

Her voice hitched.

"Take your time," I said.

"He started screaming at me, saying awful things. It was like he was unleashing every dark, violent thought he'd ever held against me. Just hurling them against the house."

The image made all of my muscles bunch up again. "Did you—?"

"Have the Glock?" she cut in. "Yes, but I grabbed my phone. And—it feels so stupid of me now. I plugged it in last night, but the charger wasn't all the way in. The battery was dead."

Which explained why my call yesterday had gone to her voicemail.

"What happened next, Dani?"

"I—I plugged it in, but then I had to wait a minute for the phone to power up. Meanwhile, Kurt was still outside screaming, but I couldn't see him. Then I realized he was circling the house, trying the doors. The dogs were going berserk. When I called 9-1-1, the dispatcher wanted to know if Kurt had made a direct threat against me." Daniela barked out a laugh. "I told her it didn't matter because he was violating the restraining order. After tapping away on her computer for what felt like forever, the dispatcher told me to hold tight, a vehicle would be here in twenty to thirty minutes. I told her I wasn't ordering a pizza—I didn't have twenty to thirty minutes!"

I noticed her voice becoming stronger as she spoke. I encouraged her to continue.

"By the time I got off the phone, I couldn't hear Kurt anymore. I looked out a window just before he disappeared down the end of the driveway. A few seconds later I heard what sounded like a car trunk open and slam shut. When he reappeared, I knew he'd just gotten something out of his car. And by the way he was walking, one arm not swinging, I knew he had it concealed in his jacket."

Attagirl.

"I got the dogs out of the room, closed the door, went back to the window, and opened it quietly. It was the office window at the front of the house, the one in that dark corner. He couldn't see me."

I nodded some more. *Thinking like a soldier.*

"I sighted on his chest and shouted that if he came any closer, I'd shoot."

Even though I already knew the outcome, I was squeezing the phone hard enough to crush it. Maybe it was because that had always been my biggest fear: despite owning a sidearm and being a decent shot, Dani was such a saint that when it came time to pull the trigger, she wouldn't have it in her. I always imagined her trying to talk to her aggressor, convinced she could tame whatever violence was raging in his mind. Especially in a case like this, where she knew the SOB.

"He reached into his jacket," she said, "and I squeezed twice."

My hand relaxed a little around the phone. "You did the right thing," I assured her.

"I wasn't sure until he fell and I saw the actual gun." She released her breath. "It landed beside his right foot. I called 9-1-1 with an update and then covered him from the window until they arrived. I didn't need to, it turned out. The detective said he was dead before he hit the ground. She also said that I was entirely within my rights. Not only did he violate the restraining order, but he'd threatened me while armed. She took my statement here."

I hit my head on the ceiling when I sat up. "You're at your house?"

This whole time I'd assumed she was talking to me from a police precinct.

"Yeah, there's a team still here." A murmured voice sounded through the phone. Daniela replied to it, then came back on. "The detective just said they'll be out of my hair in a few minutes."

I watched the activity around the front of her house. Dani was inside, literally a few dozen steps away. The police would never let me past the cordon, but if I waited until they left...

"Jason? You still there?" Dani asked.

"Yeah, sorry. How are you doing? Not physically, but you know ... with what happened?"

I was thinking about my first kill. I'd lain awake that night, wondering about the enemy soldier whose life I'd taken. But it had been his or mine. He had known that too. Still, it took several more kills before I stopped dwelling on them. They stayed with me, but I didn't let them own me.

Dani didn't have that luxury.

"I've had this fear hanging over me for the last five years," she said. "A fear, I guess, that Kurt would come back and try to hurt me. A fear I didn't even know was there." A nervous laugh. "Because the second he hit the driveway, and it was clear that, one way or another, he'd never come after me again, that fear was gone. And it's still gone. I have a counselor friend I'm going to talk to, but you asked me how I'm doing and right now I feel ... I feel good."

I suspected there was a battered woman in Central Florida who would feel just as much, if not more, relief when she learned her boyfriend had been gunned down in self defense.

But there you had it. Dani felt good. She'd go through the ups and downs just like I had done. And just like me, she'd be all right in the end. I'd be there to make sure.

"At least now you know I can take care of myself," she said.

"I never doubted that," I lied.

I started to imagine her dubious frown. But I didn't have to. She emerged onto the front porch, and I could see the frown as clear as day from across the street. She'd thrown on a white T-shirt and jeans and tied her hair up with a blue bandana. She looked amazing.

"Jason," she said in her stern voice.

"All right, I was *concerned*," I amended with a smile. "But you handled it exactly right. I'm proud of you."

"Well, I don't want you feeling like you have to worry about me."

"I'll promise not to worry about you if you stop worrying about me. Easy, right?"

"Where are you again?"

She'd been pacing the front porch, but she stopped and seemed to be staring straight at our car. I drew back before realizing she couldn't see me through the tinting. But maybe now was the time to come clean. To tell her what had happened, what I'd become, and why I needed to finish out my year away from her.

"I just completed a mission," I said. "I'm back in the country."

"Oh, is that your definition of *routine*?"

"It was last minute. There were children involved."

I watched Dani's hand go to her chest. "Are they…?"

"They're fine now."

Dani nodded and turned so she was no longer facing our car. "You're doing what you need to be doing, then." She moved the phone from her mouth to talk to whom I assumed was the detective. A police officer started taking down the crime-scene tape.

They were leaving.

My heart thundered as my gloved talons curled around the door release. I was anxious in a way I hadn't been in El Rosario. It came from the thought that Daniela would accept me for who I had become—and her acceptance would be true—but deep down she would harbor the same fear she had felt toward Kurt. Because it was a fear we all shared in the most primitive parts of ourselves. The fear of the Beast. I couldn't bear the thought of evoking that in her. And would it ever go away, even after I was restored to my human form?

"Sorry about that," she said when she came back on.

"Daniela..." I started to say, but we were moving. The car was pulling from the curb. I covered the mouthpiece and jabbed the driver's shoulder. "What the hell are you doing?" I demanded.

"Centurion wants you back in Vegas right away."

I pulled on the release, but the door was locked from the inside.

"I'm in the middle of something, *goddammit*." But as I watched the neighboring house swallow Daniela from view, it occurred to me that we might have been called to another mission. While my human eyes strained back, I felt my wolf eyes peering forward in anticipation.

"Mission reasons?" I asked.

"Something to do with Bioengineering."

"Biogen?" Had there been a breakthrough? A cure?

"Hey, Jason, can I call you back?" Daniela said. "My parents just pulled up."

"Of course," I replied distractedly, hoping the next time we talked I would have some really good news for her.

We spoke our love for one another and our gratitude that the other was all right before ending the call. As the car pulled from Daniela's neighborhood, I noticed my fingers still hooked around the door's release. When I moved the hand to my lap, it was with a guilty mixture of regret and relief.

30

I spent the next three days at the bioengineering building on Centurion's campus. I was kept in the basement, a sterile laboratory of too-bright fluorescent lights and too-white walls. I was stuck, injected, and siphoned from by faceless researchers in hazmat suits. I underwent batteries of tests while buried in a riot of electrodes and intravenous lines. My physical form never changed.

When it was over, I was released without any real explanation of what they had done or what, if anything, they had learned.

The data needed to be analyzed, I was told.

I returned to the Legion campus, glad to be out of there and back in more familiar environs. As I strode up to the barracks, I was surprised to hear grunts coming from the far side of the building. I walked around to find Takara moving around the sandy yard, cleaving the air with a variety of kicks and punches.

"Takara," I said.

"Wolfe," she responded between blows.

Progress, I thought. *Before our mission, she wouldn't have said anything.*

"How's your thigh?"

"How does it look?" she snapped, launching into a clean jump kick.

Aaand we still have a ways to go.

I peered around and sniffed the air. "Where is everyone?" The last time I'd seen the other team members was at the Centurion base outside Mexico City, before I'd jumped a flight to Houston.

"Rusty and Yoofi went into Las Vegas. The others, I don't know."

I nodded and then watched her for several moments. I found I couldn't *not* see her as the fiery red dragon that had destroyed Baboso, even though no light shone from her eyes or hand tattoos now.

"Listen—" I started to say, but she cut me off.

"I don't want to talk about what you saw in the Chagrath's realm."

"That wasn't what I was going to bring up."

She gave me a sidelong look as she kicked to the height of a tall man's head.

"I've seen your scars," I said.

She grunted a little louder with her next two blows.

"I know how they got there. August 6, 1945. Hiroshima. You were in the radius of the atomic blast. You lost your immediate family and were badly injured. I understand why you'd be angry at the ones who did that."

For the last three days, I'd had time to think about a lot of things. Among them, Takara's incomplete file. I lined up the gaps with our recent experiences. Like the dragon shifters of Waristan, Takara's dragon nature had extended her life. She was much older than she appeared—at least ninety, by my estimate. Old enough to have survived the atomic attack on Hiroshima, anyway. That was what she'd meant when she said, "read your history."

"But that war is long over," I continued. "And this past weekend showed how effective we can be when we work together."

Takara's next grunt might have been agreement. I couldn't tell.

I'd determined other things about her as well—though maybe determined was too strong a word. I *suspected* other things. For one, that when she'd healed from the blast, the survivors of her samurai clan had rejected the horribly-scarred girl. That's why she had left. Not by choice, but necessity. Internet research had shown me that the Sakuma clan still existed and also that someone didn't simply leave them, not without a death wish. Forced out, Takara had found a family among the ninjas, the samurai's mercenary cousin.

I also suspected that the repercussions of the atomic blast had gone further than scarring her body and losing her clan. It had instilled her with her dragon powers. How, I had no idea. But I'd witnessed the toll those powers could take on her, the pain they inflicted. Which led me to believe she had joined Legion for the same reason as me: to be cured.

On this last point, I had a little more evidence. While in the Biogen building, I'd picked up traces of her scent.

"Is that all?" she asked impatiently.

I knew better than to bring up any of my suspicions.

"Yeah, carry on. I'm going to drop off my things, then look for Sarah."

At the front of the barracks, I almost ran into Olaf, who was coming out. He was no longer wearing a neck brace, and his head was bandage free. He made brief eye contact with me before lowering his head and lumbering on.

I grabbed his upper arm. "Hey, hold on a sec."

He stopped and turned toward me as if awaiting a command.

"Back in El Rosario, Sarah said you requested to be included in our final push."

"Yes," he confirmed.

"Why?"

"To finish mission."

"But you were injured."

I watched his eyes closely as they stared back at me.

"Was there another reason?" I pressed.

His dull blue eyes shifted slightly, as though trying to look away.

"One having to do with the bombing in Waristan?"

This was something else I'd had time to think about in the Biogen building. Olaf's coming hadn't made sense. Injured, he was a liability—he would have known that from his own training. But not only had he joined us, he had helped lead the children out to safety. It seemed like a long shot, but *had* some part of him been trying to atone for helping destroy the Kabadi's warrior class? And had he overcome his programming to do so?

I watched a thin film of moisture grow over his eyes.

I gripped his shoulder and lowered my head. "Olaf, you can tell me."

With a face-trembling effort, he wrenched his gaze from mine. "I was assigned to mission and wanted to finish," he grunted. "That was all." He lowered his head and continued walking.

Dammit, I thought as I watched him go. *There is a living human in there.*

I dropped my stuff in my room and crossed the compound in search of Sarah. The El Rosario mission completed, we needed to get back on a training schedule. I also intended to raise the issue of Olaf and whether it was ethical keeping someone like him on our team. If Centurion was denying his humanity it was either because they hadn't looked hard enough or hadn't wanted to. That didn't make me feel good about keeping him. Unless he had the freedom to choose his path, like the rest of us, he may as well have been a slave.

Inside the main building, Sarah's office door was ajar. When I knocked, though, the voice telling me to enter wasn't hers. Like the scent, it belonged to an older man. I pushed the door open.

"What are you doing here?" I asked.

"I can't visit the program I helped develop?" Reginald Purdy looked up from a folder on Sarah's desk, already smiling. He opened a hand toward the chair facing the desk. "Have a seat, Captain."

"Where's Sarah?" I asked as I lowered myself.

"Meeting with Director Beam."

"Problems?"

Mr. Purdy chuckled. "Far from it. He's planning to use the success in El Rosario to sweeten Legion's promotional material. I'm sure he'll want to meet with you too at some point."

"So we're all good?" I asked carefully.

"That's between you and Director Beam ... though I

suspect he'll want to work out some things for future missions." He raised an eyebrow. "Such as how to take a direct order."

"You mean calling off the mission at the eleventh hour? That was a bullshit order, and you know it."

Purdy's eyes twinkled with humor. "Which is why I let you handle it."

"So you *did* get my message that day. Why didn't you call back?"

"Because I wanted to see something."

"And what was that?" I growled.

"Whether I'd picked the right man to lead the team. Director Beam and I have had our..." He circled a hand. "... creative differences, I guess you could call them. What you did is exactly what the Legion Program should represent, as I told you the other night. Our clients need to know we're behind them, regardless of costs. Especially at this early stage."

"I'm not a pawn in your boardroom pissing contest."

"Well, maybe I wanted you to see something too." He held up a hand before I could speak. "Let me ask you a question—and answer me honestly. Did you feel like a mercenary in El Rosario?"

"No," I admitted. "I didn't."

He smiled as though to say, *Well, there you go.*

"But it was because El Rosario's population was vulnerable," I added. "They needed our help. Get us more missions like that, and I'll never grumble about Legion being a mercenary outfit again."

"I'll see what I can do, Captain."

I watched Reginald Purdy, trying to decide whether or not I could trust the man. Beneath his polished surface and pinstripe suits, he was an operator. Was he only telling me what I wanted to hear? And did it have anything to do with the three days of testing I'd just undergone?

As though sensing I was trying to draw a bead on him, he touched his folded kerchief to his grinning mouth and stood. "Keep the troops sharp in the meantime. There's a developing pattern of killings up in Canada. Wolves, from the early analysis."

"How is that a supernatural issue?"

"Did I say wolves?" He chuckled. "I'm sorry, *were*wolves."

The idea of facing werewolves touched off something primal. A sudden heat erupted throughout my body, and my pulse pounded in my temples. That was the Blue Wolf talking. *Bring it,* he was saying.

But it was Jason Wolfe who finally nodded.

"We'll be ready."

The End

But get ready for another full-length Blue Wolf adventure. Keep reading to learn more...

BLUE HOWL

BLUE WOLF BOOK 3

With Jason Wolfe's ragtag team of monster hunters hardening into a lethal unit, they're ready to roll. And not a moment too soon.

In the wilds of northern Canada, something is stalking humans and leaving a trail of scattered remains. The team arrives, armed for mayhem. But how to handle an arrogant client, not to mention a killer that can't be tracked?

Meanwhile, Jason faces an inner test. His wolf nature, awakened by the vast, rugged landscape, yearns to break from the human mind tethering it. A struggle made more dangerous by Nadie, an alluring shifter intent on claiming the Blue Wolf for her mate.

With a winter storm pounding in, can Jason hold onto his command, his teammates, and his devotion to his fiancée?

Or will this mission consume them all?

AVAILABLE NOW!

Blue Howl
(Blue Wolf, Book 3)

ACKNOWLEDGMENTS

Another Blue Wolf installment, another talented group who helped bring it home.

In no particular order, thanks to my advanced readers; to Ivan Sevic and Deranged Doctor Designs for yet another inspired cover; to Aaron Sikes for his solid editing; and to Sharlene Magnarella for final proofing.

I also want to thank James Patrick Cronin for his superb narration of the Prof Croft series and now the Blue Wolf audiobooks. Those books, including samples, can be found at Audible.com.

As always, many thanks to my readers for exploring this universe with me, with a special shout out to the Strange Brigade.

Till the next one...

Best Wishes,
Brad Magnarella

P.S. Be sure to check out my website to learn more about the Croftverse, download a pair of free prequels, and find out what's coming! That's all at bradmagnarella.com

CROFTVERSE CATALOGUE

BLUE WOLF

Blue Curse

Blue Shadow

Blue Howl

Blue Venom

Blue Blood

Blue Storm

SPIN-OFF

Legion Files

PROF CROFT PREQUELS

Book of Souls

Siren Call

MAIN SERIES

Demon Moon

Blood Deal

Purge City

Death Mage

Black Luck

Power Game

Druid Bond

Night Rune

Shadow Duel

Shadow Deep

Godly Wars

Angel Doom

SPIN-OFFS

Croft & Tabby

Croft & Wesson

For the entire chronology go to bradmagnarella.com

ABOUT THE AUTHOR

Brad Magnarella writes urban fantasy for the same reason most read it...

To explore worlds where magic crackles from fingertips, vampires and shifters walk city streets, cats talk (some excessively), and good prevails against all odds. It's shamelessly fun.

His two main series, Prof Croft and Blue Wolf, make up the growing Croftverse, with over a quarter-million books sold to date and an Independent Audiobook Award nomination.

Hopelessly nomadic, Brad can be found in a rented room overseas or hiking America's backcountry.

Or just go to www.bradmagnarella.com

Made in United States
Orlando, FL
10 March 2024